"If I can knock you down, you have to talk to your brothers."

Eli raised an eyebrow in disbelief. "You can't knock me down. I'm much stronger than you. And I'm not fighting a woman."

Caroline put the boxing gloves on. "Are you chicken, Eli?"

He stood. "I'm not fighting you."

"Didn't Pa settle all your fights and disagreements this way? Put the gloves on."

He shoved his hands into the gloves and held them up. She danced in and out, taking jabs at his stomach, but he didn't move or respond. This was going to be so easy. She moved close to him, her body touching his.

Glancing up into his stubborn blue eyes, she placed her right foot between his feet, then she wrapped her arms around his waist. Eli tensed. Caroline raised her right foot, turned it, and hooked his left leg and jerked. His leg slid out from under him and he was on his butt in a split second.

He burst into laughter. "That was a trick," he said, taking off his gloves. "You knew exactly what you were doing."

"But a deal is a deal—and you're a man of your word, right?"

Dear Reader,

This book is about a Texas Ranger, Elijah Coltrane. Eli first appeared in *A Baby by Christmas* (Harlequin Superromance #1167) as a stubborn, hardworking man with a troubled past. He grew up knowing who his father was, but the man denied his existence. He has dealt with this rejection all his life—he feels like the forgotten one, the forgotten son of Joe McCain.

As an adult, Eli finds it hard to accept love, and the love he discovers with Caroline is no exception. He was a very hard character for me to write, but I learned a lot from him. I couldn't wipe away Eli's pain with the tap of my computer keys. He had to grow and learn, and it took a persistent green-eyed blonde to make him realize that maybe someone could love him.

So come along and find out if Eli can find his happily ever after.

Warmly,

Linda Warren

P.S. I love hearing from readers. You can e-mail me at lw1508@aol.com or write me at P.O. Box 5182, Bryan, TX 77805 or visit my Web site at www.lindawarren.net. I will always answer your letters.

Forgotten Son
Linda Warren

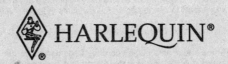

TORONTO • NEW YORK • LONDON
AMSTERDAM • PARIS • SYDNEY • HAMBURG
STOCKHOLM • ATHENS • TOKYO • MILAN • MADRID
PRAGUE • WARSAW • BUDAPEST • AUCKLAND

ISBN 0-373-71250-2

FORGOTTEN SON

Books by Linda Warren

HARLEQUIN SUPERROMANCE

893—THE TRUTH ABOUT JANE DOE
935—DEEP IN THE HEART OF TEXAS
991—STRAIGHT FROM THE HEART
1016—EMILY'S DAUGHTER
1049—ON THE TEXAS BORDER
1075—COWBOY AT THE CROSSROADS
1125—THE WRONG WOMAN
1167—A BABY BY CHRISTMAS
1221—THE RIGHT WOMAN

Don't miss any of our special offers. Write to us at the
following address for information on our newest releases.

Harlequin Reader Service
U.S.: 3010 Walden Ave., P.O. Box 1325, Buffalo, NY 14269
Canadian: P.O. Box 609, Fort Erie, Ont. L2A 5X3

While writing this book, I had the good fortune to speak with a real Texas Ranger, Sergeant Frank Malinak, and I'd like to thank him for answering my many questions with incredible patience and understanding. Any errors in this book are strictly mine, and all characters are fictional.

I asked Frank what he'd like people to know about the Rangers, and the following is his response:

"Much has been written about the Texas Rangers of the past, but probably less is known about the modern Ranger. Today's Texas Ranger is a criminal investigator called upon to assist local, state and federal law enforcement agencies with an array of cases. With the growing population of this state and the increasing complexity of criminal enterprises, Texas Rangers are called upon now with as much necessity and urgency as in bygone eras. The modern Ranger stands ready to protect the citizens of the United States against common street criminals, organized crime, public corruption, identity theft, computer crimes and domestic and foreign terrorism. In short, Texas Rangers have the training, equipment and skills to fight crime in today's sophisticated society. It has been said, 'As long as there is a Texas there will be Texas Rangers.'"

CHAPTER ONE

CAROLINE WHITTEN RUSHED into her apartment with the devil on her heels. She couldn't be late—mustn't be late. Not today. How could she forget the layout? She knew it was because she had the jitters at the prospect of meeting her father, U.S. Congressman Stephen Whitten, for lunch. The thought made her angry.

And made her feel guilty. A daughter's guilt.

Her latest photo layout was on the kitchen counter. She quickly grabbed it and counted to ten to calm herself. At two o'clock, she had an appointment with the writer and an editor for the article on Texas wildflowers. The shots she'd taken in the Texas Hill Country where the flowers grew in abundance were great. At least she thought they were.

She groaned. Now the impending lunch had her questioning her capability as a photographer. Caroline blocked the negative thoughts. She was a damn good photographer and the shots were awesome.

How she wished her parents felt the same way she did about her career choice. But the lunch was sure to be another foray into how Stephen Whitten thought she was wasting her life—and her talent.

Caroline had a law degree, like her father, but she'd done nothing with it. Instead, she'd followed her first love, photography, and she made a good living. She just didn't understand why her father couldn't be happy for her.

At least her sister, Grace, would be there to take some of the pressure off Caroline. Grace was a lawyer and worked in their father's law firm, as he had planned. She was the good daughter, while Caroline was...

Would the guilt ever leave her?

She swung around and her inner skirmish stopped, replaced by a frisson of fear. Two men stood in her doorway, two men with long hair and full beards and brown robes. She'd seen them before...when she'd taken photos of the wildflowers. They belonged to a cult hidden away in the hills, and she'd accidentally trespassed close to the high fence that surrounded their property. She'd been afraid of them then and was afraid of them now.

"What do you want?" she asked as authoritatively as she could.

"You have been chosen," one man answered.

"Excuse me?"

"You have found favor with the prophet."

That's what they called their leader. Caroline had met him briefly while she'd tried to explain why she was there. He'd looked at her in a way that made her skin crawl, and she'd been glad to get away. What were his men doing here? How did they know where she lived? And what did they want?

"If you don't leave, I'll call..."

Her words trailed off as one man grabbed her and the other clamped a foul-smelling cloth over her face. She lashed out with her arms and legs, then everything went black.

CAROLINE WOKE UP in darkness. Total darkness. Fear ran along her skin and spread through her body like a virus. It was chilling. Debilitating.

All-encompassing.

Take deep breaths. Take deep breaths, she kept repeating to herself. After a moment, her fear eased and she realized she was on a mattress. She felt its softness, then her hands touched dirt. Cold dirt.

The makeshift bed was on the ground. Getting to her feet, she groped around her with hands outstretched. She was in a small room with wooden walls, she discovered. There was nothing in the space but the mattress…and her. *Oh, God.* Where was she?

Nausea churned in her stomach and she could feel a scream rising in her throat. Then one of the walls opened and she blinked, the stream of light dazzling after the total darkness. When her eyes had adjusted, Caroline saw a woman with blondish-gray hair pulled back in a knot standing in the opening. She wore a tan, monklike robe and held a pitcher in her hand.

"I brought you water," she said.

Caroline's eyes focused on the shadowy yellow light. The woman was older, and all Caroline had to do was overpower her and run. But run where?

Caroline stepped forward. "Why have you brought me here?"

"You have been chosen to be the prophet's next wife. It is a great honor. You will be the seventh wife, the one to bear the messiah."

"What? I think that's already been done."

"Blasphemy," the woman shouted.

This was Caroline's chance and she made a dive for the opening. The woman grabbed her around the neck and flung her back on the mattress as if she were a rag doll.

Gasping for breath, she said, "You can't keep me here."

"You will get no water or food. Then you'll learn to be submissive."

"Never," Caroline screamed. "Tell your prophet he has chosen the wrong woman. I will never be his wife."

"You'll change your mind," the woman muttered. In an instant she was gone.

And so was the light.

Caroline jumped up and beat on the wall and screamed until her throat was sore. Then she sank down to the dirt. "Please, somebody. Please help me."

Please.

ELIJAH COLTRANE, Texas Ranger, found the oldest clothes in his closet and slipped them on—worn jeans with holes in both knees and a long-sleeved cotton shirt that had paint stains from when he and Tuck had painted the old house where they'd grown up. Then he found a pair of tennis shoes that had seen better days.

He stared at himself in the mirror. Dark hair curled at his collar, not too long and not too short, just right for the mission ahead of him. His blue eyes looked back at him with veiled excitement and he could feel the energy pumping through his body.

Today would be the start of an undercover operation to nail polygamist and murderer Amos Buford, alias the prophet. This time Buford would not slip through the cracks of the system. Eli would see to that.

A knock brought him out of his reverie. Eli opened the door and Jeremiah Tucker walked in. Tuck was also a Texas Ranger, and Eli's foster brother and best friend.

Tuck handed him some letters. "I picked up your mail because it was bulging out of your mailbox. Don't you ever bring it in?"

"Whenever I think about it."

Tuck thumbed through the letters. "There are three from Jake McCain."

"Throw them in the trash."

Tuck shook his head. "What's the matter with you? Why can't you talk to him? He's your half brother."

"Let it go." There was a warning in every word.

Tuck was never good at heeding warnings. "I don't understand what you have against Jake and your other half brothers. They seem like nice people."

Eli couldn't explain it to himself, never mind to Tuck. There was just something in him that wouldn't accept these men as his blood relations. The McCain brothers, especially Jake, had made several attempts to establish a connection. But Eli had spent the first thirteen years of his life being called a bastard, because Joe McCain had denied being his father. Eli wouldn't acknowledge the name now, no matter how hard his half brothers tried to make him. He realized he had a stubborn streak, but he'd rather keep his life separate from them. That was how he wanted it.

When Eli didn't speak, Tuck asked, "Do you mind if I open them?"

"Suit yourself."

Tuck's forefinger ripped through a flap and a photo fluttered to the floor. He picked it up. It was a picture of a little boy and girl. "Look, Eli," he said. "It's of Ben, Jake's son, who we rescued from Rusty Fobbs. And Ben's sister. Let's see." He glanced at the back. "Her name is Katie and she's two years old and a beauty." Tuck held out the snapshot to Eli, but he turned away.

It was Ben's kidnapping, about three years ago, that had brought Eli back into the McCains' world. He wished the family would understand that he'd only been doing his job, and would stop trying to make his role in the rescue personal.

"Put it on the coffee table," he mumbled.

"You're going to have to let go of the past at some point," Tuck told him, gingerly setting down the mail with the photo of Ben and Katie on top.

"I have other things on my mind at the moment."

"Caroline Witten's kidnapping?"

Eli rubbed his day-old beard. "Yep. I've waited a long time to get Amos Buford."

"Have you told the FBI the whole story?"

Eli sent him a look that would have made other men back off. "They asked for my help because I'd investigated Buford before. I told them everything they wanted to know, even the fact that he killed someone I cared about."

"Eli…"

"What? You think I can't do this?"

"Hell, Eli. I've known you most of my life and there ain't nothing you can't do. I don't think you're even afraid of the devil."

"Buford *is* the devil."

"That's what I'm saying. Don't make this about Ginny."

When Tuck said her name, Eli turned away and picked up his gun and badge, trying not to think, trying not to remember. But his control weakened and the image of her limp dead body, thrown into a ditch on a Texas country road, flashed through his mind like summer lightning, quick and sharp. He felt the pain for a moment, then it was gone.

But other memories lingered. Jess and Amalie Tucker were Eli and Tuck's foster parents, good people who took in kids that were in trouble and needed guidance. Tuck had been left with them when he was a baby, Eli at thirteen. It was Eli's mother, Vera who'd taken him to her uncle Jess, and ex-Texas Ranger. Even though Eli had several encounters with the law, it didn't take Jess long to adjust Eli's attitude.

Eli grew up not knowing what a real home or love was about. Vera was a waitress in a bar and worked nights and slept during the day. She'd had assistance from the state for Eli's day care, but at night he'd been shuffled from neighbor to neighbor or anyone who'd keep him. When he was four, Vera had started taking Eli to work with her and he'd slept in a back room. The smells of cigarettes and booze had filled his lungs, and stale smoke had clung to his clothes. He'd hated those smells. He still did.

But at twelve and thirteen Eli was guzzling down beer like an adult, doing anything to rebel, to get his mother's attention. He knew she cared about him, but he also knew, even at a young age, that his mother had made some bad choices.

When Eli was a little older his uncle Jess told him a bit more about Vera's life. Her mother, Adell, was Jess's sister. She'd married an abusive man who beat her and Vera. In an obvious attempt to escape her home life Vera had dropped out of school at sixteen and married a boy two years older. He'd turned out to be as abusive as her father.

After several trips to the hospital, a counselor got her out of that relationship, and Vera started a new life in Waco, Texas. She didn't have any job skills, but with the help of several state agencies she'd started working at a day care. The pay was minimal and she could barely live on it. Then she'd met a friend whose brother owned several bars, and she got a job as a waitress.

There she met Joe McCain.

And the abusive cycle went on.

Jess and Amalie—or Ma and Pa, as Eli called them—gave him everything that was missing in his life, and he grew up wanting to be a Texas Ranger, as did Tuck. They both knew they owed everything to Ma and Pa. The couple had adopted Tuck as a baby, and he carried the Tucker name. They'd wanted to adopt Eli, too, but Vera wouldn't sign the papers. It didn't matter. Jess and Amalie were his parents in every way that counted, as they were to so many children.

Ginny had been one of them.

The memory of her once again slipped past Eli's iron control.

She'd come to the Tucker's when Eli and Tuck were already gone from home. Eli had been accepted as a Texas Ranger and Tuck was working as a trooper for the Department of Public Safety.

Amos Buford had kidnapped Ginny on her way to work. Amos and his followers often begged for money on street corners, and Ginny had stopped and given a donation. One look at her blond beauty and Amos had decided she'd be his next wife—though he already had three.

According to Ginny, Buford had kept her in a dark room for two days with no food. He'd broken her spirit and tried to brainwash her, and when Ginny thought she'd lose her mind, she'd participated in the marriage ceremony.

It was another month before she was able to escape, but by then she was close to a nervous breakdown. She made it to a highway Tuck was patrolling. After she'd told her story to the police, Tuck had taken her to Ma and Pa to heal. Ginny had no family and didn't have the strength to face her friends.

When Eli first met her, she'd stared at the floor and

wouldn't look at him. Something about her attracted him immediately—as if her tortured soul was reaching out to him. He found himself going home to see her every chance he got, and eventually they started talking and laughing and sharing. Soon they were in love—something Eli had thought would never happen to him.

The police were never able to build a case against Buford because he and his followers denied ever seeing Ginny. And she had no proof of what they'd done to her. It was her word against theirs. Eli had investigated the case in his spare time, but hadn't found enough evidence to arrest Buford.

Ginny started to heal mentally, and planned on returning to work. They talked about marriage. Eli had never been so happy in his life.

Then he got the phone call… Pa told him Ginny was gone, and that he feared something bad had happened. Eli began an extensive search, and when he found her body, his world came crashing down. He knew Buford had located her and killed her.

Again, Eli couldn't prove it. But now… "I've waited a long time for Buford to make a mistake, and taking a congressman's daughter is about as big a one as you can get."

"Still…" Tuck rubbed his hands together as he sat on Eli's sofa.

Eli watched him and knew exactly what was on his mind. "You're afraid I'll kill him."

Tuck kept looking at his hands. "Something like that."

"I might want to, but I won't. I'd have to live with the knowledge that I'd dishonored the memory of the man who loved me more and taught me more than anyone in this world. I live by Pa's code of honor and I would never kill a man in cold blood. I'm going to get Buford and it'll all be legal. So stop worrying." He handed Tuck his gun and badge. "Keep these for me."

A tap at the door forestalled further conversation.

"That's the FBI," Eli said, and went to let them in. Agents Bill Caufield and Tom Mercer shook hands with Eli and Tuck.

"Are you ready?" Bill asked Eli.

"Yeah. Nothing but a couple of dollars and change in my pocket. No ID."

"Great," Tom replied. "We appreciate your help—the sheriff said you're the best. You know all about Buford and you're familiar with the area."

"Yeah," Eli said, refusing to look at Tuck.

"Congressman Whitten and his wife are beside themselves. We spent a full day checking out Buford's compound and we found no trace of Caroline Whitten."

"Did you check for secret rooms?"

"Yes. We heard that's a trademark of Buford's, but we didn't find one." Agent Caufield unfolded a map on the kitchen table. "There are five other men who live there with Buford. Buford now has six wives. Of course, he doesn't call them his wives to us. They're 'women in his family.' The other men have at least two or three women each, and we've counted forty-eight kids. That's the sad part—it's a regular commune and we can't prove a thing. The police have arrested Buford several times on polygamy charges, but he only has one marriage on record and the other women won't testify against him. So far there's not a law prohibiting a man from living with several women. But there's a law against kidnapping. We might have him this time."

"Why do you think he took Caroline Whitten?" Eli asked.

"She had a lunch date with her parents but didn't show, and she missed a meeting with an editor. She's a photographer and does work for a lot of Texas magazines. She never misses an appointment. Congressman Whitten knew something was wrong and called her fiancé, who said the last time he talked to her she had plans to meet her parents."

"So how does Buford come into this?"

"It took awhile to piece everything together. There was no forced entry, doesn't look as if anything was taken out of the apartment. Then a neighbor said she saw two bearded men in robes outside the building. Her fiancé, Colin Burke, told us that Ms. Whitten had an encounter with Buford and his followers when she was photographing wildflowers for a magazine spread. He said that they wore long robes and had full beards, and Ms. Whitten had been afraid of them."

"That's all you have?"

"That's it. This is the third day and the only thing left to do is to try and infiltrate the group."

"Maybe she's not there." Tuck spoke for the first time.

Agent Caufield shrugged. "It's the only lead we have. We checked with all her friends. No one has seen her. We're getting pressure on this and we have to find her."

"What's the plan?" Eli asked.

Tom tapped the map with his forefinger. "This is how the compound is laid out. There are six makeshift houses that have two bedrooms in each—one for the man and his women and the other for his children. That's what we're assuming. Then there's a large eating room and kitchen with a wood burning stove. All the buildings are in a circle. In the center is where they meet and pray, and there's a big area for a campfire. Everything is very primitive—

no running water, no electricity. There's a spring on the property they use for water."

He paused, then added, "Our only recourse is to get someone into the group and see what we can find. This is one of the days they beg on street corners. A police car will drop you off in front of them. They're drawn to those needing a haven, anyone who's down and out. At this time of year they're looking for strong men to help work the fields. They earn income from the vegetables they sell. So your job will be to get in there and find out what you can. We need to know where they're hiding her. Once you do that, we'll take over. Just get the hell outta there."

Bill laid a photo on the table. "That's Caroline Whitten. Take a good look."

Eli stared at the photo. Light blond hair, shoulder length, in disarray around a very pretty, almost ethereal face… Her eyes were green. Buford favored blond women.

Like Ginny.

The room was silent.

"Ready?" Agent Caufield asked.

"Yes," Eli answered. He was ready to meet Amos Buford.

He'd waited ten years.

CAROLINE DIDN'T KNOW how long she'd been here. Hours, days, weeks—everything was the same. The woman, Ruth, brought bread and water twice a day. The first and second times Caroline wouldn't eat or drink. The third time she wasn't so choosy.

Darkness was total and she felt it creeping into her soul. She'd beaten on the walls until her hands were numb. She'd screamed until her throat was raw. But nothing penetrated the blackness. Nothing eased its grip.

The air was close and dank and the room reeked. At times Caroline had trouble breathing. She had to hold on. The police must be looking for her by now, but how would they know where to find her? Colin. She'd told Colin about the cult and how she was afraid of them. He would remember. He would help her.

Please, Colin, tell my father and the police what I told you.

Colin wasn't the type of man to go charging in after the woman he loved. Suddenly she needed that—a strong man who didn't care about anyone or anything but her.

She twisted the ring on her finger. Lately she'd been having second thoughts about her engagement, and she didn't know why. She loved Colin. They had the same interests— he owned camera stores in Austin, Dallas, San Antonio and Houston. There wasn't a thing he didn't know about cameras and photography. He helped her to improve her shots and they spent hours talking about angles and light.

But their intimate relationship wasn't as satisfying, as it was comfortable. Caroline had given up on finding passion—red-hot passion. That didn't last forever, anyway. But she loved Colin. *And he was someone her father hadn't picked for her.* Was that his big attraction? God, no, this place was making her crazy.

A daughter's guilt.

Earlier—how long ago?—that thought had made her nervous and angry. Now she saw it for what it was—meaningless pride. Her father wanted to bend her to his will, and she was determined to live her own life. In this black abyss, holding on to her pride seemed an insignificant, even petty, struggle.

She'd gladly trade her pride for the sight of daylight, for fresh air and time with her father. Time to say she was sorry and to…

She couldn't breathe and she fought the suffocating feeling. Caroline was still in command of herself enough to know that the prophet was trying to brainwash her. Slowly, methodically, the darkness would eat away at her until—

Suddenly the wall opened and he stood there, the faint light like a yellow flame behind him. Caroline closed her eyes against the frightening scene. When she opened them again, Ruth was there with a white robe in her hands.

"I have brought your wedding robe," the prophet said.

Ruth held it out to her. Caroline got to her feet and took it, then threw it on the dirt and spat on it.

"Blasphemy," Ruth shouted, and grabbed the robe from the dirt.

"You have spirit," the prophet said with a sinister smile. "But that will be broken."

"You can't keep me here forever. The police will find me and you'll spend the rest of your life behind bars."

"The FBI has already been here and they found nothing."

"What?"

"If they come back, they won't find you. At least not the person you used to be. You will be one of us by then and ready to fulfill the prophecy."

"You're evil," Caroline declared between clenched teeth. "I'll never be your wife. I'd rather die."

His face hardened. "For your dishonor, you will be deprived of bread and water for a day. Then you'll learn your place."

"Never, never, never!" Caroline screamed as he disappeared through the wall and darkness engulfed her once again.

She sank onto the mattress, trying to still her trembling. Fear such as she'd never known before filled her. He was diabolical, out to kill her heart and her soul. Her body would survive, though.

To serve him.

No. No. No.

But the FBI had been here. They hadn't found her. Oh God. Where was she that even the FBI couldn't find her? *In hell,* she thought. And there was no way out of hell. She would die here in the darkness.

Or at least all that mattered would.

INFILTRATING THE CULT was easier than Eli had imagined. The police let him out of the cruiser with a few harsh words in front of Buford's followers. They immediately came to his aid. He told them he was down on his luck and had nowhere to go. They said they'd let him work for food until he got his head straight, and he could listen to the word of the prophet, who would nourish his soul.

Eli was looking forward to that.

He climbed into the bed of an old pickup and they headed out of Austin to the hills. One man, Nathaniel, sat with him; two women were in the front with Samuel, the other man. No one spoke. They turned off a highway onto a dirt road. When they turned again, it was onto nothing more than a cow trail, and the ride was bumpy and dusty. This area was sparsely populated and there wasn't a house in sight, just thick woods and brush.

Soon they stopped at a locked gate and Nathaniel got out to open it. Eli noticed the eight-foot-high barbed wire fence and the four-foot-high wire mesh that extended from the bottom up and enclosed the property. It wouldn't be easy getting out of here.

They drove into an area that had been cleared and buildings stood in a circle, as Tom had said. Eli counted six shacks and a larger structure that had to be the kitchen and eating room. Women and children were working in vegetable fields beyond the compound. They all wore brown robes.

Chickens scratched in the dirt and goats wandered freely. Behind one shack was a rickety barn of sorts. The compound had a strange feel to it—as if it was out of step with time. And there was something else about it he couldn't quite define.

As the truck pulled to a stop, the smell of smoke drifted to his nostrils. He wrinkled his nose in distaste. This wasn't cigarette smoke, though. What was it? He didn't have time to ponder the question as two women, both pregnant, and several toddlers came to meet them. The women stared at the ground and didn't speak. The children looked at him warily.

"Come this way," Samuel said, and Eli followed him to the largest of the primitive houses. Samuel tapped on the door.

"Come in, my child," a male voice called.

They walked in to find a man sitting at a table with a Bible opened in front of him. Two men stood behind him. Eli knew this was Amos Buford, and his heart hammered with anticipation, but he was careful that nothing showed on his face.

"Master, I found a needy soul and brought him to you."

Buford raised his head, and Eli was unprepared for the emotions that gripped him as he stared into those evil gray eyes.

Tuck was right. Eli wanted to kill him.

He wanted to put his hands around his throat and choke

the life out of him…as Buford had done to Ginny. But he wouldn't. Caroline Whitten's life depended on his honor as a ranger, and he wouldn't forget that.

"What is your name, my son?" Buford asked.

"Eli Carter," he replied, using the fake name the FBI had given him.

"Are you in trouble with the law?"

"I'm separated from my wife, and when I went to the house to see my kids, she called the cops and had me arrested. In the separation agreement I'm suppose to be providing child support, but I lost my job and was unable to pay her any money." That was the story the FBI had also given him. Buford hated women who tried to dominate a man.

"Women do not know their place in this world."

Neither do you, you bastard.

"Tell me about it," Eli murmured.

"All persecuted souls are welcome here. You will work for your food. There are fields to tend and goats to milk, but you can only stay if you follow the rules and the prophet's word."

"No problem."

"This is Ezra and Peter." Buford introduced the men. "They're in charge of guarding the compound…and me." He let that sink in, then added, "They will search you for any hidden devices that might harm us. Do you object?"

Eli got the feeling it didn't matter whether he did or not. "No. I have nothing to hide."

Ezra, a big somber man, gave him a thorough once-over. He nodded to Buford.

"We have to be careful," Buford said. "There are people out to hurt us."

"I just need a place to stay."

"Then you're welcome here, brother. You will not speak

to the women, though. They're off-limits to you. Do you understand?"

"Sure. A woman is the last thing on my mind."

"If you're in need of female comfort, let me know and I will arrange something."

Eli managed to suppress his shock. Did they share the women? It was too sickening to think about.

"You will have a trial period, then you'll be asked to join us in our beliefs or to leave."

"I understand and thank you."

The words tasted like sawdust in his mouth.

"We don't have extra sleeping quarters, but there are some heavy quilts you can use to sleep under the stars, or if the weather is bad, you can sleep in the eating area."

"Thanks," Eli said again.

"Brother Michael and his sons are cutting wood. Brother Samuel will take you to help them."

"Sure," Eli replied, and they left. Outside he wanted to suck fresh air into his lungs, but he resisted and followed Samuel through the woods to the chopping site.

Eli kept searching for something out of place, something to indicate that Caroline Whitten was here. The place had an eerie quiet about it. The grass and trees were green and the air was fresh and invigorating, but he didn't hear any birds or other sounds in the woods. It wasn't an eerie quiet, he decided. It was a deathlike quiet.

They reached the site. A big dead tree had been felled and Michael and his sons, Daniel and David, were cutting it up with handsaws. Two mules hitched to a wagon waited nearby. Eli was introduced and Samuel left.

Eli helped load the cut wood until his arms ached and he was soaking with sweat. Finally the last piece of wood was on the wagon and they headed to the compound. Michael drove the mules and Eli walked behind with the boys. They had to be around fourteen and fifteen and were already sprouting beards.

"That's a lot of wood," Eli commented, trying to get information. "Does it last very long?"

"Not too long," the older one, David, said. "We use it to cook."

"And we need it for the wedding," Daniel added.

"A wedding?"

"It's going to be a big one. The prophet's taking his seventh wife. It's very important 'cause—"

"Daniel!" David exclaimed in a reprimanding tone.

The youth hung his head as he realized he'd misspoken.

"Hey, no problem," Eli assured them. "The prophet helped me out when I needed it and I'd love to be at his wedding to show my support and appreciation. I don't know much about your faith but I'm willing to learn."

"My brother doesn't know what he's talking about," David said, and the boys ran toward the compound.

Eli stopped. Daniel knew what he was talking about. Caroline Whitten was marked as wife number seven. She was here. But where?

Caroline, where are you?

CHAPTER TWO

ELI KEPT HIS EYES AND EARS open, but he didn't detect any evidence of Caroline. Supper was in the eating area and the men ate at a crudely made table. The meal was vegetable soup, bread and goat's milk. After the women waited on the men, they sat on the floor and ate with the children. He noticed that most of the women were blond and young, probably in their late teens or early twenties. Two appeared to be in their thirties, and an older woman, maybe forty, with grayish-blond hair, seemed to be in charge.

One woman caught his eye. She had dark hair and eyes and looked out of place among the blondes. He wondered how she fitted in here. The other women made her do most of the kitchen work, and they shouted orders at her as if she were a servant.

After supper, the men had a meeting, and Eli was introduced to them more fully. It was clear that Samuel was Amos's right-hand man. Ezra and Peter took care of security, along with four Dobermans. Nathaniel and Michael were in charge of maintenance of the compound, which meant they supplied firewood, tended to the vegetable fields and the goats and chickens. Amos informed Eli that he'd be working with Michael, then he was dismissed with another warning to stay away from the women.

He looked around, but since it was dark he couldn't see

much. He listened at the door to Buford's house, then gave
up when he couldn't make out any of the muffled voices.
But they were making plans—plans for a wedding. He hurried away before the men came out.

Later the group met around the campfire and the dark-
haired woman brought out an ornate chair for Buford.
Everyone sat on the ground and Amos began to preach. He
spoke of hell, damnation, sinners and salvation. It was
hard for Eli to listen, but he stoically kept a rein on his emotions.

Afterward, the men hugged Buford and the women and
children bowed at his feet. This was even harder to
watch—how these women had been subdued into servi-
tude, yet praised his name the whole time.

The men retired to their huts with their wives and children. Eli watched the dark-haired woman. She didn't follow any of the men. Instead, she went to the kitchen area.
His curiosity grew, but he didn't want to cause any dissen-
tion that would get him kicked out of here—not until he
knew where they were keeping Caroline.

Nathaniel brought him two old quilts, and Eli lay under
the stars. The Dobermans guarded the compound and Ezra
was out walking them around the fence. This was Eli's opportunity to inspect the area.

He'd noticed the rickety barn earlier and now saw a cor-
ral for the mules. The chickens had gone to roost for the
night and the goats were lying around the barn. He was
careful not to disturb them.

From the light of the moon, Eli saw a wooden door on
the ground not far from the back of Buford's house. He
crept forward to check it out. The door opened easily, but
creaked loudly in the process. Waiting to make sure no one
had heard, he investigated.

He followed steps down into a dark hole—a cellar of some kind. With his hands outstretched he felt walls of dirt braced with plywood. There were shelves filled with jars.

It was a vegetable cellar—the type used in olden days to store jars so they wouldn't freeze in the winter and would stay cool in the summer. There was enough food here to last a year. And the cellar provided shelter from tornadoes and bad weather.

Eli wasn't sure how the ceiling was supported, but it had to be braced with something. He kept searching with his hands, but all he felt was wood, jars and dirt. The FBI had already checked out the room. Had they missed something? He could see nothing in the darkness, and decided to return in daylight.

Climbing the steps, Eli closed the door carefully, making as little noise as possible. A makeshift shed was used for storing feed for the animals, and he made his way there.

He saw no trace of Caroline.

Eli hurried back to his pallet before Ezra returned, feeling his frustration mounting. He fell into a fitful sleep.

The cult's morning ritual was much the same as the previous night's. Everyone was up at five and the women served breakfast after Buford gave the blessing. The prophet preached again, then everyone went to work except Buford. He asked to see Eli in his quarters.

Eli followed him to the same room as yesterday. Peter waited outside at the door, with Ezra, who was tending to the dogs.

"Have a seat, my brother," Amos said, sitting at a small table holding papers, books and a worn Bible. This furniture was not rough or crude. It had probably been brought in specially for Buford and his needs.

Eli did as instructed, wondering what this was about.

Amos folded his hands over the Bible. "You have been with us for a day and night. How do you like it here?"

"Very peaceful and quiet."

And disturbing.

"Yes. We live close to God and the earth. But we have to build high fences to keep the bigots and naysayers out."

And the law.

"You can have a home here, my brother, if you so choose."

Eli rubbed his hands together, wanting to give the right answer. "I'm out of a job, my family doesn't want anything to do with me and I'm one step away from jail. At this point, any refuge is welcome."

"Just be aware your choice will be final." The words held a warning. "Once you are accepted into our faith and its teachings, you will always belong and there will be no going back to your old way of life."

And when people leave, you murder them.

"We will feed you, give you a home and nourish you mentally and spiritually. In return you will devote your life to me and my teachings."

There it was. Buford thought he was God—accountable to no one but himself.

"What do you say, Elijah?" Buford asked. "That's what you will be called here. We use only biblical names."

"I really appreciate all you've done for me, but I'm still trying to get my bearings." Eli chose his words with care.

"What better way than to start a new life, a new beginning?"

Eli hesitated, not wanting to seem too eager.

Buford leaned back. "I have a daughter turning fifteen in a month. If you join our faith, she will become your wife."

Eli stared into his gray eyes and saw that Buford was absolutely serious. He felt sick.

"I already have a wife."

"You will leave your old world behind and everything and everyone in it. I am the law here."

"I see."

"In our faith girls are promised for marriage when they turn fifteen, then they start to bear children to fulfill the promises in the Bible—to go forth and multiply and to serve their husband and to spread the word of the prophet."

"Is it legal to marry a fifteen-year-old?"

Eli was stalling for time, to consider his responses.

"My brother, you have a lot to learn." Buford gave a slight smile. "I told you there is no law here except mine. We are not bound by society or its absurd rules."

Eli clenched his hands together. "I'm not questioning your judgment, sir, but I'm having a hard time with age fifteen. How about the dark-haired woman? She seems older." He knew he could jeopardize the whole mission, but he felt this was a way to get information.

Buford's face darkened. "Jezebel is sojourning with us. She is not a member of our faith—and *never* question anything I tell you. That is the first thing you learn here."

"Yes, sir. I'm sorry. I'm just learning."

He had to force the words out.

"Don't let it happen again."

"Yes, sir."

"Since you're new, I will be patient with you, Elijah. Let me explain something about our faith. Only pure-blood women are accepted as wives."

Eli frowned. "Pure-blood."

"Yes. Jezebel has dark eyes and hair and her bloodline

is tainted by someone with a darker skin. That is not accepted in our faith."

"I have dark hair." It was the only thing Eli could say. He was learning Buford was more of a bigot than he'd ever imagined.

"But you have blue eyes, denoting your bloodline."

"I see." But he didn't. All he saw was an evil man controlling a handful of people with his insane ideas.

There must have been something in his voice that Buford picked up on because he added, "Don't worry about Jezebel, my brother. We found her wandering the streets in search of food, and we took her in and gave her a place to stay. We are not heartless. But Jezebel has no memory. She doesn't even know her name, so we gave her one. She is happy being a servant to the wives and she asks for nothing else. When she is ready, she will leave and I will let her."

Eli's mind went into overdrive with this piece of information. He found comfort in knowing that the FBI would soon raid the compound. He would make sure they knew about Jezebel. Hopefully, they could help her—if Buford hadn't totally brainwashed her into submission.

"What is your decision, my brother?" Buford's gaze held his.

"Yes. I'd like to stay here."

He swallowed back everything else he was feeling.

"Good. Good." Buford nodded, stroking his beard. "Bless you, my brother. My head wife, Ruth, will tell our daughter, and in a month I will marry the two of you. First, you will go through a trial of learning our faith and rules. After a week, we will have another conversation, and if I am satisfied with your sincerity, I will baptize you and give you a robe. You will denounce the evils of society and from then on you will be one of us. In the meantime you will not speak to my daughter or go near her."

Why the hell would I want to?

"Yes, sir."

"You will find many rewards here, Elijah. After you are baptized, we will build a house for your family."

"My family?"

"Yes. We've needed new men for a long time. Ezra has a daughter turning fifteen in six months and she will also become your wife."

Good God.

"You are a strong man and you will help to make our faith stronger."

Like hell.

"Today you will continue to help chop the wood. We are preparing for a big celebration in our faith and you will get to witness it firsthand."

"A celebration?"

"Yes. I will be taking my seventh wife in a few days. I'm in a state of fasting from pleasures of the flesh. I have twelve daughters and six sons. My seventh wife will bear my seventh son who will be the messiah of our faith and lead my people. This came to me in a prophecy and now it will be fulfilled."

Never, you bastard.

Eli stood and held out his hand. "Congratulations, sir." He was getting close, gaining his trust. This was good.

Buford stood in turn and shook his hand. "You will now call me master."

The word stuck in Eli's throat like a wad of chewing gum, and with supreme effort he swallowed his revulsion. "Yes, master."

"Good, Elijah." Buford nodded in approval. "I could tell

when I met you that you belonged with us. You will be a great asset to our group."

"Thank you...master." He fought his distaste of the word. "What can I do to help with your wedding?"

"Just do whatever is asked of you."

The wedding was soon, so Caroline had to be close. He'd wait and watch and be a model pupil in the faith. Because Buford was going down.

Of that Eli was certain.

CAROLINE KNEW she was losing her mind. Slowly, little by little, the darkness was devouring her sanity. Her spirit was weak and her strength was waning. But she would never marry that man. She would die in this black abyss first.

Sitting cross-legged on the mattress, she leaned against the wall. Words from a hymn ran through her head. *Amazing grace how sweet the sound...* Over and over the song comforted, consoled and tormented her. *When I've been there ten thousand years...* How long had she been here?

Was this how it felt to go insane, to lose one's mind, lose touch with reality? *Think about Colin, your sister, your parents,* she told herself. But the hymn played louder.

Amazing grace...

Someone help me. Please.

THE DAY WENT THE SAME AS the one before for Eli. He chopped, loaded and carried wood until every muscle in his body ached. Being in the woods away from the compound meant he couldn't see what Buford was doing. And he had to know. Was he with Caroline?

With the wagon loaded, they headed for camp. Eli helped Daniel and David unload the wood by the kitchen.

He noticed Ruth go into the vegetable cellar. She was carrying a pitcher and something wrapped in cloth. He kept waiting for her to come out, but she didn't. He wondered what she was doing in there so long. Michael called for his help and he turned to him.

But he kept an eye on the cellar.

Soon Ruth came out with the pitcher and cloth and went into the kitchen. She was taking food and water to someone. Someone in the cellar.

Caroline.

There was nothing Eli could do now. He had to wait.

Later, at supper, Eli watched the others carefully. Buford was the only one allowed to speak—everyone was silent until he spoke to them. Even the children were quiet. The women seemed nervous, hurrying in and out of the room, serving the men vegetable soup and bread.

Buford called the men outside for a meeting, and as Eli rose, Jezebel reached for his bowl and whispered quietly, "If you want more vegetables, they're in the cellar. But the shelves are empty."

It happened so quickly Eli wasn't sure he'd heard her correctly. He knew better than to approach her, however—that could be detrimental for both of them. Buford and his men went to his house, and Eli stood outside, wondering what the woman had meant.

He bided his time, waiting for everyone to go to bed. Tonight Peter took the dogs to guard the fences from unwelcome intruders. Apparently, Ezra and Peter took turns with the nightly chore.

Eli stared up at the stars, wishing for a shower and a shave and a steak. He'd had about all the soup he could handle. Most of all he wished he could find Caroline Whitten. After a while he rolled over and glanced around. The camp was shrouded in darkness. He rose to his feet and made his way to the vegetable cellar. The moon was his only light, so he stepped carefully and quietly.

He drew back with a start as he rounded Buford's house. Three people stood at the back door—Buford, Ruth and Samuel.

"She's resisting and she's singing hymns. I think she's going insane like the other one." That was Ruth.

The other one.

"When I was in town today, I saw it was still in the papers and on the news. The congressman is offering a big reward for her safe return." Samuel's voice was low, but Eli heard it.

There was a long pause as if they were waiting for Amos's reply. "Kill her. She's become a liability and unfit to bear the messiah."

"Yes, master," Samuel replied.

"Do it later tonight and we'll dispose of her body like the others. Then we'll begin another search for my seventh wife."

"Yes, master," Samuel replied again.

Like the others.

How many women beside Ginny had that bastard killed? Eli pressed up against the house as Samuel strolled by. Buford and Ruth went inside. Time was running out. Eli could get past Peter and the dogs to alert the FBI, but that would take too much time. Caroline didn't have a lot of time left, and he still didn't know her exact location. He suspected she was in the cellar and he had to get her out—now.

Her life depended on it.

He slipped through the night to the cellar. Gingerly he opened the door, careful to keep it from creaking, then went down the steps into a pitch-black hole. He felt around with his hands and all he encountered was shelf after shelf of jars, the same as before.

The shelves are empty.

Eli remembered Jezebel's message and began to push on the shelves. They were sturdy and strong and nothing happened. Dammit. Dammit. What the hell was the woman trying to tell him?

The shelves are empty.

But the shelves were full.

He quickly searched again, then found it—an empty shelf near the bottom. He pushed and pulled, but nothing happened. What the hell did the woman mean?

Taking a deep breath, he tried to concentrate. *Think. Think. Think.*

Ruth was a short woman and Eli was six feet two. So it stood to reason that if Ruth came to feed Caroline, she had to be able to open the secret door, and the latch or mechanism would be lower than where Eli was reaching. He stooped lower, pushing and tugging until he wanted to scream with frustration.

With both hands on the empty shelf, he squatted on the dirt floor and ran his hands along the bottom, testing every nook and cranny. As his fingers touched the left corner, the shelf moved easily.

Air gushed into his lungs. He'd found it. Thank God. He hurriedly squeezed through the opening, hoping Caroline was inside.

"'Amazing grace how sweet the sound,'" a woman's voice sang.

"Caroline Whitten?" he asked.

The singing stopped, but she didn't say anything.

"Caroline Whitten?"

Still no response.

"I'm Elijah Coltrane, a Texas Ranger. Please answer me."

"Go away. Leave me alone and stop torturing me. 'Amazing grace…'"

"Caroline." He had to get her attention. "I'm working with the FBI. We've been searching for you."

"You're not real. The FBI has been here and they didn't find me. Now they will never find me. I will die in this darkness because I will never marry him. Never. 'Amazing grace how sweet the sound.'"

"I am real and I'm trying to get you out of here. Do you understand me?"

Something in his voice must have reached her because she stopped singing once more. It was so dark, though, he couldn't see a thing.

"Where are you?" she asked. "Let me touch you, then I'll know you're real."

"Here," he said, and walked into her.

Her hands trembled against him as they traveled over his body, then touched his growing beard.

She jerked back. "You're one of them."

"No. I'm not." He tried to calm her. "Feel my beard. It's short. I've been searching two days for you."

She didn't move, but murmured, "How long have I been here? 'When I've been here ten thousand—'"

"Stop it," he said in a stern voice, knowing she was close to a mental breakdown.

Her voice fluttered to a halt.

"You've been missing for four days, Caroline. Touch me again and you'll see that I'm real."

His request was met with total silence. "Caroline, touch me," he repeated, trying to gain her trust. It worked. She ran her hand over his face.

Eli caught his breath as she touched his skin, and he knew his emotions were highly charged. That was the only explanation.

"I've been growing my beard to infiltrate the group to see if you were here. I'm not one of them."

"You're real. Oh, my God. Oh, my God. You're real." Her arms went around his waist and she gripped him tightly.

He held her for a moment with her head tucked below his chin. "We have to go. We don't have much time. Can you handle a long walk?"

She drew back. "I'll do anything to get out of here."

"When we leave, be quiet, very quiet. Don't make a sound. We have to run for the fence and freedom. The FBI will be waiting, but we have to make it past Buford and his clan."

"Okay."

"Do exactly what I tell you."

"Okay."

"Caroline, do you understand me?" Eli asked, not sure if she was comprehending him or not. "Say something beside okay."

"Yes. I understand you. You're a Texas Ranger and you're taking me out of here. And we have to be quiet."

"Good." Gripping her hand, he led her from the room. He closed the shelf, then helped her up the steps and outside.

Caroline stared at the sky. "Oh my. Oh my. The stars, the moon. I thought I'd never see them again."

Eli gave her a second to adjust. "Let's go," he said, and they slipped into the woods.

They didn't get far before Caroline faltered and fell to the ground. "Oh, I'm sorry," she muttered, gasping for breath.

Eli saw how weak she was and realized this wasn't going to be easy. "Are you okay?"

She looked toward the sky again. "Yes. As long as I can see all that light, I'm fine."

Eli doubted that. He lifted her to her feet and they diligently pushed on. He had studied the compound and the people thoroughly and knew exactly where Peter was on his rounds with the dogs. He went in the opposite direction.

Caroline fell again and Eli again helped her to her feet, then they trudged on toward the fence.

Caroline stumbled once more, but this time she didn't get up. Darkness surrounded them and Eli couldn't be sure that she was aware she was out of the room. Or if she was functioning rationally. She seemed lifeless and spent, but he would not give up on her. He'd get her out of here.

He picked her up and carried her, while she whimpered in protest. He kept walking through the bushes.

Freedom wasn't far away.

Eli kept his mind and sight on that one thing—freedom. His arms ached, as did the muscles in his back, but he didn't stop. He hadn't saved Ginny, but he was determined to save Caroline Whitten.

The farther they went into the woods, the thicker the darkness became, impeding their progress. Eli moved through the brushy areas on pure instinct. Branches scraped their skin and tugged at their hair, but he didn't pause. He stepped into a hole and almost went down, but managed to stay upright with Caroline in his arms.

Just when the journey seemed endless, Eli saw the silver fence glistening in the moonlight. He stopped beside a fallen log and sank down, loosening his hold on Caroline, who eased to his side.

"You okay?" he asked, taking a deep breath.

"Yes."

"The fence is about fifty feet in front of us. It's eight feet high and made of barbed wire and mesh. You have to climb over it. Do you think you can?"

"I'll try."

Eli shook his head. "No. You have to do better than that. Ahead is freedom and behind is Amos Buford. If you don't make it across, he'll kill both of us."

She trembled. "I'm so weak and my head's fuzzy."

"I know, and I'll help you all I can, but you have to help yourself. You have to make it over the fence. When you reach the other side, run as fast as you can. Don't look back and don't wait for me."

She wrapped her arms around herself.

"Do you understand?"

She nodded, but Eli wasn't so sure she did. It didn't matter. He'd literally carry her across if he had to.

"Rest for a bit, then we have to go," he said.

"What did you say your name was?"

He was taken aback for a moment, but pleased. She was asking questions. That meant her mind was functioning.

"Elijah Coltrane, but everyone calls me Eli."

"Thank you, Eli, for getting me out of that room."

"You're welcome," he replied, loving the way she said his name, soft and low with a husky undertone.

"I lost part of myself back there—my pride, my dignity and my self-esteem."

"It's called brainwashing. Buford and his cult are very good at it."

She shivered and tightened her arms.

"It's almost over. We just have to get over the fence." He paused. "Are you ready?"

She took a ragged breath. "Yes."

He stood and cocked his head, hearing a sound in the distance. The Dobermans were coming. Damn. Buford knew they were gone, and the dogs were on their trail.

Their time had just ran out.

"What is it?" she asked in a worried voice.

"They're coming. I can hear the dogs."

"Oh no!"

"Remember what I told you. Get over and run, and don't look back."

He grabbed her hand and they sprinted for the fence. Eli heard the yelps of the dogs, getting closer and closer.

CHAPTER THREE

AT THE FENCE, Eli caught her around the waist and lifted her in the air. "Reach for the wire and start to climb. Even if the barbs cut you, keep going."

Her bare feet brushed against him. "Dammit. Where are your shoes?"

"Back there," she replied, grasping a wire.

There was nothing he could do about that now. He climbed behind her, acting like a shield as he boosted her up. He'd forcefully shoved her to the top when, out of the corner of his eye, he caught movement as the dogs charged toward the fence.

Caroline was over. "Run, run, run!" Eli shouted.

He made to swing over the top, but one of the dogs leaped into the air and clamped its teeth on his right arm, banging him against the fence. Suspended in air, the canine fiercely held on to his prey. Eli struggled to dislodge it, but the dog's jaws were strong.

Caroline turned and saw Eli struggling with one of the dogs. She ran back. The Dobermans saw her and switched their attention to her, lunging against the fence. This broke the other dog's concentration and it fell to the ground, freeing Eli, who also tumbled to the ground—but on the right side of the fence. He quickly jumped to his feet and grabbed her hand. They hurried into the woods as the first clan member reached the fence, yelling unchristian words at them.

Eli kept running, pulling Caroline behind him. On and on they raced through the thicket. Eli's arm burned, but he didn't pay any attention. He had one goal—to get them to the country road and safety before the clan caught up with them.

They passed through thicket after thicket, then into a valley lined with tall grasses, and into dense woods again. Eli kept a firm grip on Caroline. She was holding up well and he admired her spirit. His own legs grew tired and his chest was tight with exhaustion, but he never wavered or stopped. He wasn't sure if Buford and his men would follow, so he wanted to get them far, far away.

Finally, Eli tripped, and they tumbled in a heap on the spring grasses. Neither moved—they were too exhausted. Caroline lay on top of him for a moment, then moved to his side to lie on her back.

He sucked air into his starving lungs. "You okay?" he gasped.

"Yes," she breathed, panting, then pointed to the sky. "Look, Eli, look."

He glanced up and saw the sun peeking above the tree-tops, heralding a new day. He took joy in that. He'd found her and they were out. Buford would not control or ruin her life. Eli took joy in that, too.

"That's the most beautiful sight I've ever seen," she said, her eyes shining as the morning sun chased away the night, the darkness.

He looked at her and saw her clearly for the first time. Her blond hair was dirty, as was her skin and clothes, but her green eyes were bright with wonder.

"Isn't it, Eli?"

He lost the gist of the conversation, but quickly recovered. "Yes," he answered, his eyes never leaving her face.

She brushed back her hair and he caught sight of her hands.

He sat up and reached for them. "Oh, my God." Both palms were scratched and bleeding, the blood caking with the dirt on her skin.

"They're okay," she said, pulling her hands away and sitting up.

His eyes traveled to her bare feet, then he lifted a foot to stare at the bottom. He closed his eyes briefly. The sole was one bloody mess, and he knew she had to be in a lot of pain. Dammit. He should have carried her when he realized she didn't have any shoes on. But after the encounter with the dogs, he'd just wanted to get her to safety. He unlaced his sneakers.

"What are you doing?" she asked.

"You need something on your feet."

"Your shoes are too big for me."

"I know," he said. Pulling off his socks, he gently slipped them on her feet. "That's not much, but it should help."

"Thank you." She touched his arm. "You're hurt, too."

His right sleeve was torn and bloody. "It's just a scratch." He put his sneakers back on and got to his feet. "We'd better make it to the road."

He bent to pick her up, but she pushed his arms away. "No, you're not carrying me."

"You can't walk on those feet."

She stood. "Watch me."

He grunted. "God, you don't take orders very well."

"No. Now let's go." Her eyes held his. This woman was a fighter, a survivor. Buford and his clan would never have been able to brainwash her. She would have died in that dark hole of a grave. Eli wondered about the "others" that Ruth and Amos had mentioned. How many women had died in that makeshift tomb?

Eli shook his head and started walking. Caroline followed. Even though he was perturbed at her stubbornness, he admired her courage. That courage would help her in the days ahead.

After another long walk, the road at last came into view. They sat in the bushes, out of sight in case Buford was looking for them.

"We'll wait until a vehicle comes along so we can get help."

"Okay." Caroline was glad to rest, and she stared down the blacktop road toward a bend in the distance. She hoped someone would come soon, but as long as Eli was with her she could wait. Her hands and feet burned and her clothes were torn and filthy, but freedom was an exhilarating feeling.

Eli had saved her life. Her sanity.

She was out of the darkness, and her thoughts weren't so disoriented or confused now. Fresh oxygen had cleared away the cobwebs, the near insanity, and she knew this was real. The man beside her was real.

She glanced at him and took in this extraordinary person. He was tall, his features prominent and sharp, as if they'd been carved from stone. He had an aura of strength that would deter anyone from daring to change anything about him. She didn't know him, but she instinctively knew that Elijah Coltrane did not take well to change.

"How are your hands?" he asked, watching the road.

"They're burning a little, but they'll be fine."

He turned his head caught his left sleeve with his teeth and jerked. The fabric tore at the seam. With his right hand

Eli unbuttoned the cuff and gathered the cloth, which he continued to rip into strips with his teeth. She watched in awe.

Without a word, he took her hand and wrapped some strips around it. He did that to the other one, and she knew better than to tell him it wasn't necessary.

When finished, he asked, "How's that?"

"Better," she had to admit. "The burning isn't so bad."

"You couldn't have done all this on the fence."

She swallowed. "When I was scared, I'd beat on the wall of that room with the palm of my hand, then my fist, hoping someone would hear me. I just wanted out of there."

"You're out now and you'll soon get medical attention." She couldn't see his eyes, but she knew he was upset.

"My hands feel much better now," she said again, to reassure him.

"Good." He turned his attention to the road.

Caroline watched his unyielding face. He hadn't removed his shirt, because he didn't want her to see his right arm. She had a feeling it was bad. Maybe he didn't want to see it either—not yet.

They sat in silence. A squirrel ran across the road and a crow landed in a tree with a frantic squawk. Everything was peaceful—another spring day in the Texas Hill Country.

But it was so much more to Caroline.

"Did you volunteer for this job?" she asked.

"The FBI asked for my help, since I know the area."

"Why didn't an agent volunteer?"

"The agents went in with a warrant and searched the place, but found nothing."

Goose bumps popped up on her skin as she remembered the prophet's chilling words and the devastating effect it had had on her.

"How did you know where to find me?"

"A woman in the group gave me a clue. They call her Jezebel, but she's not one of them. Buford said they found her wandering the streets and they gave her a home. They treat her like a slave."

"You have to get her out of there, too."

"I plan to, but right now you're my top priority."

The words had a soft, sincere ring to them. She just wanted to keep hearing his voice.

"So the Texas Rangers help the FBI?"

"When they ask. The FBI was getting a lot of flak from Washington and they needed something done quickly. The sheriff knew I had investigated Buford before, so the FBI called me."

"And you agreed to go undercover?"

"Yes."

"Why would you do that? You don't even know me."

"Usually it's my job to investigate, but I have personal reasons for wanting to get Amos Buford."

"Does he know you?"

"No, I'd never met him until two days ago."

"Then…"

"He killed someone I cared about."

"I'm sorry."

"It happened a long time ago."

She licked her cracked lips. "Was it a woman?"

"Yes. My fiancée."

"Oh."

"His men grabbed her from the street because the bastard chose her to be his next wife." Eli glanced at Caroline. "She wasn't strong like you. She lasted two days in the room, then agreed to marry him. After a month, she managed to escape."

He took a long breath, hardly able to believe he was telling her this. But he couldn't seem to stop. "Then I got the call. She was missing, and I found her not far from our ranch, in a ditch, strangled to death."

"Oh. I'm so sorry." Caroline touched his arm. "Why isn't Buford in jail?"

"The police couldn't prove anything. It was her word against theirs, and there was no evidence Ginny was ever in the compound. They never found a secret room like Ginny said there was."

"Ginny was her name?"

He swallowed, struggling with his emotions. "Yes."

"Since Buford is free, I'm assuming they couldn't prove he killed her, either."

"No. There wasn't one shred of evidence, but the FBI were able to close down his camp. He just moved on to these hills, terrorizing other women."

"I don't understand how that could happen," Caroline said. "Why hasn't the law done something?"

"They will this time. Buford screwed up by kidnapping a congressman's daughter."

"I've hated that title most of my life. Today it feels good." Her gaze swung to the road. "My parents are probably very worried."

"Yes. Your father has posted a big reward for any information leading to your whereabouts."

"How is Colin, my fiancé, taking this?"

"I don't know. I haven't heard anything about him."

She bit her lip. "We were having problems. He wanted to get married right away and I didn't. Now I can't remember exactly why I was against it. At thirty, a woman should be ready to get married." She paused. "Are you married?"

"No."

"I'll be glad to see Colin." She glanced at Eli. "Thanks to you, I will."

"I'm just doing my job, ma'am."

Blood trickled down the side of his face into his beard. She reached out with her bandaged hand to touch it. "You've scraped your face."

He wished she wouldn't keep doing that—touching him. He had to keep this on a professional level, and when she touched his skin, he found that difficult. All he had to do, though, was close his eyes and see Ginny's face, and everything was fine.

"It's nothing," he murmured, trying not to pull away.

She let it drop and he was glad. His arm was on fire, but he couldn't let her see he was in pain.

"It's early, but the FBI is patrolling this road, so someone should be by soon."

She studied her bandaged hands. "I probably won't see you again after they arrive."

"Probably not."

"I want to thank you again for getting me out of that place."

He shifted uncomfortably. "As I said, it's my job."

"But you did it for Ginny, didn't you?"

"Yeah," he admitted. "That bastard deserves to be put away for what he did to her and probably many other girls."

Caroline put both arms around his neck and hugged him. "Thank you, Eli."

Dammit. Did she have to keep doing that? He closed his eyes, but he couldn't see Ginny. That scared him. It was the first time that had happened. He was just exhausted physically and mentally, he told himself. He had to hold on to Ginny, but all he could see and feel was Caroline Whitten.

A hum in the distance was a welcome relief. He pulled away. "A car is coming. Stay put and I'll check it out. Don't stand on your feet."

He stood and walked to the edge of the road, recognizing the car immediately. It was Tuck. What the hell was he doing here? He had his own job to do. Then again, Eli was glad to see him.

Tuck pulled over and jumped out.

"Call the FBI and an ambulance," Eli shouted.

Tuck dashed into his car and was back in a minute. He stopped short when he took in Eli's appearance, especially his bloody arm. "What happened to you?"

"It's a long story and I don't have time to get into it."

"You found Ms. Whitten?"

"Yes. She's over here." They walked toward the bushes. "What are you doing here?"

"Surly as ever—still the same old Eli. For a moment there I wasn't sure. But to answer your question, I offered my help. The lieutenant and captain agreed that the FBI could use all the help they could get."

"What happened to one riot, one ranger?"

"Well, it took one ranger to get her out of there, and Congressman Whitten will want answers as to why the FBI didn't find her days ago."

That would certainly come up in the investigation that was to follow, but right now, Eli's main concern was still Caroline.

They walked up to her. "Caroline, this is Jeremiah Tucker, and Tuck, this is Caroline Whitten."

"Howdy, ma'am." Tuck tipped his hat, staring at her bandaged hands.

A string of cars came roaring down the road, and Eli reached down and lifted Caroline into his arms.

"Put me down, Eli," she ordered. "You can't carry me with your arm like that."

He didn't oblige, but just kept walking.

"Eli," Tuck called after them.

Eli didn't pay any attention to him, either. He seemed to stroll effortlessly toward the road, but she knew he had to be in a lot of pain.

Tom and Bill ran up to them.

"We need an ambulance," Eli said.

"It's on the way," Bill replied, his eyes on Caroline. "Are you okay, Ms. Whitten?"

"I am now."

"Where did he have her hidden?" Tom asked.

"In the cellar."

"We checked there."

"One of the walls moves in slightly, just enough for a person to squeeze by, and it's very hard to detect."

An ambulance pulled up, followed by a black car. Paramedics jumped out with a gurney and rolled it up to Caroline. Eli gently laid his burden on it. Before the paramedics could take her away, she grabbed Eli's left arm.

"No," she cried. "Eli has to come, too. He's hurt and he needs attention."

"Caroline, just go and get taken care of. I have things to do."

"No," she said again, and held on tight even though her hand was hurting like hell.

Bill was looking at Eli's blood-soaked sleeve. "That arm does look bad. We're going in to make the arrest, and you're not any help to us in that condition. Go to the hospital and take care of your arm. We'll check in later and get a full report. Your job here is done."

Eli gritted his teeth. He wanted to go back and arrest Buford himself, but knew that wasn't going to be possible. "The dark-haired woman isn't one of them, so go easy on her. She helped me find Caroline."

"Okay," Bill said. "We'll make sure she gets special attention. I'm just hoping this goes peacefully. Did you notice any weapons?"

Eli shook his head. "No. I searched a lot of places and never saw any type of weapon, but they're good at hiding things so be careful."

"You take care of that arm," Tom interjected. "Great job—now relax and let us handle the rest."

Stephen Whitten got out of the black car, ran to his daughter and embraced her. Still Caroline did not let go of Eli's arm.

"Oh, Caroline," the congressman said, his voice cracking. "What have they done to you?" His gaze swept over her. "You need medical attention."

"I'm fine, Dad," she said. "And, yes, we're on the way to the hospital."

"We need to get going," a paramedic said to no one in particular.

"Go to the hospital," Tuck whispered, and Eli wanted to punch him like when they were kids. But he didn't have any strength left and knew it was time to give in. It wasn't easy.

"You can let go of my arm," he said to Caroline. "I'm going."

She complied and the paramedics pushed the gurney into the ambulance. Eli took a seat on the side. Stephen stood at the doors, talking on a cell phone.

"Where's Colin, Dad?"

Stephen clicked off. "I'm not sure, Caroline. The press

will be at the hospital. Don't say a word to anyone about what happened. Your mother, Grace and I will meet you there."

Why wasn't he going in the ambulance with her? Eli wondered. And why in hell was he worried about the press? Caroline needed her family, but Congressman Whitten went back to his car and his bodyguards. Eli saw the hurt look on Caroline's face and suspected it had less to do with the congressman than with the fiancé. Where was he?

In the ambulance, a paramedic was taking her vital signs and another was taking his. "I need to remove your shirt, sir," the man said. "Or what's left of it."

Eli unbuttoned his shirt and removed it, trying not to flinch as he pulled the bloody fabric from his arm.

The man glanced at the wound. "What happened?"

"A dog, a Doberman to be exact, tried to keep me from going over a fence, and almost succeeded."

"Then this was done by a dog?"

"Yep."

The paramedic moved and Caroline saw Eli's arm. "Oh, my God. Can't you do something?" she cried to the paramedic.

"We're almost at the hospital, where a doctor will take care of it. I'll wrap it in the meantime."

Eli hadn't looked at his arm and he knew he had to. Big, fearless Elijah Coltrane was afraid. But fear never had much of a hold on him for long. He turned his head and forced himself to look down at where the dog's teeth had sunk into him, pulling flesh and muscle from the bone. He wasn't sure how he was still using his hand.

He'd never been sick a day in his life. The cold and flu bugs always got Tuck, but never him. Pa used to say Eli was tough—even germs were afraid to live in him. But what if his arm was permanently injured now? And it was his right arm….

No. His arm was fine. It would heal in no time.

The paramedic bandaged him and he shifted his thoughts elsewhere. The other technician was attending to Caroline.

"How are her feet and hands?" he asked.

"Scraped, bruised and cut. No deep lacerations, so they should heal without a problem."

That's what he wanted to hear. She would be fine.

"Eli," she said in a soft voice. "Are you upset with me?"

He knew what she was talking about—her refusal to let go of his arm. "No, Caroline. I just wasn't thinking too clearly. I've waited a long time to put handcuffs on Amos Buford. I didn't want to miss that, but I'm in no condition to put handcuffs on anyone."

"They'll get him."

"I just hope the arrest goes smoothly."

There was silence for a moment and he heard a whimpering sound.

He frowned. "Are you crying?"

"No. Yes," she sniffled. "And I don't know why. I'm out of that place and I should be happy but…"

"It's an emotional reaction," he said, the sound twisting his gut. "You've been through a lot. Soon we'll be at the hospital and you'll see your fiancé, your family, and you'll feel better."

"I don't think so," she mumbled. "I feel as if I'm never going to be the same again. Somehow I'm different."

"Give it time." But he felt the same way. For years he'd held on to Ginny's love, her memory. That was enough.

Until now. Now…

He closed his eyes, forcing the feeling away, striving, struggling to see Ginny's face. No matter how hard he tried it wasn't there. Caroline's was. That frightened him more than the damage to his arm. Caroline was seeping into his system and he didn't like that. He didn't want it. He barely knew her, but he was powerless to change whatever was happening.

He didn't like that, either.

CHAPTER FOUR

WHEN THEY REACHED the hospital, things happened fast. Reporters and TV crews were everywhere, with the police trying to push them back. Attendants whisked Caroline away, and above the noise Eli heard her call out to him.

He didn't respond. She needed her family now—not him. Stepping out of the ambulance, he saw an orderly with a wheelchair. His first response was to object. Then he glanced at all the people clamoring to get a statement from him. He sank into the chair without protest, wanting to get away from the crowd as quickly as possible. Reporters were shouting questions at him and flashbulbs were going off, but he ignored them.

The orderly quickly took him to a bed in the emergency room. Eli stood and lay down there, feeling totally spent.

"The doctor will be in here shortly," the attendant said.

"Thanks," Eli replied, and stared up at the fluorescent ceiling lights. Had the arrest been made? He hoped this wouldn't take long because he had to get out of here and give the FBI a full report. They had to know everything he'd learned as soon as possible. Where in the hell was the doctor?

A doctor who barely looked old enough to be playing in Little League came into the room. Eli knew he had to be much older, or at least hoped he was.

"I'm Dr. Fisher, Mr. Coltrane. I'm going to look at your arm."

"Sure. Stitch it up or whatever you have to do because I have to go. I have an investigation to finish."

"Yes. I heard," the doctor said, unwrapping his arm. "It's been in the news all week and the hospital is inundated with reporters. Everyone is very relieved Ms. Whitten was found alive."

"Yeah. Me, too." Eli watched as he examined his arm. "How long is this going to take?"

The doctor made a grunting sound. "I'm not sure. I have to get a surgeon down here."

"A surgeon! What the hell for?"

"Your arm needs special attention, Mr. Coltrane."

"That's why I'm here. Stitch the damn thing up so I can go."

"It's not just the skin that's been damaged—muscles and nerves have been ripped apart and it will take a specialist to put it back together."

That still didn't deter Eli. "It can't be that bad. See? I can move my hand." He raised his arm—it was beginning to feel heavy—and moved his fingers.

"Look closely at your fingers," the young doctor said patiently. "They're starting to swell and so is your arm. With this type of injury, surgery needs to be done as soon as possible so you can maintain full mobility."

"Are you saying if I don't have the surgery, I'll lose the function of my right hand?"

"Yes. That's what I'm saying."

There was silence as Eli battled with what he had to do and what he wanted to do.

"Surely you're not thinking about not having the surgery?" The doctor was clearly shocked.

"How long will the operation take?" he asked instead of answering.

"The surgeon will be able to tell you that."

"Well, get him in here. I don't have a lot of time."

Dr. Fisher gave a long sigh. "Mr. Coltrane, you're not going anywhere for a while. It would be best for you if you started thinking in those terms."

"And it would be best for you if you got the damn surgeon in here."

The doctor was scribbling in a chart and he didn't look up. "I'm attributing your bad attitude to the pain you're in. I'll have the nurse give you something."

Eli took a deep breath. "I don't want a damn thing for the pain. I just want to get this over with."

"Yes. I think we've established that." He closed the chart. "The surgeon will be in soon, Mr. Coltrane, so please try to relax."

Dr. Fisher walked out and Eli knew he was being an ass, but he couldn't help himself. He'd never been badly injured before and he wasn't handling it well. Closing his eyes, he tried to relax as the doctor had suggested. This would be over in no time and he could finish the job he'd started. They had to have arrested Buford by now, and he wished someone would come and tell him how it went. He had to know Buford was in jail.

"Mr. Coltrane."

Eli opened his eyes to see an older, bald-headed man reading his chart. "I'm Dr. Jim Stiles. I hear you've had an encounter with a mean dog."

"Yes. You could say that."

"Let me take a look." He laid the chart down and moved to the right side of the bed, where he picked up Eli's arm and examined it. "Mmm. Mmm. Mmm. A lot of damage has been done. We need to get you to surgery now before the swelling gets any worse. Has your wife been called?"

"I'm not married."

"Family?"

"My brother's working the same case that I was and he'll be here as soon as he can."

"We have papers that need to be signed. Do you think you can sign them with your left hand?"

"I can sign them with my right," Eli said.

The doctor stared directly at him. "Ranger Coltrane, I hear you've been giving the intern a hard time. But you and I are of the same caliber—tough, determined men—and if you want me to save that arm then you'll have to cooperate. That's the bottom line for me—cooperation. My time is too valuable to waste on a man who is too stubborn to realize he needs help."

Eli didn't waver under that intense gaze. "Dr. Stiles, I've always been a survivor and a fighter, and I learned discipline, respect and honor from a man I worshiped. He taught me how to take a punch like a man, how to give in without giving up, but he never taught me how to handle anything like this. So you'll pardon me if I'm not on my best behavior."

Dr. Stiles picked up the chart. "It's all over the news that the Whitten woman was found alive by a Texas Ranger. Something the FBI hadn't been able to do."

"I was working with the FBI."

"Don't know how to take praise, either, do you?" The doctor scribbled something in the chart.

"Guess not."

"Let's go fix that arm so you can pin on that medal they're going to give you."

"Just do it as fast as you can."

"I'll do the best job I can in the amount of time it takes," Dr. Stiles retorted.

"You don't cooperate very well, do you, Doc?"

The doctor smiled. "I said I demand cooperation. I didn't say I gave it. I'll see you in surgery."

After that Eli relaxed. He didn't have much of a choice. They removed the rest of his clothes and gave him a hospital gown to wear. A nurse started an IV and he signed papers with his left hand, and another doctor came in to explain what was going to be done to his arm. Soon he was rolled to the operating room, where the anesthesiologist explained how he was going to put Eli to sleep.

Eli stared up at the bright lights, realizing he'd never felt so alone in his life. He had no family, what with Ma and Pa gone. It was just him and Tuck.

A man should have a family. He shouldn't be alone. Where had that thought come from? He'd always been a loner. Maybe it was the drugs starting to flow through his system. Maybe it was his age. Maybe life had just caught up with him.

It would be nice to have someone here, though—someone to wake up to. Caroline's face swam before him and he squeezed his eyes tight. *No.* He didn't want to see her. Then he pictured Jake McCain. *No.* He didn't want to see him, either. But Jake was his brother, his half brother. He was family. He was blood. *No.* Eli wasn't a McCain. Joe McCain had denied his existence, and Eli would never admit that the man's blood ran in his veins.

Never.

That thought lasted a second, then everything went black.

CAROLINE LAY QUIETLY as the doctors and nurses attended to her wounds. She wondered where her family was.

Where was Colin? She felt so alone in this roomful of strangers. They quickly took her to a private room, and Caroline kept looking for her mother, father, Grace and Colin, but all she saw were people she didn't know.

She had an IV in her arm because the doctor said she was dehydrated. They'd given her something for pain and she was beginning to feel woozy and disoriented. But she had to stay awake and find out how Eli was.

Her hands and feet were bandaged, and a nurse removed her clothes and helped her put on a hospital gown. After making sure she was comfortable, the woman left the room.

Caroline licked her dry lips as tears gathered in her eyes. She felt alone and abandoned and she wanted to touch Eli—to feel his strength. She didn't even know him, yet she felt a connection she couldn't explain.

Her eyes grew droopy and she forced them open. She wouldn't close them. She never wanted to see darkness again—not ever. "Amazing grace" hovered at the back of her mind and she wanted to give in and sing to block everything out.

She heard voices in the hall and that weakness dissipated. Grace was here. She'd know her sister's voice anywhere. The door burst opened and Grace ran in and grabbed her.

"Caro, Caro," she cried, holding her tight. "Thank God you're okay. Thank God you're alive."

"Yes. I'm very lucky."

Grace drew back and brushed away a tear. The sisters looked very much alike, with the same blond hair and green eyes and body shape, except Grace wore her hair pulled back while Caroline's was usually loose. Their personalities were so different, though, that people often said they didn't resemble each other.

Caroline was soft and giving, but had an inner strength. Grace was studious, career driven and very much like their father, whom she spent most of her life trying to please. Caroline was just the opposite—needing to be on her own, needing to be her own person.

"My," Grace said, "look at you. You have scratches on your face and arms, and the doctor said your hands and feet have bad lacerations."

"They'll heal."

Grace frowned. "Couldn't that Texas Ranger who found you have done more to keep you from getting hurt?"

"I'm *alive*," Caroline stressed. "I'm alive. If not for him, I'd be dead."

Grace shivered and ran her hands up her arms. "Don't say that. We've been so worried and I—"

"Where's Mom and Dad?" Caroline asked, before they both started bawling like babies.

"You know them. Dad's giving a news conference and Mom is right beside him, as always. It makes good politics—gets the sympathy of the voters, and that's top priority—the voter."

Caroline heard the bitterness in her voice. "Do you think we'll ever get past the resentment of not having normal parents?"

"Probably not." Grace sat on the bed beside her. "But, you're thirty and I'm twenty-nine so we should probably try."

"Yeah," Caroline answered quietly.

Grace rubbed Caroline's arm. "Are you okay?"

She smiled at her sister. "Yes. I'm a little shaken still, but I'll be fine." She glanced at the door. "Where's Colin? I thought he'd be here waiting for me. I'm anxious to see him."

Grace looked away.

"Grace, where's Colin?"

"He should be here soon."

Grace was trying not to tell her something.

"Why isn't he here now?"

"You know he had that new store opening in Houston."

"Yes."

"The opening was today."

"And he went!" Caroline knew the answer before Grace spoke.

"Yes. We'd been waiting for days, and like I said, we were so worried. I think he just needed to do something. The wait was getting to all of us. Mom called him and he's on his way back."

"Oh. I guess that makes it all right then." She couldn't keep the anger out of her voice.

"Caro, please don't—"

"I'm so tired." Caroline cut her off. "I want to go to sleep, but I'm afraid to close my eyes. They kept me in a cellar with nothing but bread and water. There was no light." She had to take a deep breath as the suffocating memory filled her. "I think I went insane for a while. I sang hymns and I want to start singing again. That way I can stay awake. I feel as if I'm losing it. I can't…"

"Shh," Grace murmured, stretching out beside her. "Remember when we were kids and I was afraid of the dark and I'd sneak past the nanny to sleep with you?"

"Yes."

"Now I will protect you from the dark." She snuggled against her. "Just close your eyes and go to sleep. I'll be right here and I'll leave all the lights on."

"I don't think I can sleep. I can still feel the terror of that room—of him."

"Caroline, try to put it out of your mind."

"I can't. He picked me to be his seventh wife—to bear his seventh son. If he had touched me in that way, I would have died. I couldn't have lived through that."

"It's over. Try to think of something pleasant."

Eli was pleasant and nice and…

"Shut your eyes," Grace coaxed. "I'll be right here."

"Sisters first," Caroline mumbled, remembering a pact they'd made when they were nine and eight years old. Her eyes closed.

"Sisters first—always," Grace echoed, as Caroline let go and drifted into a restless sleep.

She didn't know how long she'd slept, but she woke up screaming. Grace quickly calmed her. "It's all right. You're in a hospital. It's all right."

"Oh, God," Caroline whimpered, feeling the remnants of the nightmare about Amos Buford. "I could see him so clearly, as if he was in this room with me."

"He's not. I'm the only one here."

Caroline scooted up in bed. "I can't sleep. I just can't."

"Okay." Grace pushed up beside her. "Then we'll talk. There's a new chick flick out—the mushy, happily ever after stuff that you love. We can go see it as soon as you feel up to it."

"Okay," Caroline mumbled.

"And, oh, there's a new suit at that little dress shop we love. It's a light mint-green with a lacy camisole. Absolutely fetching. I love it, but its kind of bright and I wanted to get your opinion. Tell you what, I'll buy the suit and you pick out something equally charming and we'll dress up and go out to a movie and dinner."

Caroline rested her head on Grace's shoulder, relaxing at her easy, nonsensical chatter. "Keep talking."

"I was thinking about joining one of the fitness places for women. I don't get much exercise and at my age I should start thinking about that. I hate getting all sweaty, though, and I haven't figured out a way around that. Maybe you could join me and we…"

The thought of Grace exercising was hilarious—Caroline couldn't even picture it. She'd join just to get a glimpse of her sister working out. Grace's voice drummed on and Caroline smiled, letting go of the fear and easing into sleep once more.

CAROLINE AWOKE TO VOICES, familiar voices, and saw that her mother and father were in the room. Joanna was sitting in a chair talking on a cell phone and Stephen was pacing back and forth, talking on his own cell phone. Grace sat by Caroline's bedside, holding her bandaged hand.

"You're awake," Grace said. "Feeling better?"

Caroline didn't get a chance to answer as her mother jumped up and ran to her. "My baby, my baby," she cooed, brushing back Caroline's hair. "Don't worry about a thing. You're going to be fine. I'm making arrangements to fly you to Washington to a private clinic, where you'll get special attention and a qualified therapist to help you deal with this."

What was her mother talking about? She wasn't going anywhere.

"Caroline." Her father came to the bed. "You look much better. Agent Caufield is outside waiting to speak with you. You can handle it, right?"

He didn't ask how she was, or if she was up to facing anyone. He wanted her to do it because he expected her to. Stephen Whitten's daughters always did what was expected of them.

She pushed herself into a sitting position and winced.

"Stephen, I don't think she can do this right now." Her mother spoke up.

"Yes, I can. I want to tell them what happened."

"See?" Stephen said. "She's made of strong stuff."

Her father opened the door and two men came in. Her father introduced them as Agents Tom Mercer and Bill Caufield. She remembered them from the road where the ambulance had picked her up. Tom sat and began to ask her questions. He took down her answers, recording everything she said about what had happened after the men took her from her apartment.

"That's good, Ms. Whitten," Tom said.

"Have they arrested him?"

"Yes. Amos Buford and his men are in jail. The women and children are in another location, and several agencies have been called in to help gather information. We're hoping to place the children with relatives—we just have to locate them."

"I hope Amos Buford won't be able to do this to another woman."

"Amos will not be on the outside for a while," Bill promised.

"You make damn sure they put him away forever," her father ordered.

"We'll do our best, Congressman Whitten."

Her father's eyes narrowed. "Sometimes your best isn't good enough."

"How is Eli?" Caroline asked, before her father could demean the agent more than he already had.

"He's in surgery," Tom answered, as Bill turned away.

"Surgery?" She sat up straight. "Oh, no."

"The dog did some damage to his arm and a surgeon's repairing it."

"Will he be okay?"

"Now, Caroline," Stephen interjected. "Don't upset yourself. I'm sure the man will be fine."

"Will Eli be okay?" She spoke to Tom, ignoring her father.

"The doctor is very confident, but Eli will be out of commission for a while, at least until his arm heals. I'm not sure who's going to be brave enough to tell him that, though."

Caroline smiled a tremulous smile. "No. He's not going to take that well." She could see his stubborn face, and it was so uncanny that she could do that. She felt she was never going to forget that face. They were two strangers, yet...

"I will be taking my daughter back to Washington," her father was saying.

Tom's lips tightened. "I know you want to do that, sir, but it would be best if Ms. Whitten stayed here awhile longer. The prosecutor will need her testimony to get an indictment."

"That can be done from Washington. I'll speak with the U.S. Attorney's office."

"I'm not going anywhere, Dad," she said, not able to let this go on any longer. "I'm staying here."

"You need medical attention and—"

"I know what I need. I'm not a child."

The room filled with a thick tension.

"We'll check in later, Ms. Whitten," Tom said. He and the other agent quickly left, but Caroline barely noticed. She was concentrating on her father's anger, which she could feel sucking all the oxygen out of the room.

"This is just like you, isn't it, Caroline," Stephen charged. "Always needing to defy me. Do you even realize how worried your mother, Grace and I have been? We thought you were dead, killed by this insane cult leader. And now that you're back we want to take care of you, but you're throwing it all in our faces."

"But you will not be taking care of me," she pointed out, with as much calm as she could manage. "You'll hire someone to do that, and I'd rather recuperate here close to Grace."

"Maybe she's right, Stephen," Joanna said. "The girls have always been close."

"Do you know what this is going to look like in the papers?" Stephen turned on Joanna.

"Oh. I hadn't thought of that."

"Well, you'd better. We have an election coming up."

Caroline lay back on the pillows. It always came down to that—the next election, the votes. Nothing else mattered, not even their daughters' health or happiness. She wished they'd go away and leave her alone. Loneliness was preferable to this.

The door opened and Colin rushed in. He went directly to Caroline. "You're okay? I was so worried." He kissed her cheek and she tried not to pull away.

"It's awful big of you to show up, Colin," her father said.

Her mother picked up her purse. "I think we need to leave the two of you alone. I'll make arrangements for you to stay here if that's what you wish. Your father and I will delay our plans until tomorrow. That will give you time to think about it."

"Thank you, Mom."

"I'll be outside," Grace said.

Joanna and Grace kissed her and walked out. Stephen glanced at her briefly, then followed.

"I'm so glad you're okay," Colin said.

She took a deep breath, knowing she couldn't take much more that day. "I'm really tired and I just want to rest."

"Sure. I understand, I'll stay until you wake up."

"No. I'd rather that you left."

"Caroline…"

"How did the opening go?"

"Great. But I couldn't concentrate on what had to be done for worrying about you."

"Then why did you go?" Try as she might she was unable to keep the hurt out of her voice.

He touched her face. "Please don't be angry. I just couldn't sit around one more minute." He kissed her forehead. "I love you."

Did he? She didn't think so. He didn't love her the way she wanted to be loved—completely and passionately, like Eli loved his Ginny. When he'd talked about her, Caroline had heard the love in his voice even after all the years she'd been dead. Colin and she didn't have anything close to that.

She wanted to be the most important person in his life and she wasn't. That's what had bothered her about them getting married so soon. She wanted more than what she and Colin had. The ordeal she'd just been through proved that they didn't have that special magic to make a marriage last forever. And she wanted that—one man, one marriage, forever.

"I left my ring in that room they kept me in," she said, trying to think of something else.

"Doesn't matter. I'll buy you another one."

She didn't have any strength left to deal with Colin and everything she was feeling about their relationship. She turned away. "I need to rest."

"Sure. I'll come back later." He kissed her cheek, but she didn't respond.

When he left, she began to cry. Tears ran down her cheeks to her neck and gown and she didn't try to stop them. She cried for everything that had happened, for all the changes in her life and the changes that were to come.

And she cried for Eli.

CHAPTER FIVE

ELI WOKE UP FEELING strange. His right arm was on fire and it took a moment for everything to come rushing back. He was in a room, attached to machines. Good God, was he dying? Turning his head, he glanced at his arm. It was bandaged and looked as big as a log. How bad was it? he wondered.

Tuck was sitting in a chair with his long legs stretched out in front of him, his hands folded across his chest, his head against the back of the chair. He was asleep. Tuck could fall asleep anywhere. Eli had teased him about that for years. He was never so glad to see anyone in his life.

Eli moved his legs and Tuck was instantly on his feet. Another thing about Tuck—he was a light sleeper.

"How are you?" Tuck ran both hands through his hair in a nervous gesture.

"Did they arrest him?" he asked instead of answering. He was surprised his voice sounded so hoarse, but then he remembered the anesthesiologist saying something about putting a tube down his throat.

"Yeah. They arrested Buford and his followers."

"Good," Eli murmured, and drifted back to sleep.

When he woke up again, he wasn't feeling so strange. Tuck was still there and got to his feet when Eli opened his eyes.

"You're awake," he said, coming to the bed.

"Yes," Eli replied, his throat still dry. "You said they arrested Buford?"

"Sure did. They were sitting around a campfire praying when we arrived. The FBI called for a bus and they went peacefully. One of the dogs got out of control and attacked an agent and the dog was shot. The other dogs are at the pound and they've been checked out. They're clean, so you don't have to worry about that. But they'll probably be put down because they've been trained to kill."

"What about the dark-haired woman called Jezebel?"

"She can't remember anything before Buford's followers picked her up on the street. Child Protective Services is helping with the children, and several other agencies have been called in to help. The FBI is making sure Jezebel gets help, too."

"Good. Did forensics get all the evidence they needed from that secret room?"

"No."

"Why?"

"There wasn't a room when we got there."

"What the hell are you talking about?" Eli moved in agitation but quickly calmed himself when pain shot through his arm.

"The vegetable cellar was caved in and the ground leveled. All the jars of vegetables were stacked against one of the huts. They scattered chicken feed and goat feed over the area and the animals were busy scratching and eating. I'm not sure how they did that so fast, but obviously it was built that way—to cave in easily."

"Buford's a smart son of a bitch."

"Not smart enough this time," Tuck said. "Caroline

Whitten is alive and the feds are hoping to make a case on her testimony and yours."

Eli shifted uneasily, needing to move, but his body wasn't cooperating. "How is Caroline?"

"She's fine. Tom and Bill have been getting her account of the events and they said she's doing very well."

Eli listened to the humming of the machines in the room as the things Tuck had told him ran through his mind.

"You know, Tuck, that's what Buford did when he held Ginny captive. She said she was kept in a secret room, but the police could never find it. He caved it and the evidence in, and the police couldn't prove she wasn't making it up."

"I thought about that, too, but I don't think anyone's going to doubt Ms. Whitten."

"He chose the wrong woman to kidnap for his next wife," Eli said, then grew silent.

Tuck watched him. "You got him, Eli. He's not getting off this time."

"That doesn't bring Ginny back."

"But it makes me feel a hell of a lot better, and I know you do, too."

"I'd feel better if Ginny was here," he said quietly.

"Eli…"

"I've been obsessed with this for a decade. Ten years I've been waiting to get him, and my life has slowly slipped by. I'll be forty-two years old and I should have a wife and a family. A man should have a family."

"You have a family."

"I'm not talking about you," Eli snapped.

"I wasn't, either," Tuck retorted. "I was talking about the McCains."

"Well, you can forget that. I'm talking about my own family—a wife and kids. I've been holding on to Ginny's memory and I haven't even looked at other women or even wanted to, but it's time to let her go, to let her rest in peace. I think I can do that now."

"Because Buford is behind bars?"

"Partly. But when I was waiting for them to take me into the operating room, I felt alone—really alone. It would have been damn good to have someone special with me. And before you say anything, I'm not talking about you or the McCains. I'm talking about a woman, someone I can touch instead of someone in my head."

"I think I'll go see if I can find out what they did to the Eli I know, because you're not talking like the one I grew up with—the man who never needed anyone or anything."

"They say trauma changes people. Maybe I'm changing." He glanced at Tuck. "Don't you want to get married? Have kids?"

Tuck's face tightened. "I'm never getting married."

Eli had heard this many times. "Because you don't know who your parents are isn't going to matter to someone who loves you. Ma and Pa were your parents in every way that matters."

Tuck scratched his head, watching Eli. "We're getting in a little deep here. Is that medicine they gave you triggering some deep thinking, or is it Caroline Whitten?"

Eli frowned. "Why would you say that?"

"She was holding on to you on the road, and I could see it affected you."

"I saw what Buford did to her. That's all."

"If you say so."

They were silent.

"Aren't you going to ask about your arm?" Tuck queried in a cautious voice.

"Why? Is there something I should know?"

Tuck smiled. "Okay. Now the old Eli is back. For a minute there I was worried."

"So what's the verdict?" he asked, not able to put it off any longer. He had to know.

"Dr. Stiles said the surgery went fine. He was able to repair everything, but you're not going to be able to use your arm for a while."

"Like hell." He raised himself up from the bed and the room swayed. He lay back. Oh, he hated this. He knew he wasn't going to be a nice person to be around for the next while. He'd never been weak and he didn't like the feeling. Nor did he welcome it. "I need to see Tom and Bill."

"They're waiting to talk to you. I'll go get them."

Eli took a long breath, trying to deal with this situation. He'd gotten Buford, he kept telling himself. That was worth a little pain, discomfort and helplessness.

Tuck came back. "Bill's taking a call, then they'll be in."

"When can I get out of here?"

"The doctor will check you this afternoon and if everything looks good, he'll take you off these machines. In the morning he'll check your arm, and if it still looks good, he said you can go home."

"Good."

"But you have to recuperate, take it easy and not use your arm."

"Not until I'm finished with this case," Eli said, his eyes narrowed.

"Talking is about all you'll be able to do," Tuck pointed out. "So tomorrow after they release you, I'll take you out to the ranch and you can recuperate there."

"I'm not living with you. I'm used to living alone and I like it that way."

"You just said you didn't want to be alone."

"What the hell do I know? I'm on medication."

Tuck laughed. "When Tom and Bill get here, I'll head to the ranch to get things ready."

"I'm not staying with you," Eli insisted with a touch of anger. "You'll mother me to death. I know you." He grimaced as he tried to shift around in the bed. "Besides, I want to stay close, to keep tabs on what's happening."

"Then I'll go clean up your apartment," Tuck said, not deterred for a second. "Although I might need a face mask to do that."

"Stay out of my apartment. When I leave here, I'll be walking and driving, and I don't need someone to fuss over me. I can take care of myself."

"Oh, yeah." Tuck grinned. "The old Eli is back."

Tom and Bill walked in and Eli wanted to sit up. He fumbled with his left hand until he found the controls on the bed. He pushed a button to raise himself.

Tuck and the agents watched, but didn't offer to help. They knew better.

"Is there anything you'd like me to bring you to eat?" Tuck asked as he reached for his hat.

"A thick, juicy hamburger."

"That ought to clog those arteries right up," Tuck said, going out the door.

Tom and Bill took seats.

"How are you feeling?" Bill asked.

"Ready to get out of here," Eli replied.

"Yeah." Bill pulled out a pad and pencil. "The doctors and nurses feel the same way."

"I don't know what they're talking about. I've been a model patient." Eli was surprised he could say that with a straight face because he knew he'd been a pain in the ass.

"Yeah, right," Tom said. "Now let's get down to facts. Do you feel up to telling us what happened?"

"Damn right I do." For the next thirty minutes he told them everything, trying not to leave out any small detail. "When Buford, Ruth and Samuel were talking outside Buford's quarters that night, Buford said to kill Ms. Whitten and dispose of her body like the others. I believe there are young women who didn't succumb to the brainwashing, or died in that room. They could be buried on the property."

"We'll check it out," Tom said.

"He gave orders to kill Ms. Whitten—is that why you didn't get out and call us first? Is that why you decided to take her with you?" Bill started firing questions.

"Yes. Buford said to kill her before dawn, and that only gave me a few hours. I didn't know how long it would take me to get out, what with the dogs and the fence. I wasn't taking a chance of us coming back and finding her dead. And I didn't know exactly where Caroline was. They were preparing for a wedding—even Buford told me that. The dark-haired woman whispered a clue to me at dinner, so I knew for sure that Caroline was in the cellar somewhere. When Buford said Caroline had to be killed, that didn't leave me much choice."

"You did a great job," Bill said.

"Why do you say it like that?" Eli couldn't miss the hesitation in his voice.

"Only because Buford is telling a much different story."

Eli's eyebrows rose. "And you believe him?"

"Hell no," Bill replied. "But it might have been easier for us if you had emphasized your personal interest in this a little more."

"Personal interest?"

"Ginny Barker."

Eli frowned. "So? You knew I investigated Buford because of her murder."

"She was your fiancée, though, and now I'm thinking we should have taken that into consideration."

"Why?"

"Because things are going to get rather sticky."

Eli clenched the bed rail with his left hand, feeling the anger rising inside him. "The congressman wanted you to find his daughter and I wanted to get something on Buford. I did everything within the confines of the law and within my ethics as a ranger. If you guys have a problem with that, then—"

"Hey." Bill stopped him. "I just want you to be prepared."

"For what?"

"For a lot of questions."

"I can handle that," Eli told him.

Tom joined in. "You haven't heard Buford's story."

"Which is?"

"He says he met Ms. Whitten while she was taking pictures, and she later asked to become a part of their faith. His men went to get her as she requested, and she agreed to go through the ritual of fasting and isolation to rid her body of the poisons of society. When she was brought out to meet the flock, you became infatuated with her and later removed Ms. Whitten from isolation against her will and fled with her. They were praying for your soul when we arrived."

Eli forced down his angry retort. "And you're buying this story?"

"No way in hell," Tom said. "But that's what we meant by being prepared. Once Buford learns you have a personal interest in getting him, he'll milk it for all it's worth and so will his lawyer."

"Who is—?"

"No one, yet," Tom answered. "He refused counsel, saying he had nothing to hide and could speak for himself. But that's going to change—probably by this afternoon."

"The Wessell family."

"Yeah." Tom looked surprised. "You know them?"

"I have two cardboard boxes in my office with files on Amos Buford. His first wife, Cynthia, the only one he's legally married to, lives in Dallas with their four children. Buford's father was a Baptist preacher, and when he passed away Buford tried to take over the congregation with his weird religious beliefs. He was asked to leave. He did so without his wife and children.

"He took up residence in a small town outside Houston and met Ruth Wessell. She and Buford became involved and he performed his own marriage ceremony. He's not licensed to do that, but that didn't stop Buford. He makes his own laws and finds people to follow him. He and his followers never stay long in one place because they're always asked to leave."

Eli took a breath. "The Wessell family has money, and they tried to get Ruth away from him, but never succeeded. Over the years they've given Ruth money, hoping she'd come home. Instead Buford courted Ruth's sister, Naomi, and she became his second wife in his so-called faith. The Wessells kept giving the women money—money that Buford took. He bought the land in the hills with Wessell money, and I'm sure the Wessells will be here to post their daughter's bail."

"Yes," Bill told him. "We've already gotten the call. According to Ms. Whitten, Ruth is the only person she saw besides Buford, and the two men who abducted her. Ruth will probably be the only woman charged. We've contacted the families of the other women and they were glad to hear their daughters were alive, but they were shocked at the situation. Four were runaways—one seventeen, two eighteen and one nineteen. They'll be released into the custody of their parents. The other women will also be released to family members."

"What about Jezebel?"

"The people at the hospital have changed her name to Jane Doe for their records. We're keeping her away from the others and she's talking very little. She's afraid, but we're not sure of what. The men, women and children are all telling the same story as Buford—that Ms. Whitten was there of her own free choice and you took her against her will." Bill glanced at Eli. "They all say that Ms. Whitten's isolation was in Buford's home, not a dark room."

"Goddammit." The curse erupted from his throat. "And, of course, there is no room."

"No," Bill said. "But we have people out there digging, trying to find evidence that there was."

Eli shook his head. "Buford is good at covering his tracks, but you can't let him get away with this."

"We're trying," Tom stated. "It's just startling how all these people tell the same story verbatim, even the kids."

"What about Jezebel—I mean Jane Doe. Damn, couldn't they've come up with something better?"

"We're hoping to identify her, but she won't talk. When she does, she says she doesn't know anything, and she always looks at the table, not at us."

"All the women are like that," Eli said. "Buford has demoralized them and they take it. The ones that didn't are dead."

"Yes." Tom got to his feet. "Now we have to build a case

against him, and the congressman is pushing for a speedy trial."

"Have you told Caroline all this?" Eli asked.

"Yes." Bill said, also standing. "We just came from her room, and she's taking it very well. As long as yours and Ms. Whitten's stories match, the prosecutor feels he can get an indictment. Ms. Whitten knows that and she's being optimistic. She's a very strong person."

"Yes," Eli murmured. He wanted to ask how she was physically, but he wouldn't. Caroline would be fine—now that she was away from Buford and his clan.

"Someone from the prosecutor's office will be by to get a full statement, but then you know the drill."

"We'll talk to you later." Bill shook Eli's left hand, as did Tom. "Don't be too hard on the nurses."

Eli lay back and thought about this development. He wasn't surprised. He should have known that Buford wasn't going to make this easy. Eli hoped Caroline stayed strong, because she had to testify and put Buford away. He had to get better fast to help with this investigation—to help Caroline.

Whoa! Where had that thought come from? He wasn't sure. His job was to help build a solid case against Buford.

And that was all.

"ARE YOU OKAY?"

"Sure." Caroline answered her sister for the third time. "Why do you keep asking me that?"

"You seem a little down since the FBI agents were here yesterday."

She was better, but the terror was still there. She was trying to deal with it, for the present, the future and the trial. "I just keep thinking that Amos Buford is not going to get away with what he did to me. Not like he got away with killing Eli's fiancée."

"You don't know anything about that case."

"I know what Eli told me, and he's a man who doesn't lie."

"Caroline," Grace sighed. "You don't know anything about Ranger Coltrane, either."

"He risked his life to save mine—that's all I need to know."

"Okay. I'm not going to argue with you. I'll leave that to Mom and Dad." Grace picked up a suitcase. "I brought your things. Do you want to change out of that hospital gown?"

"Yes." She swung her feet over the edge of the bed and sat up, glad her sister wasn't going to argue. Grace couldn't possibly understand what she was feeling.

Her sister pulled a lavender negligee out of the case.

Caroline's eyebrow shot up. "Why did you bring that?"

"It was in your drawer and I just grabbed several things." Grace looked at it. "What's wrong with it?"

"Didn't you notice that it's very revealing?"

"No. Not at the time. I just wanted to get out of your place. It had an eerie feel about it and I don't think you should go back there."

Caroline fingered the lavender silk. "I bought this to wear when Colin and I went to Houston for the opening of his new store. We planned to stay a week, and I was going to say yes about getting married as soon as we could."

"And now?"

"Now I can't see myself marrying him at all."

"Caroline, don't do something you'll regret," Grace warned. "You've been through a horrendous ordeal. Give yourself some time and talk to Colin."

She didn't need time. She knew what she wanted—someone to love her the way Eli loved his Ginny, and until she found that she wasn't marrying anyone. But she wouldn't tell her sister that. Grace was a very practical person and she didn't believe in happily ever after. Caroline did, and she would find the perfect love—one day.

She slipped the gown over her head and quickly reached for the robe to cover herself.

"I see what you mean," Grace said. "It is very revealing, but the robe covers you up."

"Yes. I guess it will do."

"I don't even own a gown like that," Grace said out of the blue.

Caroline eyed her sister, whose life, she knew, revolved around her career and their father's law firm. Grace had never tapped into her feminine side, and Caroline wasn't sure if she ever would. She made a mental note to spend more time with Grace.

"When I get home, you can have this one," Caroline said.

"Please." Grace rolled her eyes. "Where would I wear it?"

"To bed."

"No, thank you. I'm comfy with my cotton gowns."

Caroline wagged her head. "We're going to work on you."

Grace lifted her chin. "No, we're not. I have better things to do than to waste my time."

Grace handed her a hairbrush and Caroline began to brush her hair, letting the subject drop.

She was surprised that her hands were so much better. The bandages were off, with just a few strips over the deeper cuts. The bandages on her feet were also mostly gone. For a couple of days she was supposed to walk only when necessary. After that, the doctor said, she would be fine.

"Are you sure you're okay with me staying at your place?" Caroline asked. She couldn't go back to her apartment just yet, and she wasn't going to Washington.

"Yes. I'm positive. I guess I should warn you, though."

Caroline stopped brushing. "About what?"

"Mom and Dad are on the way up, and Dad's hired a nurse and a bodyguard. Mom has also booked some sessions for you with a therapist." She took a deep breath before adding, "That's their concession in letting you stay here."

Caroline didn't have time to respond, for just then their parents came into the room. Joanna came over to her. "Oh, darling, you're looking so much better."

"Thank you, Mom."

"Your father and I have to fly back to Washington and we've made some arrangements for you."

"There's no need," she answered in a stiff voice. "I'm capable of making my own arrangements."

"We know you are." Joanna stroked her arm. "But we'd feel better knowing you're in good hands. We've hired some people to take care of you—that way we won't worry."

Caroline chewed on the inside of her lip. When she'd been in that awful room, all she'd wanted was to see her parents, to talk to them. That urge had grown out of fear. Out of her guilt, too. She'd learned a long time ago, though, that talking to her parents was like trying to touch the sun—impossible. And she usually got burned in the process.

"I don't need a nurse. I'm able to take care of myself, but if it will put your mind at rest, then by all means hire the guard."

"Thank you, darling," her mother said, reaching into her

purse and pulling out some appointment cards. "A therapist will help you to deal with this. Dr. Roland will come to Grace's condo. Everything's been arranged."

Caroline took the cards. *Don't get angry. Don't get angry,* she kept repeating to herself.

Her father stepped closer. "If you need anything, just call."

"I will," she replied, but she knew she wouldn't. Her parents didn't understand her and she didn't understand them. She loved them, but had nothing in common with them. They wanted to make sure she was taken care of—she understood that. But she wondered if they ever thought that she might need them, their love and time, and not some stranger's.

Her mother hugged her. "I'll call tonight."

Stephen hugged her, too. "I've spoken with the prosecutor and he said this could be a long, drawn out trial. I've also spoken with Hal Gooden, a criminal attorney, and he will help you with your testimony."

She gritted her teeth. "I don't need help."

"Don't be naive, Caroline." Stephen's voice rose. "To get this man you have to know what to say and when to say it."

"I—" Grace squeezed her hand and Caroline bit her tongue. Grace hated confrontations with their father, and today Caroline couldn't deal with it, either. She just wanted to be left alone.

"I'll do whatever I have to to convict Amos Buford."

"Good girl." Stephen patted her shoulder and soon their parents were gone.

Caroline looked at Grace. "Go get a wheelchair, please."

Grace reached for her purse. "You want to go to the coffee shop or to the cafeteria?"

"I want to go visit Eli."

"What?" One of Grace's eyebrows almost disappeared into her hairline.

"Go get the chair or I'll walk to his room," she threatened, knowing that was the only way to get Grace's cooperation. "I have to see how he is—with my own eyes."

Grace slung her purse over her shoulder. "You're becoming obsessed with this man."

"Until you've been held in a dark room for four days and nights with occasional bread and water, you don't have a right to judge my actions. At the very least, I owe the man a polite inquiry about his health."

Grace flounced to the door, then turned back. "I hope this isn't going to be a pattern of our living together—you giving orders and expecting me to obey them."

Caroline held up her right hand. "I'll be a docile roommate."

"Uh-huh."

Caroline smiled as her sister disappeared out the door. The smile soon faded.

What would she say to Eli? She knew he didn't want to hear another thank-you or any questions about his health. So what could she say? *And in this ridiculous negligee.* Oh God. She'd forgotten what she had on. She was still going, though. Grace thought she was acting irrationally and she probably was.

But she was going.

CHAPTER SIX

ELI SAT ON THE EDGE of the bed, his bandaged arm in a sling. He was dressed and ready to go. It took a few minutes to get his boots on, but he managed. Tuck grumbled the whole time, and Eli was glad he was going back to his apartment. He'd been on his own ever since he graduated from college and started working for the Department of Public Safety. Injured or not, he wasn't about to let someone mother him now—even Tuck.

Tuck had also left home, but returned when Pa died so Ma wouldn't be alone. She'd complained a lot about him doing that, but Tuck did it anyway. The house wasn't far from his office and it worked out well.

When Ma passed, Tuck continued to stay at the ranch. The house was his and the land had been split between him and Tuck years ago. Eli had planned to build a home on his land for him and Ginny, but that was before Pa and Ma had died. They'd loved Ginny and he'd wanted her to be close to them when he was away. Those plans never materialized and he'd never build that home.

He was thinking about family and he wasn't sure why. He was basically a loner and always would be. Maybe it was the medication.

"The nurse is bringing a wheelchair," Tuck said, zipping up an overnight bag.

"A wheelchair!"

Tuck turned to him. "It's hospital policy. You're not going to be difficult about this, are you?"

"I might."

"Let me put it to you this way." Tuck drew in a deep breath. "I'm wearing a gun and you're not."

"Point taken." Eli tried not to grin because Tuck was so serious. He and Tuck were closer than any two brothers and they knew each other so well. Tuck knew that Eli's pride sometimes flared up, but it never got in the way of doing what was right. Being a ranger kept him focused on that.

Someone tapped at the door.

"Ah. There's the nurse now," Tuck said, then called, "Come in."

Eli watched as a wheelchair was rolled in, but it wasn't empty. A woman was in it—a very beautiful woman with blond hair and green eyes.

Caroline. His stomach tightened. What was she doing here?

He found he couldn't look away. She wore a lavender silky thing and her skin glowed and her eyes sparkled. She didn't resemble in the least the terrified woman he'd rescued from Buford.

"Ms. Whitten." Tuck stepped forward, shook her hand gently and echoed Eli's own thoughts. "You look great—nothing like the woman I saw the other day."

"Thank you. I feel much better." Her soft voice played over Eli and he could almost feel her touching his skin. "This is my sister, Grace."

"Nice to meet you, ma'am," Tuck said. "I'm Jeremiah Tucker. Everyone calls me Tuck."

"Why?" Grace asked, her frown adding emphasis to the rudely spoken word.

Tuck seemed taken aback for a second. "That's the nickname my father gave me and it stuck."

Eli could see that the women looked a lot alike, but the sister was uppity—that's what Ma would call her. From Tuck's expression, it was clear he felt the same way.

"I'm sorry," Grace said when she realized her faux pas. "It's really none of my business."

That's what Eli was thinking, until his brain went haywire as Caroline's eyes caught his.

"I wanted to come by and see how your arm was."

Eli clenched his left hand. "It's fine," he said in a low voice. "I'm going home this morning."

"Yes. I guessed that from your clothes. I'm hoping the doctor will release me tomorrow." Caroline took in every facet of his appearance, from his longish brown hair to his clean-shaven face and gorgeous blue eyes. She felt she knew his strong body very well. At night when the darkness surrounded her and a suffocating feeling engulfed her, she'd think of his strength and she'd calm down.

His lips were tight, his expression closed, telling her he did not appreciate this visit. In that instant she realized Grace was right—she was attaching too much importance to Eli. Clearly he did not want her thanks again. Now she had to make a graceful exit.

"How are the hands and feet?" he asked.

"Great. I should be walking in a couple of days."

"That's good."

"Yes. I'm very grateful I came out of this with only a few cuts and scratches."

They were talking stiltedly—like strangers, which was what they were.

"I'd better go," Caroline said, looking directly at him. "Thanks again."

His gaze didn't waver and though she saw something flicker in his eyes, he quickly disguised it. "You're welcome."

She bit her lip, wanting to get away. Grace turned the chair just as there was a knock on the door.

"Come in," Tuck called.

Three men walked into the room and everything became very quiet. Caroline caught a glimpse of Eli's dark face and knew he didn't want to see these men, either. They were all about the same height, with dark hair and eyes. One wore slacks and a pin-stripe shirt, one wore a suit and the other was a Texas Ranger. She knew that by the badge, gun, boots and light-colored hat. Who were these men? Why did Eli not want to see them?

The ranger held the door open and soon she and Grace were in the hall.

"I wonder who they are?" Caroline asked, looking at the door.

"It's none of our business," Grace said. "Let's go to the coffee shop. I could use a double mocha latte."

"Make that decaf," Caroline replied.

"Make it with a shot of bourbon."

Caroline smiled slightly at Grace's nervousness, but her thoughts were on Eli.

Who were those men?

TUCK SHOOK Jake McCain's hand. "It's good to see you. How's Ben?"

"Better than we ever expected. He's keeping up with the other kids in his class. Of course, Elise works with him constantly and she makes it fun so Ben doesn't even know it's work," Jake replied. He was the oldest brother and a farmer. He ran the farm that Joe McCain had—the farm that had been in the family for years.

"Your wife sure loves that little boy."

Eli clamped his lips tighter, letting their words go over his head. He didn't want to see the McCains, his half brothers. But obviously they'd taken it upon themselves to come anyway. That made him uncomfortable and angry.

He tried to block out the conversation, but found himself listening for news of Ben. Three years ago it had been an odd twist of fate that he'd been the one to help rescue Jake's son, who'd been kidnapped by Ben's biological mother. Ben was a preemie and had developmental problems, but Elise and Jake were working hard to help him overcome his difficulties.

From what Eli understood, Jake hadn't even known Ben existed until the boy was three years old. By then Jake had married Elise and they were planning their own family. Things were rocky for a while, but they'd worked out their problems.

Ever since the incident with Ben, Jake had been trying to contact him. Eli had sent back letters and ignored the phone calls. They might have the same father, but that didn't mean a hell of a lot to Eli. He had to get that across to the McCain brothers. Again.

"How's the new baby?" Tuck asked, and Eli wanted to hit him. Why was he being so damn friendly?

Jake smiled. "Katie holds my heart in the palm of her hand and she doesn't even know it."

"She has us all wrapped around her little finger." Beau spoke up, shaking Tuck's hand. He was a lawyer and the middle son of Althea and Joe McCain.

"You're a lucky man, Jake," Tuck said.

"We tell him that every day," Caleb said, also shaking Tuck's hand. Caleb was the youngest and a Texas Ranger. Eli had heard he'd been accepted, and wasn't pleased. He didn't want to deal with the McCains in his work. He just wanted them to stay out of his life.

"Congratulations on making the rangers." Tuck couldn't stop socializing.

"It's been a dream of mine for a long time and so far it's everything I thought it would be. I've been asked to help out with the Amos Buford case. They need investigators to help place some of the women back with their families." He looked at Eli. "When my brothers heard I was headed to Austin, they wanted to come and see how you were doing."

Jake took a step toward Eli. "I know we're invading your privacy, but we'll only stay a minute. How are you?"

"I'm fine," Eli mumbled.

"I never got the chance to thank you for what you did for Ben."

"It was a job." Eli stared at Jake, his eyes dark. "I told you that at the time."

He'd known this man since they were boys. They'd gone to the same school, in the same class, yet Jake never knew they were half brothers. Eli had. His mother made sure he knew, hoping that Joe McCain would one day leave his wife and kids and marry her.

Joe had used Vera as a diversion when he grew bored with his wife. As Eli grew older he saw what was happening, but his mother never did. She'd loved the man till the day she died.

As a young boy, Eli had rebelled and got into fights and trouble at school. It escalated to the point where he'd been facing juvenile hall. That's when his mother had called her uncle, Jess Tucker, and it was the best thing she'd ever done for him. He'd found a home and a family and it had saved him.

He'd left the McCains behind and he didn't want them

back in his life. He knew he was being hard-hearted, but it was the way he felt. Nothing was ever going to change that.

"Yes. You did." Jake broke through his reverie. "And I apologize for this intrusion." He took a step closer. "But you, Beau, Caleb and me are brothers bound by blood. I understand you have bad feelings about the past. I did, too. I had brothers I didn't know about until I was grown, because I believed in a father who didn't deserve my trust. But I learned to forgive. Without forgiveness there's not much happiness in this world. I learned that, too." He took a breath. "If you ever reach that point, you know where to find us. Hope your arm gets better soon."

The three men walked out.

Tuck shook his head in frustration. "I don't get it. Why do you hate them so much?"

Eli stood. "I'm ready to go."

"Yeah, Eli. Block it out. Ignore it. That helps a lot."

Eli glared at him. "If my right arm wasn't bandaged, I'd knock you on your ass."

Tuck blinked. "What the hell for?"

"For being you, dammit."

"That doesn't make sense. Who do you want me to be?"

Tuck was right. Eli wasn't making any sense. But he knew why he was angry. He wanted to be as friendly as Tuck had been to the McCains, but he couldn't. He couldn't just wipe out a past that had molded, shaped and scarred him, and become one of them. For the first time he wanted to, but he'd never be able to make that transition.

He took a long breath. "Just your aggravating self is enough."

"I think we need to write this down somewhere." Tuck

waved his hand, as if jotting something in the air. "Do not give Eli medication. It makes him crazy."

Before Eli could respond, a nurse came in with a wheelchair, and within minutes they were on the way to Eli's apartment. When Eli walked through the door, he stopped short. The place was immaculate—not how he had left it.

"You couldn't resist, could you?"

"Nope."

He sank onto the sofa. "I'm not even going to get angry."

"That's a first." Tuck carried the overnight bag into the bedroom. "I stocked the refrigerator, so you're set for a few days."

"I'm going to work in the morning."

Tuck hurried into the living room. "Does the captain know this?"

"He hasn't told me not to."

"He told you to recuperate. I'm not sure what that means to you, but to everyone else it means stay at home and rest."

"I can't," Eli said. "I have to help with this investigation."

"The attorneys and the FBI will handle it now."

"I can still help them. Buford is saying Caroline was there of her own free will and I can't let him get away with that."

"They'll sort it out," Tuck insisted.

"Not without my testimony."

Tuck sighed in frustration. "A ranger has to be physically fit to perform his duties to the best of his ability. You're not even in the ballpark, so take the rest you need."

Eli glared at him. "Dammit, I'm not going into a gun battle. I'm just planning on finishing my paperwork so the FBI can have all the information they need to nail this case shut."

"You can't use your hand," Tuck pointed out.

Eli gritted his teeth. "I can dictate."

"Once a ranger, always a ranger." Tuck muttered the familiar ranger saying. "Just take it slow and easy." He sat in a chair facing Eli, propping his feet on the coffee table. As particular as Tuck was, he'd still do things like that. It was incongruous for a man who took such good care of everything. "You haven't said anything about Ms. Whitten's visit."

"She has a very uptight sister."

Tuck laughed out loud. "Yeah. Grace Whitten is wound tighter than an eight day clock. Caroline is different, though. She seems very nice."

Eli didn't say anything.

"Click. The shutters close," Tuck said.

Eli frowned. "What the hell are you talking about?"

"Whenever I mention her name, that's what you do—shut her out of your thoughts."

"Tuck…"

"You said you were ready to let Ginny go. Well, this is how you start—by admitting you feel something for Caroline. I'm not saying it's love, but it's interest and it's something to build on."

"She's a witness on a case I'm working," Eli reminded him. "That's it. Anything else would be unethical on my part."

"She's also going through a rough time and could use a little understanding."

Eli's frown deepened. "Don't you have to go to work?"

"Yes." Tuck set a small bottle on the table. "I had the

prescription filled for pain pills. You might need them to-night."

"I won't."

"Want me to help with your boots before I leave?"

"No."

"Anything you want me to do?"

"Go to work," Eli growled. "And stop annoying the hell out of me."

Tuck stood. "I'll bring something back for supper."

"No," he snapped. "Go back to your life and stop fussing over me. I can take care of myself. If I need anything, you'll be the first person I call."

"Okay." Tuck headed for the door, but turned back. "Did you notice the hurt look on Caroline's face when you treated her as if she was contagious?"

"No. I didn't notice a thing."

"You're lying."

"Go to work before I—"

"I'm gone." The door slammed shut.

Eli rested his head against the sofa and tried to erase the image in his head, but it wouldn't go away. He saw Caroline's face clearly and the hurt look in her eyes. The memory curled his stomach into a knot and he cursed himself. But how was he supposed to have acted? He couldn't see him and Caroline becoming friends or much of anything else.

Besides Ma and Pa, Ginny was the only person who'd understood him. She'd accepted his bad moods and rough edges and loved him in spite of them. She knew he carried deep wounds from his childhood that kept him shackled to a past that controlled his emotions. And she'd loved him anyway. She'd made him laugh and...

He closed his eyes, trying to see her face, but all he saw was Caroline.

Dammit. This was crazy. He hardly knew the woman. Dammit.

GRACE FLUFFED PILLOWS and hovered around Caroline. "Do you need anything else?"

"No, Grace. I have everything I need," Caroline said, propped up on the sofa with her laptop, books, phone and TV control. Magazines were displayed in an orderly fashion on the coffee table.

"You don't have to worry. The guard is outside the door."

"I know."

Grace watched her. "Are you still upset?"

"About what?" Caroline looked up from flipping through a photo magazine.

Grace heaved a sigh. "About Ranger Coltrane not being too friendly yesterday."

She laid down the magazine. "That's just Eli." She brushed it off, but she was hurt and wasn't hiding it well.

"If you say so," Grace said. "I was just glad to get out of there. I can't believe I spoke so rudely."

"You were a bit tactless."

"When Ranger Coltrane's friend said his name, I immediately questioned it and I'm not sure why. I'm not usually that blunt. But Jeremiah is a very beautiful name and if I ever see him again I'm calling him that."

"I don't think you have to worry about seeing Tuck again. He'll probably stay as far away from you as possible."

Grace grimaced. "I seem to have that effect on men."

"Not Byron Coffey."

Byron was senior partner in the law firm, and since his wife had passed away, he'd taken an interest in Grace.

She rolled her eyes. "Please. He's twenty years older than me."

"But he has a big crush on you. I've noticed that when I've visited you at your office. He's always hanging around being nice and helpful."

"Yes. But I can handle it."

"Just relax a little and have some fun," Caroline advised. "You're too structured." She waved a hand around the room. "There's nothing out of place in this apartment. There's not even any trash in the trash cans or dishes in the sink or dishwasher. I'm going to drive you nuts in a week. I like clutter."

"I'm aware of that. There are photos all over your apartment. Do you ever put them away?"

"Yes. I have a filing cabinet, but sometimes I like to look at them for a while to see if I can improve the shot."

"You really love photography, don't you?"

Before Caroline could answer, Grace glanced at her watch. "I've got to get back to the office or Byron will be calling."

"Dad made you head of the law firm, so why would Byron be calling you?"

Grace picked up her purse. "He's been with Dad for many years and I respect his place in the firm." She slipped her purse over her shoulder. "Do you need anything?"

"Go to work, Grace."

"Call if you need anything." She hurried to the door as the doorbell rang.

Caroline heard Colin's voice. She clenched her jaw, not wanting to see him but knowing she had to.

Colin came in and kissed her forehead. "How are you?" he asked, sitting at the end of the sofa.

"Better."

Colin was blond and blue-eyed—more boyish than handsome. He was sharp and intelligent, a stickler for quality and detail, yet he was very patient with her idiosyncrasies. She'd loved that about him. She tried to dredge up that feeling but it wasn't there anymore. His going to Houston without knowing if she was dead or alive had killed the feelings she had for him. She was aware that she was still experiencing an emotional upheaval, but she knew without a doubt that she and Colin could not get back what they'd once had.

He ran his hand up her shin. "You're upset with me. I understand that, but I was going crazy not knowing who had you or what they were doing to you. I had to get away."

"I know." She took a deep breath, pulling her leg away from his hand. "Now I'll tell you how I feel. If you really loved me, you would have been thinking more about me than yourself. You would have stayed in touch with the police, with my family, and you would've wanted to be there when they found me—whether I was dead or alive. That's what love is and that's how I want to be loved—by someone who'll put me first just like I would put him first. We don't have that type of commitment. I'm not sure we ever did."

He paled. "Don't say that. You've been through so much. You just need some time."

She shook her head. "No. I don't need any time. I know how I feel."

"I won't accept this. I can't." He stood. "I have to go to Houston for a few days. When I get back, we'll talk again."

She wasn't getting through to him and she didn't want to hurt him. But he wasn't leaving her much choice. "We won't talk again. I'm sorry, but it's over."

He stared at her as if he couldn't believe what he was

hearing. "I'll call you when I get back." Saying that, he walked out of the room.

"Colin," she called, but he didn't stop.

She curled up on the sofa and wanted to cry, but she wouldn't. Their relationship was over and he had to accept that. She had. A tear trickled down her cheek and she brushed it away, feeling weak and tired. They'd made so many plans, and they were over, too.

Right now she had to concentrate on her testimony and the trial ahead. She had an appointment with the federal prosecutor to go over her story. She was sure Eli had to do the same thing. Would she see him? Probably not, and that was for the best. She had to put her life back together—by herself, without Grace or her parents. Without Eli's help.

A couple of days were all she planned to stay with Grace, then she'd return to her place. Her life. With all that had happened, it was hard to focus on anything. Fear was her constant companion.

As much as she tried to push Eli from her thoughts, he was always there. She wasn't sure why he'd been so cool when she visited him, but reminded herself that they were strangers, as she'd admitted to herself in his room. He was just doing a job; he'd told her that. But she felt a connection to him she couldn't explain. He'd saved her life and she couldn't forget that.

And she couldn't forget Eli.

CHAPTER SEVEN

THE NEXT DAY Eli went to Dr. Stiles's office to have his arm checked.

"Everything looks good," the doctor said. "How's the pain?"

"I can handle it."

"Are you taking the pills?"

"No."

Dr. Stiles grunted. "I'm not sure why I asked. Just be careful with the arm and watch for excess bleeding."

"Will do," Eli said, and left to go to work. He spent most of the day going over details of the case with Tom and Bill, who constantly badgered him to go home. By five o'clock he was drained and finally did so. He fell into an exhausted sleep, hating that he felt so weak.

For the next few days, he paced himself and knew he was getting better. The doctor removed the stitches and Eli started therapy, but he never lost sight of the Buford case. It was the main reason he was doing so well. Tuck said it was his stubborn pride. Whatever the reason, Eli wanted to help the FBI close up all the loopholes.

Herbert and Cora Wessell arrived in Austin with Emory Lansing, a high-powered defense attorney. Lansing had Ruth and her sister, Naomi, out of jail in a matter of hours. Ruth talked her father into hiring Lansing to defend Buford, but getting Buford released wouldn't be so easy. Lansing had a lot of tricks up his sleeve, however, and Eli knew they had to be ready.

Most of the other women and their children had been turned over to their families. They would still be available for questioning, though. Two eighteen-year-old runaways and their four children were left. Their families didn't want them back and Child Protective Services had found a place for them to stay.

The woman now called Jane Doe had been moved to a hospital for a thorough examination. Caleb was handling her case. Eli hadn't seen him, but since they were working the same case, he knew it was going to be hard to avoid him. He could keep their relationship professional, though.

Why? That little word hung in his mind, demanding an answer—an honest answer. He wanted family—Caleb was family. But Eli wasn't ready.

There wasn't anything he couldn't handle. Pa had told him that. But Ginny's murder had been the first dent in that armor of strength. Ma and Pa's deaths had been another. Now it was his arm. Little by little, life's blows were getting to him.

Again he wished he could be like Tuck, open and friendly, accepting of the hand that life had dealt him. But something in him wouldn't allow him to do that. Maybe he was protecting himself from another blow. Whatever it was, he felt better away from the McCains.

ELI MET WITH TOM AND BILL at the federal building.

"Has anyone had enough nerve to tell you that you shouldn't be working?" Bill asked.

"My captain is pressuring me," Eli replied. "But I'm not taking a break until we have all the loose ends tied up."

Bill and Tom exchanged a glance. "That might take awhile."

"What do you mean?"

"Buford and his men are sticking to their stories, and now that Lansing is involved, well, we need something to challenge Buford—something to make him slip up."

"Like what?"

"We were hoping you'd pay Buford a visit at the jail. When he sees you, he might become so enraged at what you'd done to free Ms. Whitten that he could slip up and say something to help our case."

"Buford is sharp and he's not going to make any slips." Eli didn't know why he was hesitating, but he didn't want to encounter Buford again unless it was in a courtroom.

"So you're not willing to help?" Bill waited for an answer.

What was the matter with him? He never took the easy way out. He usually faced everything head-on.

"No. I'll see him," Eli answered. "What do you want me to try and get him to say?"

"Admitting to Ms. Whitten's kidnapping would be great," Tom replied, tongue-in-cheek. "But we'll take anything that will shake his story."

"Okay. I'll head over to the jail now."

When he got there, the FBI had the visit already set up. Eli waited in a small room and they brought Buford in with handcuffs on. He still had long hair and a beard, but he now wore prison orange.

He sat across from Eli with a calm expression on his face—no anger, no emotion, but a faint smugness. "I forgive you, Brother Elijah," he said.

Eli was taken aback, but only for a second. "For what?"

"For betraying the prophet, but do not worry, my

brother. I have prayed for mercy for your soul. You did not know what you were doing."

Was he for real? Eli let him talk. It seemed to be what he wanted to do.

"You should have never taken the woman."

"I'm a Texas Ranger and I was there to find her because you had kidnapped her. You were going to kill her—that's why I took her." Eli looked directly into his cold gray eyes and saw nothing but a wasteland of hypocritical rhetoric.

"You took Mary because she was beautiful. You wanted her for yourself, but Mary knew her destiny. That's what you didn't understand, because you are so unwise in the ways of our faith. You did not know that we meant Mary no harm. You are forgiven, Elijah."

"Mary?"

"The seventh wife of the prophet. The one to bear the messiah who will bring peace to the world."

He was talking about Caroline. Evidently her name was to be Mary. Eli tried to gauge if Buford believed what he was saying or yanking his chain. He decided that Amos knew exactly what he was doing within the confines of that warped mind. The man was deluded, almost insane. He believed in his religious world, in himself and his purported powers—that's why he could convince people to follow him. The fact that he committed crimes in the name of God made everything all right in his eyes.

Eli leaned across the table. "Her name is Caroline Whitten and she doesn't want to be one of your wives or bear you anything."

"Elijah, you do not have faith."

"I have faith, Amos," Eli told him. "In my faith a woman has rights—she has the right to say no."

"You do not know of what you speak, but it doesn't matter. The prophecy will still be fulfilled. I will be released soon and my people will be back with me and we will carry on with our mission. We have been persecuted before, but we will triumph. It is God's will."

That was it. Amos was planning on convincing a jury of his persecution. He'd done it before and he was counting on doing it again.

Eli leaned back. "Or is it the prophet's will?"

Amos smiled. "Elijah, they are one and the same. Don't you realize that by now?"

"Yes, Amos. I do." He held his gaze. "How many other young women have you killed?"

"Many lives will be lost before the prophecy is fulfilled."

Eli stood before he actually hit the man. "No, Amos, you're wrong. No more lives will be lost. You'll be in jail for a very long time. I'll make sure of that. That's Elijah's will."

He walked out of the room feeling a small measure of victory. He wanted that victory for Ginny, and for Caroline.

In the hall, he met Tom and Bill. "He didn't budge on his testimony," Eli told them.

"Yeah. We heard," Tom said. Bill and Tom had listened to the whole conversation. "I'm sure Lansing's going for the insanity plea, and he'll be right on target."

Eli wasn't so sure. "He's very calm and I get the feeling Amos wants to tell his story to a jury so they can see a persecuted man. He's hoping to gain sympathy and he's counting on freedom."

"I just think he's insane and I'm sure Lansing does, too," Bill added.

"Amos has a psychology degree and he knows how to work the mind, how to get what he wants. He's very charismatic and he can play to a jury." Eli paused. "We need more proof. I know there are bodies on that property somewhere."

Tom sighed. "We have people checking—so far nothing. Right now we have to concentrate on the kidnapping charge. That's going to put him away for a while."

"Let's hope it turns out that way."

CAROLINE WALKED a little more each day and she was getting stronger. She was also trying to gain control of her life. She had a bit of an argument with her father when she dismissed the guard, but he eventually accepted her decision.

She spent most of the week settling in with Grace, which was an accomplishment in itself. Everything in the condo was neat and clean, as Grace liked it, but Caroline was miserable there. She couldn't be herself. Sometimes she didn't want to make the bed when she got out of it, sometimes she left her coffee cup on the table or in the den, and heaven forbid, she occasionally liked to put trash in a trash can. When she did, Grace immediately emptied it into the larger can in the garage.

Caroline was a guest in her sister's home, though, and she respected her wishes even if she thought they were off the wall at times. From an early age it was clear that she and Grace were different, but that didn't keep them from being close. Growing up, with their parents gone so much, they'd depended on each other. Caroline comforted Grace when she was afraid of the dark. Grace helped Caroline pass many tests by helping her study the night before. Grace was on the debating team while Caroline was on the tennis team, and when one sister had an event, the other never missed it.

Even though their father had pushed both of them to

study law, the choice had been right only for Grace. Caroline had seen her sister in a courtroom, and she was brilliant when she was fighting for someone else. She thrived on confrontation, except when it came to their father. It was hard to fight him—Caroline knew that well.

Maybe it was time she grew up. Maybe it was time she joined her father's firm and practiced law as he wanted her to. Then she'd be more miserable than ever and that would accomplish nothing.

She wandered around the apartment, going stir-crazy. She liked being outdoors and on the go. That's why she loved photography—it allowed her freedom and expression and excitement. But no one understood that—not even Colin. He didn't understand how she could get so sidetracked with a shoot that she'd forget their dinner date. That was a big clue about the problems in her relationship, one she hadn't seen before. They were not soul mates or she'd never forget a date, and if she did, he would try and understand.

Sitting on the sofa, she picked up the remote control and turned on the TV to a talk show. It featured a man caught between his wife and his mother. The wife complained that the mother interfered in their lives, and the mother complained that the daughter-in-law was selfish in not allowing her free time with her son.

"Get a life," Caroline said to the TV, and turned it off. How did women watch this every day? It was drivel. She got to her feet, feeling restless. It was time to go back to her own place. She was going nuts here.

She hurried to her room and grabbed a suitcase. Throwing a few things inside, she refused to listen to the voice in her head. But eventually she had to.

What about the night?

She wasn't afraid of the dark, but if she fell asleep and woke up in darkness, for a split second she was paralyzed with the memories of that underground room. Now she slept with the light on. And Grace was always near. When Caroline couldn't sleep, they watched movies until she drifted off. They talked, argued, laughed, forgave and loved like sisters. But she couldn't keep clinging to Grace. She had to go home and face her future.

She heard the front door open. "Caroline, where are you?"

"In the bedroom," she called.

Grace stopped in the doorway at the sight of the open suitcase. "What are you doing?"

"Packing."

She walked into the room in a navy suit, heels and pinned-up hair. "Are you sure about this?"

"No. But I'm going crazy." Caroline turned to her sister. "I have to get back my life."

"But you're still sleeping with the light on."

"I know." She sank onto the bed.

Grace sat beside her. "Give it a few more days."

"No. I have to do it now. I'll leave first thing in the morning."

"I'll miss you," Grace said in a weak voice. "It was nice coming home to someone."

Caroline wavered, but she had to do this. "I have an idea."

"What?"

"A man—you need a man in your life."

Grace grimaced. "I see men all day long and when I come home, I do not want to see another one."

"Then you're not seeing the right man."

"That'll never happen for me. You know how I am. No man will ever be able to put up with me." Grace smoothed her skirt. "When we were small and we'd go outside to play, you'd run around and get your dress all dirty. I wanted to do that, but I couldn't—just like I can't make myself change now."

"Sure you can," Caroline said. "You're older, wiser."

"I don't know."

Caroline grabbed her purse and pulled out the therapist's cards her mother had given her. She hadn't thought of them until now. She handed them to Grace. "Use these."

Grace looked horrified. "I can't."

"Why not?"

"I know what my problem is and I have to solve it myself."

"Okay, then." Caroline jumped up. "Let's do something you wouldn't normally do."

"Like what?"

"Let's eat spaghetti in your white living room, watching TV." Eating was not allowed in the living room.

Grace swallowed hard and looked at Caroline. "You don't think I can do that?"

She lifted an eyebrow. "Can you?"

Grace stood. "Yes. I'll change my clothes.'

Caroline caught her arm. "Don't do this with a knot in your stomach. Do it for fun—silly girl fun. Otherwise it will only make you ill."

Grace thought about it. "I don't think I've ever done anything silly." A grin spread across her face. "Except that time we were at Daddy's cabin on the lake and the boy next door was really cute. I put on my bikini and sunbathed."

Caroline remembered. "And he came over and talked to you, then you went swimming with him."

"We had a good time," Grace said, her eyes wistful.

"Yes. Sometimes you can have a good time by letting go."

"Then let's have spaghetti in my perfect, tastefully decorated living room." Grace headed for the door. "I'll change."

"Put on jeans and a T-shirt," Caroline called after her. "Get comfy."

Thirty minutes later they had the spaghetti ready—laughing like two ten-year-olds. Caroline carried the plates into the living room and placed them on the coffee table. "Mmm. I think we need some wine. A merlot maybe."

"Definitely a merlot." Grace was getting into it, but Caroline sensed her actions were forced. She was trying, though.

"I'll open it." Caroline popped the cork and poured two glasses. She handed Grace one and they settled on the sofa.

Caroline held up her glass. "Here's to change."

"Change," Grace murmured, and gulped down a big swallow.

After two glasses, Grace was laughing and so was Caroline. It felt good to be silly.

Caroline held up the empty bottle. "Someone drank all our wine."

Grace hiccupped. "I think we did."

"And not one drop on this white sofa."

"Yay." Grace held up her empty glass. "Here's to…what the hell are we toasting?"

"Beats me."

"Oh, Caro, I'm going to have a big headache tomorrow."

"Yeah."

Grace stretched out on the sofa. "Do you think we need to do the dishes?"

"Wow! You have had too much wine."

"Are there polka dots on the ceiling?"

Caroline glanced up. "I don't think so."

"Good." Grace snuggled into the sofa. "Caro?"

"Hmm?"

"Do you think I need to apologize to that man with the weird name?"

"You mean Tuck?"

"Yes. Jeremiah."

"Since we're never going to see the man again, I don't think another apology is necessary."

Grace didn't answer and Caroline knew she was asleep. She picked up the plates and carried them into the kitchen. Putting dishes in the dishwasher, she found a tear trickling down her cheek.

No, Grace, we'll never see Tuck or Eli again.

The thought made her very sad.

THE NEXT MORNING Caroline moved back to her apartment. She and Grace both had hangovers and it dulled the fear in her. Grace went to work as usual and they hugged tightly before Grace left. Caroline knew if things didn't work out at her own place, she could always come back.

But she wouldn't.

She spent the day cleaning and airing out the place. When she picked up her camera, she didn't feel the excitement she always did when she touched it. It would come back, though. She just needed time.

Tomorrow was her birthday and her parents were flying in to have lunch with her. She wasn't jittery. She knew she'd get another lecture on her irresponsible behavior, but she was prepared. Or numb. Trauma seemed to have that effect.

In the afternoon she had an appointment with the federal prosecutor, and she had another at two o'clock the next day. They'd gotten an indictment and now they were preparing for the trial.

Buford and his followers were sticking to their stories, and Caroline hoped a jury wouldn't believe them. That's what it would come down to—the decision of a jury.

She hoped she would see Eli, but she didn't. That was okay, too. She was moving forward.

Lunch with her parents and Grace went smoothly, mainly because her parents were on their cell phones most of the time. They gave her a day at a spa for her birthday and she thanked them, knowing she would use the gift. A day of pampering would be nice.

Grace gave her a bottle of merlot and a book of photos by a famous photographer. All in all her day was going well. She arrived for her meeting with the attorneys on time and spent two hours going over her testimony. They said they would get Buford and for her not to worry. She was worried, though.

She couldn't explain exactly about what. She just had an uneasy feeling. It had a lot to do with fear. If Buford's attorney persuaded a jury of his innocence, then "the prophet" would be a free man. Free to hurt other women. Free to hurt her again. That was a big part of her worries. How would she deal with that?

Distracted, she hurried down the hall and bumped into a solid wall of human flesh. She immediately started to apologize, but the words froze on her lips when she saw who it was.

"Eli." Her heart picked up speed as she took in his tall frame, cowboy boots and cream-colored Stetson. His hair was now cut short in traditional ranger style.

He tipped his hat. "Caroline."

"I'm sorry. I wasn't watching where I was going."

"It's okay," he said.

"I didn't hurt your arm, did I?" The bandage and sling were gone and there were strips of tape over the healing scars.

"No. I'm much tougher than that."

She knew that he was—as tough as they come.

"How is your arm?" she asked.

He flexed his fingers. "Better every day."

She saw the end of jagged cuts that would leave scars—a reminder of the day he'd rescued her from hell.

He glanced at her low heels. "Guess your feet have healed?"

"Oh, yes. I'm back to normal," she replied. "I've just been visiting with the attorneys."

"Then you're leaving?"

"Yes."

"I'll walk out with you."

That was a surprise. She'd thought he would make a point of getting away.

She smiled. "I'd like that."

They walked outside to a beautiful May day. The sun was shining, birds were singing and the magnificent colors of spring enhanced the landscape.

She turned to face him, her eyes centering on his badge. "I've never seen a Texas Ranger badge before." It was a circle with a cut out five-pointed star inside. His name was written across the top of the circle and Texas Rangers across the bottom. His rank—sergeant—was printed in the middle of the star.

He lightly touched it. "It's made from a Mexican five peso silver coin. The oak leaves on the left represent strength and the olive branch on the left signifies peace. The cut-out star symbolizes the Lone Star of Texas."

She heard the pride in his voice. "And it's worn over your heart as a sign of integrity and honor."

"Something like that."

"You're very proud to be a ranger, aren't you?"

"Yes. The most honest, decent man I ever knew was Jess Tucker. I wanted to be just like him. I'll never reach that goal, but I'm a better man for just having known him."

The wind blew Caroline's hair and she pushed it away from her face, thinking Eli was the best man *she'd* ever met.

"I feel as if I should thank you again, but I know you don't want to hear it."

"No. You've already covered that."

"But you saved my life and it's really hard for me to forget that."

There was that expression again—the closed one. The one she was beginning to recognize.

"At the very least let me buy you dinner." She rushed on before she could halt herself.

His expression didn't change, but it didn't stop her. "It's my birthday. You're not going to refuse me on my birthday, are you?"

His eyes narrowed slightly. "Aren't you eating with your fiancé?"

Was that it? He thought she was still engaged.

"Colin and I broke up."

"Oh. I'm sorry to hear that."

But he wasn't. She could see it in his eyes and his expression changed. Things were looking better.

She cocked her head to one side. "I bet you're a steak man."

His mouth twitched and it was the closest thing she'd ever seen to a smile on his face. "You'd be right."

"Then do we have a date?"

"Okay." He glanced at his watch. "I have to go back to my office, but I can pick you up in about an hour."

"Or I can pick you up?"

The twitch became more noticeable. "I drive. I always drive. I don't make a very good passenger."

"Then you can pick me up at my apartment. It's—"

"I know where it is," he interrupted. "I'm just surprised you're staying there."

"I was staying with my sister and I love her very much, but living with Grace can be trying on my nerves."

"I can imagine."

From his tone, she knew exactly what he was talking about. "She's real sorry for what she said about Tuck's name. She didn't mean it to sound the way it did."

"Don't worry. Tuck has a very thick skin."

"Okay." Caroline took a step toward her car, hating to leave but knowing she'd see him soon. "I'll see you in an hour."

WHAT WAS HE THINKING?

He chastised himself all the way to his car. When Caroline smiled, he couldn't think too clearly. She had a smile that rivaled the sun for brightness and warmth, and he felt its heat in a way he hadn't for a very long time. He tried to remember Ginny's smile and failed. That didn't upset him. He had to move on. Ten years was long enough.

He closed his office and hurried home to shower and change.

He was shaving when the phone rang. It was Tuck.

"Sorry. I can't come over and watch the baseball game tonight. I have to get ready to go to Oklahoma on a murder investigation. I'm leaving tomorrow and I'll be gone for a couple of days. Could you feed the horses, as well as Samson and Delilah?"

"Sure. No problem." He'd completely forgotten about the game.

"Eli?"

"Hmm?"

"You're very quiet. Something wrong?"

"No. I'm fine. I'll talk to you when you get back."

He was better than he'd been in a while and the truth of that ran through him like the call of a whippoorwill—tempting, appealing and mystifying in its intensity.

CAROLINE RUSHED INTO her bedroom, yanked open her closet door and started pulling out clothes. What was she going to wear? Something casual? Something nice? What? What? What? She didn't have a lot of time. Something casual, yes—black slacks with a mint-green knit top. That would work.

As she headed for the shower, the phone rang. She talked to Grace as she removed her clothes.

"I spoke to your friends Abby and Dani, and we thought we'd go out tonight and celebrate your birthday."

"Thanks, but I have other plans."

"Like what?"

"Don't be nosy. Tell Abby and Dani thanks and I'll call them and we'll arrange something later."

"Caroline—"

"Bye, Grace. I'll talk to you tomorrow." Before Grace could protest further, she hung up. Caroline didn't mention her date with Eli because she didn't want to hear how unwise it was, or how she was fixated on him, or how she was on the rebound from Colin.

She was aware of all those things and she knew what she was doing. After tonight she'd probably never see Eli again, except in the courtroom. But tonight she planned to enjoy herself and to get to know the man who'd saved her life.

She showered, then did her hair and makeup, all the while watching the clock. While she was applying lipstick, the doorbell rang. She grabbed her purse and went to let Eli in.

And she'd never felt so excited in her life.

CHAPTER EIGHT

THEY DECIDED ON a steak house and talked as if they'd known each other forever. They discussed the trial and their fears that Buford might find a way to get off. They were so absorbed in each other that they didn't seem to notice the other people in the room.

Their food came. Eli had ordered steak and a baked potato, and Caroline had grilled chicken breast with vegetables. She started to ask if he wanted her to cut up his steak, but saw that he could use his right hand very well. She had a feeling Eli did everything well.

"How is Jezebel, the woman who helped you find me?" Caroline asked, cutting up her chicken.

"They're now calling her Jane Doe," Eli replied. "She's in the hospital and they're running tests to see if they can determine the cause of her memory loss."

"That has to be so frightening."

"Yeah." Eli took a swallow of tea. "The agents say she won't talk, so they're giving her some time to adjust before questioning her again."

"No one knows why she was in the camp?"

Eli finished off his steak and wiped his mouth. "We don't know anything about her except that she's not one of Buford's clan. She was more or less a slave."

"How horrible." Caroline laid down her fork. "Those

hills are so beautiful and vibrant with color in the spring. I never imagined something so ugly was hidden away there."

The waiter brought the check and Caroline quickly handed him a credit card. She had it in her pants pocket, readily at hand, because she'd sensed Eli was going to resist her paying.

"No, no. I've got it." Eli immediately pulled out his wallet.

Caroline placed her napkin on the table. "No way. This is my treat." The waiter left with the card before Eli could stop him.

He frowned.

"Tough," Caroline said, trying hard not to laugh at his expression.

"What?"

"It's really tough when a woman buys your dinner." Unable to stop herself this time, she laughed.

He laughed, too and the sound was awesome—deep and robust. "It just doesn't feel right."

She raised her right hand. "I won't tell a soul."

He scooted back his chair. "I guess I'm not a modern man."

"What type of man are you?"

His eyes held hers. "I don't think I'll answer that."

She knew what type of man he was—a man of honor, ethics and high standards, and she'd never met anyone like him before.

Neither said anything as they made their way out to the car. She turned in her seat to face him. "To make you feel better, I'll let you buy me an ice cream cone."

"Okay. What flavor?"

"Rocky Road with chocolate sprinkles on top."

They stopped at an ice cream shop and he got out to get it. When he came back, her eyes opened wide. He'd bought the biggest one they had.

"I can't eat all that," she said with laughter in her voice, staring at his own choice. "Why is your vanilla cone so small?"

"That's what I wanted."

"I think you're trying to pay me back for buying dinner."

"Nah. I wouldn't do that. Beside, it's your birthday." He finished his cone in record time and started the engine.

"Uh-huh." She tackled the ice cream with gusto and thoroughly enjoyed it, but she still wasn't finished when they reached her apartment. They sat for a few minutes parked under a streetlight until she did. She licked her lips. "Now I think we need some exercise."

He watched her tongue dart in and out. "Like what?"

The innocent question and his gaze created a sexual tension that hummed through her veins with a lazy languor.

She shook it off and answered, "Walking."

Hurrying out of the car, she met him on the pavement. He'd left his hat in the car.

"You don't walk by yourself at night, do you?"

"Relax, Mr. Ranger," she teased. "I never walk at night, but I figure since I have a big lawman with me, I'll be safe."

They set off down the sidewalk in comfortable silence. It was a beautiful moonlit night and the sky was brilliant with stars.

"Can I ask you a question?" she murmured.

Silence. No "sure." No "go ahead." Only silence. But that was Eli. He was a man who didn't like to answer questions. She already knew that about him.

"So you don't like questions?"

"No," he replied. "Especially if they're personal."

"How do you know it's personal?"

He glanced at her. "Isn't it?"

She inhaled deeply, loving the fragrant scent of blooming roses drifting through the air. "I was just going to ask who the men were that came into your room the day I visited you."

There was a noticeable pause before he said, "They're my half brothers. We have the same father."

"Oh." This was an answer she wasn't expecting and it threw her for a second. "You weren't glad to see them."

"No. I'm a Coltrane and they're McCains."

"But you said you have the same father."

"Joe McCain never claimed me. He said I wasn't his."

This time she didn't know what to say. She was sure he didn't want to hear that she was sorry, so she said nothing.

When he continued, she was surprised. "My mother worked in a bar in Waco and we lived in a two room apartment not far from it. Joe McCain was always there even though he had a wife and kids. He was seeing my mom before he even married Althea McCain. Althea never knew and neither did Jake, the eldest. I'm a few months older than him and he never knew we were brothers. But I did."

Caroline still didn't say a word, letting him talk because she had a feeling that Eli didn't speak about himself often, if ever.

"Althea finally left him and my mom thought he'd marry her then, but he didn't. I was around ten and I hated him. I heard him tell Vera, my mom, many times that I wasn't his—that she slept with other men so I had to be someone else's. Vera never saw other men. Joe McCain was the only man in her life as far back as I can remember."

"Then you've never had a relationship with your brothers?"

"No. As a kid I was always in trouble, fighting and skipping school. Finally I stole a car and the police caught me. Vera called her uncle, Jess Tucker, a retired Texas Ranger. He came to Waco and told the judge that if I was released into his custody, he'd make sure I stayed out of trouble. That saved me from a life of crime."

She couldn't even imagine Eli being anything but law abiding and her heart ached for that little boy whose life had been so turbulent.

"If you haven't had any contact with the McCains, why did they want to see you?"

"A few years ago Jake's son was kidnapped by his biological mother, who was a drug addict, as was her boyfriend. Tuck and I just happened to be in Waco at the time and we heard the news of the kidnapping. We'd had a lot of encounters with the boyfriend, Rusty Fobbs. When I worked for the DPS, I stopped him more times than I cared to remember. Tuck had, too. We tried to help him, but Rusty was one of those kids who tried but could never stick to much of anything. He'd rather steal than work."

"So what happened?"

"I tried to talk him into releasing the boy, but Rusty was never one for listening, either. The mother knew he was going to kill Ben so she pushed him out a window. Rusty then shot her and himself before we could get into the trailer."

"Oh. How sad."

"Yes. But Ben, the boy, is fine. He's about six now." Eli took a breath. "Ever since then Jake had tried to contact me, wanting to talk. I'm just not interested. I'm not part of their family and I never will be."

"But they *are* family." Even as she said the words she

wanted to take them back. "I'm sorry. I shouldn't have said that," she murmured, not wanting to ruin the pleasant conversation they were having.

"Sometimes I tell myself that, but I can't get past those wounds from my childhood."

"You want to. I can hear it in your voice."

"Maybe. Maybe not," he admitted, and she could feel his eyes on her in the darkness. "My turn to ask a question. Why did you break up with your fiancé?"

"We just couldn't…" Lightning split the sky as a thundercloud burst, and raindrops splattered their heads. "Oh, my goodness."

Eli grabbed her hand and they ran for the car. He unlocked a door and retrieved her purse, then they made a dash for her apartment just as it began to rain in earnest.

Caroline quickly inserted her key and pushed the door opened. Eli caught her arm. "Did you leave the lights on?"

"Yes." She always left the lights on now. She couldn't face coming home to a dark apartment.

They hurried inside, both of them wet and dripping. Caroline ran to the bathroom and brought back towels. Eli's hair was plastered to his head and she realized hers was, too. Their clothes were drenched.

"Let me have your shirt and slacks and I'll put them in the dryer."

"That's fine. I'll just dry off and head home."

"It's early," she said. "Please don't go."

Eli didn't miss the plea in her voice and knew it had something to do with her leaving the lights on.

"I don't have anything to put on," he replied, looking for a way to leave, but really not wanting to.

"I have a man's bathrobe you can wear until your clothes dry."

A man's bathrobe.

Her fiancé's, probably. Eli didn't want to wear the man's robe, but found himself saying, "Okay."

"It's my dad's," she said, and that made him feel better. "They spent a night here when their house had termites. Grace was in the process of moving so they stayed with me. They flew to Washington the next day and it was a welcome relief for all of us. Dad left the robe behind and it's in the utility room, on the back of the door. I'll go get out of these wet clothes. Just leave your things in there and I'll dry them."

Eli walked to the room, found the robe and removed his clothes. The robe didn't fit all that well. It was silk and had the congressman's initials on the pocket. Eli wasn't used to wearing robes like this, but it covered him. He placed his boots and belt on the counter and put his clothes in the dryer.

"You didn't have to do that," Caroline said, standing in the doorway in a T-shirt and pajama bottoms. Wet tendrils hung around her face and he thought she looked beautiful. Fast on that thought came the realization that the situation was getting a little too intimate.

"I've lived alone for a long time and I know how to use a dryer." His words came out sharper than he'd intended, and he hated himself when he saw that flicker of hurt in her green eyes.

"Coffee is ready." She turned toward the kitchen. "How about a cup?"

He followed her. She stopped at the coffeemaker and glanced at him. "Do you want to pour your cup or do you want me to?"

Amusement dripped from every word, and despite himself, he grinned. "Point taken. I was a bit crass because…"

"Because you're a man," she stated.

"Yep. That about sums it up."

"Piece of advice, Eli. When a woman offers to do something for you, let her."

"Mmm. I like my coffee black and strong and I'd like it in the den." On that he marched into the den, but not before he saw her smile.

He sat on the sofa and looked around. The sofa was tan with maroon and dark green throw pillows. The drapes were floral. Photo magazines were scattered on the coffee table and the room had a homey feel. He liked it.

Caroline came in and handed him a cup, then sat cross-legged on the end of the sofa not three feet from him.

"Thanks," he said.

"Did it hurt?"

"What?"

"Letting a woman do something for you."

He took a sip. "No. It actually feels pretty good and the coffee is great."

"Thank you."

"People that know me say I don't need anything or anyone. I'm self-sufficient. Tuck tells me that at least once a week." Eli couldn't imagine why he was telling her so much. Sharing things about himself wasn't like him at all.

"You and Tuck are very close."

"Yeah. He's the only family I've got."

Caroline twisted her cup and couldn't resist saying, "You have blood brothers."

"Hmm." He stared into the dark liquid, not at all angry she'd said that. "You know how you get a scrape or a cut—like my arm? Those scars heal, but the inner scars from my childhood haven't healed. I'm not sure they ever will." ·

"Do you resent that the McCains had a father and you didn't?"

He shrugged. "I never liked Joe McCain because of the way he treated my mother, and me, too. He was a very controlling man, but I'm not sure what kind of father he was. When Althea left, Beau went with her, but Jake refused. He stayed with his father."

"Why?"

"I don't know that part of the story. I just know he stayed with Joe, because we were in the same class at school."

"What about the other son?"

"His name is Caleb, and Althea was pregnant with him at the time."

Caroline frowned. "That's odd that she'd leave when she was pregnant."

"There was a lot of talk around them, but I ignored it."

"But now you want to know."

He shrugged and said the same thing he had on the sidewalk, "Maybe. Maybe not."

She scooted closer. "I think it's a definite maybe."

"And I think we're talking too much about me." He knew she was right, but it would be a very difficult step to take. He thought it was time to change the subject. "What happened with your fiancé?"

She stared at a picture on the wall. "Colin and I had a lot in common. He owned camera stores and I was a photographer. There's not anything he doesn't know about cameras and how they work. He happened to be in the store one day when I was purchasing a new camera. I was asking the salesperson all these questions and he came over and explained in more detail. He gave me his number and said if I had problems, to just call. We talked several times on the phone about the camera, then he asked me out. We dated for six months and he asked me to marry him. I said yes because we had a good relationship and I knew we could have a good marriage."

She stopped speaking.

"You don't now?" Eli asked.

"No. Love to me is putting the other person before yourself and being there no matter what." She set her cup on the coffee table. "Colin kept pressuring me to set a date for the wedding. He wanted to get married as soon as possible. I was reluctant and I wasn't sure why. I'm thirty years old and I thought I was ready for that kind of commitment. Colin had a store opening in Houston and I was going to go with him. I had decided to set the wedding date and I was going to tell him then. But I was kidnapped and…"

She stopped again. "When you rescued me, I was so anxious to see Colin, but he wasn't there. He went to the opening in Houston not knowing if I was dead or alive. I tried to understand his reasons—the wait was getting to him and he had to do something—but I can't understand and I never will. I just don't want to marry someone who doesn't put me first in his life."

Eli couldn't imagine a man doing what Colin had done, and he could see how much the man's actions had hurt Caroline. Eli thought it best to get off the subject.

He placed his cup beside hers. "Why do you leave your lights on?"

She shifted uneasily. "I'm having a hard time with the darkness now. As long as its daylight and the lights are on at night, I'm fine."

"What do you do when you go to bed?"

"Leave the light on." She linked her fingers together.

"That first night when I was in the hospital, I woke up to darkness and thought I was back in that room. I felt as if I was suffocating and I don't want to feel that again, so I leave the light on."

"It was fresh in your mind," he told her. "It may not be that way now."

She shook her head. "It's always going to be fresh in my mind."

Eli watched her for a moment. "Are you afraid, Caroline?"

She nodded.

"Don't let Buford do this to you. Don't let him control your emotions."

She tucked a strand of wet hair behind her ear. "I'm not sure how to stop it."

"By turning the light out tonight when you go to bed."

She bit her lip. "I don't know if I can do that."

Seeing her bent head twisted something deep in him. "I'll help you."

She raised her eyes to his. "How?"

"I'll stay the night. Maybe if someone is here it will be easier for you."

Her eyes opened wide. "You'd do that?"

"Sure. After that dog ripped open my arm, I only took enough time off to get treatment at the hospital, because I was determined to help the FBI gather all the evidence. But now we've reached a lull in the investigation. We're waiting for the prosecutors and defense attorneys to do their jobs. So my captain has ordered me to take some time off, starting tomorrow. I don't have to worry about going in to work." He looked down at the robe. "And I'm ready for bed."

She smiled. "Yes, you are."

"Consider it a birthday present. We'll turn off the lights. I'll sleep here on the sofa and you go to your bed."

"Okay." The dryer buzzed and she stood. "I'll get your clothes or—" she glanced at him "—do you want to do that?"

He grinned. "You can do it."

She hurried to the utility room, removed his slacks and shirt and put them on hangers, then went to the hall closet and got a blanket and a pillow. She carried them to Eli.

He took them. "You can do this. Do not sleep one more night with the light on. You're stronger than that. I know you are."

"Okay. I hope you'll be comfortable here. I used to have a spare bedroom, but I turned it into a darkroom."

"Don't worry. I'll be fine. Now go to bed."

"Good night, Eli." She leaned over and kissed his cheek.

"Night."

Eli held a hand to his cheek as she ran to the bedroom. Soon the light was out, and he lay on the sofa and stretched out. He didn't have a clue as to what he was thinking anymore. He should be on his way to his place, but somehow he couldn't leave her. She had to conquer this fear or it would control her forever. He'd seen what fear had done to Ginny and he didn't want another woman to go through that, especially not Caroline.

THE RAIN PEPPERED the window and Caroline tossed and turned. She had to go to sleep but recognized she was doing everything to keep from doing that. Darkness was all around her and if she closed her eyes she would be completely submerged in it. And that horrible suffocating feeling would be there. No, she couldn't do this. She needed more time. She got up to turn the light on, but her hand paused over the light switch. Eli was framed in the doorway.

"Don't do it," he said in a low voice.

"I—I…"

"Come," he said, and took her hand and guided her back to bed. "I'll sit here until you fall asleep."

She crawled into bed and reached for his hand. If she could touch Eli, feel his strength, then she might be able to conquer this fear. "I'm afraid to close my eyes."

"I know. Think about something else."

"When Grace and I were small, she used to be scared of the dark, especially when our parents were away. She'd come to my room and sleep with me. I'd tell her that the darkness was nothing to be afraid of and that I was much meaner than the darkness and I would protect her. It's so strange that now I'm the one frightened of the dark."

"It's still nothing to be afraid of. I'm here and I *am* much meaner than the dark."

"You're nice. Sweet and compassionate, too."

"Don't tell anyone who knows me that."

There was silence for a moment, then Caroline said, "Eli?"

"Hmm?"

"You will be here when I wake up?"

"Yes, Caroline. I will be here. Happy birthday." He put his other hand over her eyes. "Close them."

She felt his fingers against her eyelids and they fluttered shut without a trace of fear. She went to sleep with the feel of his skin against her face, lulling her into peaceful dreams where there was no darkness.

Just Eli.

CHAPTER NINE

CAROLINE WOKE up to darkness, but she wasn't afraid. Eli lay beside her, her hand in his. She scrambled to her knees, embracing the darkness with her arms outstretched, and she'd never felt so liberated in her life.

Eli sat up.

"You're awake," she said.

"Yeah. I've been for some time."

"I slept all night and I feel wonderful. Look." She pointed to the blinds covering the window. "Daylight is tiptoeing in and I haven't been breathlessly waiting for it. Thank you, Eli. Thank you." She threw her arms around his neck and hugged him.

He breathed in the scent of her hair, her skin, and his arms slipped around her waist. She rubbed her cheek against his stubble and he turned his head and captured her mouth. Their lips met in a kaleidoscope of emotions fueled by the need in both of them. Eli opened his mouth, needing more, and Caroline reciprocated with an urgency that surprised her. She wanted to taste and feel every part of him, and her hands and lips heeded that message.

Eli lost control the moment she touched him, and he wasn't fighting too hard to regain it. Her touch and skin were as soft as she was, and he didn't want to stop the feelings she was bringing to life in him. He lay back, taking her with him, and she rested on top of him, molding her soft curves against his hardness. Nothing else mattered but this moment, holding Caroline, loving Caroline.

Through that newborn pleasure a thread of reason penetrated.

This is wrong. This is wrong.

He tried to push it away, but his ethics were stronger than the man in him, and he slowly pulled his lips away.

"Eli." She kissed the side of his face.

He hesitated for a second before slipping from her arms and getting out of the bed. "I can't do this." He tightened the belt on his robe.

"Why?"

He ran both hands through his hair. "Because I only wanted to help you fight the fear—that's all. You've been through a traumatic ordeal and a broken engagement. We don't need to complicate things. Besides, you're a witness on a case I'm working."

"I see."

She looked so sad sitting in the middle of the bed with her hair in disarray and her eyes glistening with a pain he'd just put there. But he'd done the right thing. She would realize that later.

"I'll get my things and leave." He paused at the door, finding it hard to walk away. "Are you okay?"

She swallowed. "Yes. I'm fine."

But he could see that she wasn't. It took every ounce of strength he had to walk out the door. He quickly changed into his clothes and within minutes was in his car, heading toward his place, feeling lower than a snake's belly.

But he'd done the right thing, he told himself again.

Neither of them was ready for a casual affair. Neither of them was ready for a commitment, either.

Then why did he feel so down?

CAROLINE HEARD THE DOOR close and burst into tears. "I am not fine, Elijah Coltrane," she shouted, then lay back, wiping her eyes.

What was she doing?

Throwing herself at a man who didn't want her. She tried to figure out what she was feeling—why she was so attracted to Eli. And she was. She wouldn't have stopped if he hadn't. Four weeks ago she'd been in love with Colin, planning a life with him. Today she wanted a stranger to make love to her. To say she didn't know what she was doing or thinking was probably an understatement.

Her fingers touched her lips, where she could still feel Eli's kiss. It didn't feel wrong. It didn't feel like a stranger's. It felt right. She might be confused about a lot of things, but of that she was certain.

The doorbell rang and she ignored it. She didn't want to see anyone. The ringing stopped, then she heard pounding. She got up and made her way to the door.

"Caroline, let me in," Grace called. "I know you're in there."

She swung open the door. "Good morning, Grace."

"What took you so long?" Her sister walked into the living room, impeccably dressed in a business suit and ready for work.

Caroline lifted an eyebrow. "I was in bed. It's six o'clock in the morning."

Grace took in the cups on the coffee table and the blanket and pillow on the sofa. "Oh. Colin is here. I'm so sorry to have intruded."

"Colin's not here," Caroline said before Grace got carried away.

"But he was here last night—that's why you didn't want to go out?"

Caroline shook her head. "No. He wasn't here."

"You went out with someone, though."

Caroline sighed in frustration. "Grace, when did you become my mother?"

"I'm just worried about you," she retorted.

"Pull in those worry antennas. I'm fine." Caroline sank onto the sofa, thinking if she had to say that to one more person, she was going to scream.

Grace sat beside her, staring at the cups. "Don't you have coasters?"

"Yes."

"Why didn't you use them? That's going to leave a—"

"Grace, don't get on my bad side this morning."

"You're very testy."

"Yes, I am, so don't push your luck."

There was silence for a second and Caroline took a moment to gather herself, but she knew her sister. Grace wasn't going to let this drop. Her next words proved her right.

"So who was here last night?"

Caroline didn't even pause. "Eli."

Grace's eyes widened. "Ranger Coltrane."

"Yes."

"Did he come to discuss the case?"

"No. I took him out to dinner as a thank-you for rescuing me, and we came back here for coffee."

Grace glanced at the blanket between them. "What's the blanket for?"

She drew her knees up and rested her head against the

back of the sofa. "If you weren't my sister, that question would make me very angry."

"Caroline, you're not getting involved with him, are you?"

She raised her head. "No. I can honestly say that I'm not getting involved with Eli. I threw myself at him and he rejected me."

"Oh, Caro." Grace hugged her.

She brushed away a tear. "Go ahead and tell me how crazy I am—how fixated I am on him."

"I would, but I can see how upset you are. Do you feel something more than gratitude for this man?"

"I'm not sure. I enjoy being with him and talking to him. He makes me feel like I'm important and that I matter. I'm happy when I'm with him. No man has ever made me feel that way, not even Colin."

Grace watched her with a skeptical eye. "Why don't you go back to work?" she suggested. "That might help you get everything into perspective."

"I haven't even been able to pick up my camera."

"That's my point," Grace exclaimed. "You're still dealing with the kidnapping and the impending trial. It's not good or rational to use Ranger Coltrane to forget Colin."

"I'm not doing that."

"Caroline…"

"Go to work, Grace."

Grace glanced at her watch. "Oh. I've got to run. I have an early appointment." She got to her feet. "Let's have dinner tonight."

"No. I'm getting dressed and taking my camera and walking through the city, hoping something will inspire me to take some photos. I intend to keep searching until

I start taking pictures again, and I don't want to have watch the clock. I'll call you when I get back, so don't worry."

"Okay." Grace gave her a quick hug. "But give Mom and Dad a call before you go."

Caroline phoned her parents and talked for a few minutes because she knew they were worried about her. Everyone was. Even Eli. Last night had been a big mistake. She could see that clearly. She'd told herself that she had to put her life back together by herself. But she'd clung to Eli as she'd clung to Grace. That wasn't progress, that was denial. Now she had to do something about her fears—alone.

She showered and dressed. Taking her camera, she walked until she was exhausted. Four hours later she was back in her apartment without snapping one shot. She was disgusted with herself, and for the first time thought her mother might be right about her needing to see a therapist.

No. She could put her life back together. Tonight would be the test. If she could go to sleep with the lights off, then she could make it. And she had to make it without Eli. She just wished she could stop thinking about him, because he was not part of her life—just a nice man she'd met along the way.

A man she would never forget.

ELI WAS AT THE HOSPITAL at eight so Dr. Stiles could run some tests on his arm. The whole thing took about two hours. Dr. Stiles said his arm was healing perfectly, but to keep up the therapy for three more weeks. Eli felt good about that. His arm was going to be fine—just a few scars to show for the day he'd rescued Caroline.

As he waited for an elevator, Caleb McCain walked up. "Morning, Eli," Caleb said.

Eli nodded and took the stairs, running down them two at a time. On the bottom one he sank down. What was wrong with him? Why couldn't he speak to his... He exhaled a deep breath and made himself say the word. His *brother.* Caleb, like Jake and Beau, were his brothers.

He thought about that fact. He couldn't change it, had to accept it—some way, somehow.

He'd told Caroline that she had to face her fears. He was running from his and he wanted to laugh at the thought. He'd never run from anything in his life, but he was running now. Running scared.

There was only one thing to do. He had to face it—face the McCains. Getting to his feet, he walked into the hall and headed for the entrance. Next time he would speak to Caleb. Next time...

He stopped when he saw Tuck coming into the hospital. Tuck walked directly to him, his expression worried.

"Where have you been?" he asked. "I called and called last night and even went over to your apartment this morning, but you weren't home. Are you okay?"

No way was he telling Tuck where'd he been. It was none of his business. "Yes, Tuck, I'm okay," he replied. "I just had a visit with the doctor and my arm is okay, too, so you can stop worrying now."

Tuck eyed him strangely. "Not going to tell me where you were, huh?"

"Nope. I thought you were on your way to Oklahoma."

Tuck frowned. "Had a bit of a delay. I need a damn cup of coffee. I left the house early trying to catch you and I didn't take time to make any."

"Let's go to the hospital coffee shop and I'll buy you a cup," Eli offered.

They got coffee and sat at a small table. Eli took a swallow, knowing they had to get something straight. "Tuck, when did you become my guardian?"

Tuck placed his hat on the table. "Since you had surgery and started talking weird."

"I'm fine now."

Tuck looked at him over the rim of his cup. "Are you?"

Eli couldn't lie to Tuck for any length of time. They were too close. He told him about Caleb. "I don't understand why I have such a hard time accepting the McCains," he confessed.

"They say memories from childhood stay with us forever."

"Yeah," Eli agreed. "But Caleb had nothing to do with my childhood."

Tuck smiled.

"What?"

"That's the first time you've admitted that."

Eli realized it was. That had to be progress.

"Remember when we were kids and always getting cuts and scrapes from being boys?"

"Sure."

"Ma used to put Band-Aids on us and I'd wear mine until it washed off—I never liked the feel of removing it from my skin. But you'd rip yours off without flinching. That's what you have to do now—just do it, and I bet you won't even flinch."

"You have it all figured out, huh?"

Tuck drained his cup. "You're making this hard when it isn't. Let go of the past. Just rip it away and see what happens."

Eli gave him a dark look, but knew he was right.

Tuck stood. "I've got to run. Don't forget to feed the animals at the ranch. We'll catch a baseball game when I get back. See you later."

As Tuck walked away, Caleb came in. Eli saw them shake hands and talk for a minute. Tuck left and Caleb got coffee and sat at another table. He didn't look Eli's way.

Eli knew what he had to do. As in Tuck's damn Band-Aid story, it might hurt, but… He got up and made his way over.

Caleb looked up. "Hello, Eli," he said, as if Eli hadn't been extremely rude earlier.

"Hello," he answered, and shook the hand Caleb extended. It was so easy and painless.

"The arm looks great."

"Yeah." Eli twisted his hand. "The doc says I'm a fast healer."

"Do you have time for a cup of coffee?" Caleb asked. "I'd like to talk about something."

Normally Eli would say no and go about his business. "Sure," he replied. "I'll get another cup and be right back."

Within seconds he took a seat opposite Caleb and braced himself for this conversation. He'd been avoiding it for years, but after speaking to Caroline last night and Tuck this morning, he felt he was ready to talk about the past. He just had to do it—as Tuck had said.

"The FBI has basically turned over Jane Doe's case to me," Caleb said. "They want me to place her with her family, and that's like finding a needle in a haystack. She doesn't remember a thing and she won't talk much. She reminds me of a trapped animal and I'm not sure how to help her. She's afraid of me and everyone that comes into her room. Since she tried to help you find Ms. Whitten, I was hoping you might talk to her."

Eli wasn't expecting this. He'd thought Caleb would

want to talk about family, and he couldn't imagine why he was disappointed.

"Sure. I'll talk to her."

"I just came from her room and she'll be having tests all day. How about tomorrow morning?"

"That'll be fine."

Caleb watched him. "You thought I wanted to talk about something else, didn't you?"

Eli took a swallow of coffee. "Yeah."

"Be patient with Jake. He just wants us all to be a family, like we should have been years ago."

Eli looked directly at him. "But I'm not part of the McCain family."

"Neither was I until a few years ago."

"What do you mean?"

"When my mother left Joe McCain, she was pregnant with me. Joe said I wasn't his. My mother was friends with Andrew Wellman, a man at our church, and Joe accused her of sleeping with him. He said I was Wellman's bastard. Jake was ten and Joe told him those lies, and Jake wouldn't leave with my mom and Beau. Joe continued to poison Jake's mind and he refused to have anything to do with us. It broke my mother's heart and I watched her yearn for her eldest son most of my life."

Eli gripped his cup. "I didn't know this."

"When Jake found out he had a son of his own and might lose custody of him, he swallowed his pride and asked for Beau's help. Ben brought us together as a family and he brought you back into our lives, too."

Eli's hand felt numb from gripping the cup, and he was feeling numb inside, too, because his brothers' past was so different than he'd ever imagined. For the first time he wanted to know more.

"You said Joe never claimed you?"

"No. I was Wellman's bastard to the day he died."

"I know the feeling," Eli confessed. "He always accused my mother of sleeping with other men."

"He put my mother through that hell, too, until she found the courage to get out."

"Didn't your mother eventually marry Wellman?" He'd heard that somewhere, but he wasn't sure where. He kept news of the McCains to a minimum.

"Yes," Caleb replied. "My mother and Andrew's relationship sort of evolved. He was always there making sure we had everything we needed. Andrew never had children of his own and when I was born, he doted on me. I couldn't have asked for a better father, but all his love and all his caring couldn't take away the stigma that Joe McCain denied who I was."

"I know that feeling, too."

Caleb nodded. "If you want to hate Joe McCain, go right ahead. I hated him for more years than I care to remember. But hate is a destructive emotion. I see it every day in my line of work, as you do. Life is too short to waste it hating. If you want to get to know us, all you have to do is ask. But it's up to you."

Eli stood. "I don't see that happening. I'm sorry." His words belied the faint glimmer of hope within him. He didn't push it away, nor did he accept it. But for the first time he felt a kinship to his brother. Maybe…

"Don't be. You can't change the way you feel." Caleb got to his feet and Eli noticed they were the same height. They had the same dark hair, too, but Eli's eyes were blue. He had Joe McCain's eyes.

"I'll see you in the morning," Caleb added.

For a minute Eli lost track of what Caleb was saying,

he was so consumed with everything he was feeling. "Yes. I'll be here tomorrow." He strolled away, the past closing in on him so fast that he felt out of breath.

ELI DROVE TO his apartment and changed into jeans. He needed to go to the ranch to feed the animals, but he also needed to go there for himself—it had been his haven since he was thirteen years old. All the things Caleb had told him kept running through his mind. He'd had the Mc-Cains pictured as a very loving family, but it seemed things were different. All the sons had suffered because of their father. Eli was not alone in that.

Maybe that's what had been bothering him all these years, like Caroline had said. They were a family and he was an outsider, the bastard, the one to bear the sins of Joe McCain. But it wasn't like that at all. Jake, Beau and Caleb's lives had been torn apart and they were now struggling to be a family. Eli had an open invitation to join them.

He went to his desk and picked up the letters from Jake. Some he'd sent back, but these he'd thrown on the desk. The only letters opened were the ones Tuck had read. Eli sat down and read through all of them. Jake told of his life and the lies fed to him by their father. He told of finding his mother again and the relationship he was building with his brothers. There were pictures of Ben, one of Katie the day she was born and several more over the years.

Eli got up and propped two of the photos on his desk. He took a long breath, staring at his nephew and niece. They were his family. He could actually admit that without the destructive emotions taking control. He had a family. Just saying the words to himself was a start. For the moment that was all he could do. It would take time for the next step.

He wanted to share this news with someone, and Caroline's face swam before him. No. He had to leave her alone to get on with her life. He didn't like hurting her, though, and he had this morning. He'd done the right thing in stopping, but he realized at the very least he owed her an explanation.

A few minutes later he was sitting outside her apartment debating whether to go in or not. He had to apologize. He had to explain how he felt and he wasn't sure she wanted to hear it. Still…

CAROLINE WAS DETERMINED to take some shots today even if they were of nothing. She rested for a while, then grabbed her camera bag to go out again. The doorbell rang. Damn. She didn't want to see anyone, and if it was Grace… Standing on tiptoe, she looked through the peephole. Eli. Her pulse pounded loudly in her ears.

She swung open the door.

"Hi," he said in a husky voice. "Can we talk?"

"Sure." She moved aside to let him in. He walked to the sofa and sat down, placing his hat on the table. "I'm sorry about what happened this morning."

"Yes. I got the gist of that," she said, not able to keep the hurt out of her voice.

He watched her closely. "But you're upset."

"Rejection is hard for a woman to take."

"Caroline," he sighed. "There's something happening between us but it's happening too fast and for all the wrong reasons."

She sat in the chair. "You feel something happening between us?"

"Of course. I'd be lying if I said anything else, but we have to take it slow and we have to keep things platonic."

Why? was her first thought, but then she knew why and

realized he was right. Just this morning she'd admitted to herself that she didn't know what she was doing, and work would help get her life into perspective. That hadn't happened, though.

"You're a witness in a case I'm working. If anything happened between us it would be unethical for me. Please understand that."

She brushed back her hair. "You're right. I'm feeling adrift at the moment. This morning I went out to take pictures with the thought that work would help me."

"And?"

"I didn't snap one shot. I didn't have the desire, and I blamed you for clouding my mind with other thoughts."

"I'm sorry for that and—"

"I understand about your conflict," she interrupted, her voice rising. "I'm a little mixed up right now, but wanting to make love with you seemed very right."

"I think you mean have sex with me." His eyes held hers and she stared back at him with everything she was feeling.

"No. I don't."

His eyes narrowed. "Caroline…"

She held up a hand, stopping him. "Just go away."

He stood, but other than that he didn't move. She looked up to find his eyes on her.

"What?" she asked at the unspoken question there.

"I have a feeling you could break my heart—badly."

"Is that what you're afraid of?"

"After Ginny, I swore I'd never get involved like that again and I haven't. It's called protection and I'm good at protecting my heart. It's easier that way, but it's not so easy for me to hurt you."

Her gaze delved into his. "I'm a little afraid myself. I've

never had these kinds of feelings so fast before. Grace says it's just gratitude, but I don't know."

That wistfulness in her voice got to him. She needed someone. He was here now and he could keep things on an even keel without compromising his ethics. He'd helped people before and he could help her. He just had to guard against letting a situation get too intimate, like last night.

He saw her camera bag on the table. "Do you have plans for this afternoon?"

She blinked in confusion. "I was going out with my camera again."

"I know where you can get some great shots."

"Where?"

"Tuck is away and I have to go out to the ranch and feed the animals. It's very tranquil and scenic."

"Are you asking me to go with you?"

He took a deep breath. "Yes."

Suddenly the world took on a brighter glow, and Caroline knew she was starting to have strong feelings for Eli. He'd said that she could break his heart, but that worked both ways. He could hurt her like she'd never been hurt before. Could she handle that? Could she handle it if Eli never loved her the way he'd loved Ginny?

The word *no* hovered on her lips. Things were too intense, too emotional, and she needed space and time. On the other hand, she wanted to spend time with him to see if what she was feeling was real or a result of gratitude, as Grace had said.

Caroline got to her feet. "You don't have to do this," she said.

"I know, Caroline. What's your answer?"

"Yes. I'd love to go. I'll just get my camera and purse." She headed for the bedroom, knowing that any time spent with him was better than being alone. Maybe he felt the same way. He was a loner, a rebel, and in many ways she was, too. This time together could be what she needed to discover why she felt about him the way she did. It was probably just a result of the trauma she'd been through.

But she didn't feel it was.

CHAPTER TEN

DRIVING OUT OF AUSTIN, they headed toward Round Rock, turning onto a hardtop country road. Neither said much during the drive. Caroline was enjoying the rolling, sunlit countryside of live oak trees and green grasses, small farms and ranches. The wildflowers were all gone now and soon the heat of summer would dull the lush landscape.

Eli turned off the road and crossed a cattle guard. White board fences lined both sides of the drive, running all the way to the rambling farmhouse and around it. A barn and a couple of outbuildings were visible in back of the house. He drove into a two-vehicle carport and parked beside a silver pickup truck.

"That's Tuck's," Eli said. "Pa bought it for him when he graduated from high school. It's his pride and joy. The truck has some years and miles on it, but it runs like brand-new. Tuck takes very good care of it."

"Did you get a truck, too?"

"Oh, yeah," he answered, opening the door. "It's in the barn. We use it to haul hay and feed. I'm not as particular as Tuck."

Caroline got out and walked around the front of the car, gazing at the neatly cut grass and flower beds. Roses were vining on a fence—bright red, pink and yellow roses. They were beautiful.

Eli was watching her face. "Those were Ma's. She loved those roses."

"Don't tell me," Caroline said, laughter bubbling inside her. "Tuck takes care of them."

"You bet."

"I think Tuck should meet my sister. They have a lot in common."

"He already has," he remarked dryly.

"Oh, yeah." Caroline grimaced. "I almost forgot. Bad idea."

A frenzy of barking broke the abrupt silence and a small, mixed-breed white dog with brown spots hurled himself at Eli. He looked like a terrier.

"Hey, Sam." Eli knelt down and rubbed the dog's head with affection. "Are you hungry?"

Sam barked louder and jumped up and down in excitement, obviously understanding what Eli meant.

"Okay. Okay. I'll get your food."

Eli opened a side door and they went through a utility room into a large kitchen with a big oak table. He flipped on a light, revealing that everything inside the house was kept as neat and clean as the yard.

"I like this farmhouse," she said. "Lots of space and room and ambiance. It's really homey and comfortable."

"There's a long porch with cedar columns in the front and in the back. When you sit outside, you can smell the cedar." Eli took down some canned dog food and two cans of cat food from a high shelf. "There are two bedrooms upstairs and two downstairs. Tuck and I shared a room and the beds upstairs were used for the kids who needed help."

"It takes a special kind of person to reach out to others like that."

"Ma and Pa had very big hearts. They made every kid

that came here feel special. Some stayed overnight until relatives could be located, some stayed a week, others months. Tuck and I were here for the long haul."

She could hear the love in his voice when he talked about his foster parents—it was the same kind of love he radiated when he talked about Ginny. That kind of love was everlasting.

"Is there a cat, too?" she asked, eyeing the cat food, that Eli was spooning into a dish.

"Oh, yes. Her name is Delilah and she appears when least expected."

"Come on, boy." Eli led Sam outside and Caroline followed. He placed the food by some water bowls. Sam immediately dug into his. Suddenly something leaped from the roof to the ground, and Caroline jumped back in alarm.

"It's okay," Eli said. "It's only Dee."

"Oh. I think my heart stopped beating for a moment."

"Dee always makes a dramatic appearance."

Caroline looked closely at the cat that was crouched over her food bowl. "It's a Siamese. She's gorgeous."

"She just showed up one day and Tuck's been feeding her ever since. She's great company for Samson."

"They're Samson and Delilah?"

"Yes, they're very close. Watch."

Both animals were now eating out of Dee's bowl, then they quickly turned together to finish off Sam's food. Caroline expected a growling fight to start, but it didn't. Sam curled up on the grass and Dee rubbed against him, finally resting on the dog's back.

"I have to get a picture of this," she said, and ran to the car. She grabbed her camera and was back in a minute. She squatted down, looked through the lens and started snapping. Finding something beautiful and meaningful to photograph had suddenly become so easy. Why had it been so hard before?

Pausing for a moment, she sank back on the grass and stared up at Eli. Her stomach tightened at the look in his blue eyes. For a second neither spoke.

He cleared his throat. "I've got to feed the horses. Want to come with me?"

"Sure." Scrambling to her feet, she followed him to the barn. Caroline took numerous pictures of him dumping feed into a trough. Horses fretted around him and he rubbed them with a cajoling hand. They whickered in response. He was so caring, so gentle. She captured it all through her lens—once she started she couldn't seem to stop. Eli made a very good subject.

Later they walked down to the pond, Sam and Dee tagging along. She captured the ducks frolicking in the water. A couple of deer came to the edge to drink and she snapped as many shots as she could, trying to capture every facet of the beautiful creatures. When the deer ran into the woods, Caroline sat in the grass beside Eli in comfortable silence.

"Thank you," she said. "This is what I needed. It's very tranquil and picturesque, like you said."

"Yes. It is," he replied, his eyes locked on her face.

The sun began to go down and they slowly made their way back to the barn. Eli closed the door to the storage shed and Caroline sat on a bale of hay watching him. Sam barked frantically at the hayloft and she looked up to see Dee strutting around on the rafters.

Caroline patted Sam's head. "It's all right, she'll come down."

"Sam gets upset because he can't go after her," Eli said. "We had a ladder to the loft but Tuck took it down 'cause Sam tried to climb it. Tuck was afraid he'd break his legs."

Dee jumped down onto the hay and curled up. Sam barked at her a couple of times, then lay beside her.

"It must have been wonderful to grow up here." Caroline could envision two young boys enjoying the outdoors and learning about life from two incredible people.

Eli eased down onto the bale of hay and once more, like the night they went out to dinner, opened up to her about his past. "It was unlike any place I'd ever been. I didn't know what discipline or rules were. My mother let me do whatever I wanted, and I did. She had no control over me. Here there were rules and I resisted them with everything I had in me."

"You did?"

"That first night I planned to run away. As soon as Uncle Jess and Aunt Amalie—that's what I called them then—went to bed I was going to steal some money and leave. No one could tell me what I had to do. I was thirteen years old, with a big chip on my shoulder."

"But you didn't leave?"

"No." He looked down at his hands. "At supper that night I didn't say thank you, or please, or yes ma'am, or no sir, and Pa said that in his house table manners were observed. I told him to go to hell and that he couldn't keep me here."

Eli had a faraway look on his face. "I can still hear his chair scraping back as he got to his feet, saying in that deep voice, 'To the barn.' I told him to go to hell again and that I was leaving. He caught my arm and dragged me out the door. Tuck looked horrified and Ma was wringing her hands."

"What happened?"

"See those boxing gloves on the wall?"

She followed his gaze and saw them hanging from a nail. "Yes."

"Once we got out here, he yanked them off the wall and threw a set at me. He said if I wanted to leave so bad that I'd have to fight my way out. I asked what he meant. He said since I like to fight so much, all I had to do was knock him out and I was free to do whatever I wanted. I thought, hell, he's an old man, and I could put his lights out with one punch. I was big for my age and thought I was ten feet tall and bulletproof, so I agreed. Then he told me that if he won, I would abide by the rules and give them a chance. I don't think I really heard that part because there was no way that old man was going to beat me."

She waited with bated breath for him to continue. "I quickly put my gloves on and we danced around each other. I couldn't wait to show him how tough I was. I didn't even see his right coming. The next thing I knew I was on my ass looking up at him. I jerked to my feet, thinking he'd got in a lucky punch, but again I was on my ass before I knew it.

"Again and again I went down. I got so angry that I just ran at him, trying to drive my fists into his stomach. He wrapped his arms around me and held me. I buried my face against his chest and started to cry. I never let anyone see me cry, but that night I sobbed like a baby. He just held me and told me everything was going to be all right. Then I dried my tears and we sat out here and talked for a long time. He told me about the rules and what was expected of me. He said a man always keeps his word. He told me *I* was a man and he would trust me to keep my word and not run away."

"Did you run away?"

He rubbed his hands together. "Whenever I thought about it, I could hear Pa saying he trusted me and that I was a man. I always put off running until another day. I wanted him to know I could keep my word, and I wanted him to be proud of me. By then Ma had started to work her magic with her sweetness and gentleness and, oh, could she cook. I teased her when I was older that the reason I never ran away was because I loved her cooking. She'd say it was them that I loved, and she was right. No one had ever loved or cared about me before, and as days passed I never wanted to leave."

"Since Tuck was their only child, did you get along with him at first?"

Eli looked at her with a puzzled frown. "Ma and Pa didn't have any kids. Tuck was adopted. He was left in a cardboard container at their mailbox."

"Oh, my. And Jess Tucker gave him his name?"

"Yeah. Ma told me that when the adoption was final, Pa said, 'We now have a little Tucker.' They called him little Tucker for a long time, then shortened it when he got older to just Tuck."

"Knowing that, I can't believe he was so nice about Grace's reaction to his name."

"He just brushed it off."

"Still, Grace should apologize again."

Eli glanced at her. "Let it drop—that's what Tuck would want."

"Okay," she replied, feeling a little giddy from the warm look in his eyes.

"Then Tuck doesn't know who his parents are?"

"No, and as he gets older it bothers him."

They were silent for a moment. "To answer your question, at first I hated him—but then I hated everybody so that wasn't unusual. But it was hard to keep hating someone who's so nice. That's Tuck—those first few days I said some hurtful things to him, but it didn't phase him. He kept trying to help me. Tuck was a scrawny kid, small for his age, and I found myself becoming his protector. No one picked on him when I was around. At fourteen he shot up and filled out. He's still tall and lanky, while I have more muscle. I could always take him in a fight—"

"Let me guess," she interrupted. "Every fight had to be settled with those boxing gloves."

Eli smiled. "Yep. Sometimes I let him win, though. Tuck and I know everything about each other and we're closer than most brothers."

He became thoughtful and she knew he was thinking about his real brothers. "I talked to Caleb today," he blurted out.

She caught his arm. "Oh, Eli, that's wonderful."

He stared down at her hand for a moment before telling her what he and Caleb had discussed.

"So Joe McCain didn't claim him, either?"

"No, and all of a sudden I felt a kinship to him. We were the unwanted sons, the forgotten ones, and that threw me. I thought I was the only one who lived through that kind of pain."

"But Caleb understood."

"I suppose."

"Now you can talk to Jake and Beau and get to know one another as brothers."

"It's not that easy," he mumbled.

"Why isn't it?"

"I can't just wipe out the past."

Her fingers tightened, and in an uncanny way she knew what his problem was. "Are you afraid if you accept the McCains as family that you will somehow lose the feelings you have for Ma, Pa and Tuck?"

He didn't answer. He just kept staring at her hand.

"Eli, you will lose nothing, and you won't tarnish your foster parents' memory by accepting the McCains as your family. They will just be an extension of what and who you are. A relationship with your brothers might ease the heartache you've felt for so long and give the wounds inside you a chance to heal."

He took a deep breath. "I don't know if I can do it."

"Sure you can."

"Caroline…"

She got up and went to the boxing gloves and removed them from the nail. She carried them to him and handed him a pair.

"If I can knock you down, you have to talk to your brothers."

Eli raised an eyebrow in disbelief. "You can't knock me down. I'm much stronger than you! And I'm not fighting a woman."

She put the gloves on. "Are you chicken, Eli?"

He stood. "I'm not fighting you."

"Didn't Pa settle all your fights and disagreements this way?"

"Mostly."

"Then that's what we'll do." She hopped around in front of him. "If I can knock you down, you'll speak with your brothers. Deal?"

"No."

She stopped hopping and glared at him. "I'm not asking you to fight me. You're big and strong even with your hurt arm, but if little old me can knock you on your butt then that's a sure sign that Ma and Pa would want you to embrace your brothers. Deal?"

"This is crazy." But she felt his resolve weakening.

"Deal?"

"Deal," he growled.

"Put the gloves on." She hopped around him again.

He shoved his hands into the gloves and held them up with a complacent expression. She danced in and out, taking jabs at his stomach, but he didn't move or respond. This was going to be so easy. She moved close to him, her body touching his. He still didn't respond.

Glancing up into his stubborn blue eyes, she placed her right foot between his feet, then wrapped her arms around his waist. He tensed. She raised her right foot, turned it and hooked his left leg, then jerked. His leg slid out from under him and he was on his butt in a split second.

He burst into laughter, the sound filling the barn. She fell down beside him, laughing, too.

"That was a trick," he said, catching his breath while removing his gloves. "You knew exactly what you were doing."

"You made it so easy. You should have fought back." She slipped her hands out of the gloves.

He sobered. "Not on your life. I would never hurt one hair on your head."

They stared at each other for endless seconds, then he cupped her face and drew her toward him, kissing her long and deep. Her arms encircling his neck, she gave herself up to whatever he wanted.

The kiss went on and on as each of them held nothing back. They stretched out in the hay and Eli's hands slipped beneath her blouse, caressing, stroking. Her hands were also at work, feeling the heavy muscles of his shoulders and back. The world spun away as they found pleasure in the basic, most simple needs.

Sam barked several times before they heard him. Eli pulled his lips away and buried his face in her heated neck. "He thinks we're fighting," he said in a ragged tone.

"Silly dog." She stroked Eli's back.

He lifted his head and she saw the torment in his eyes. "Caroline, what are we doing?"

She arched an eyebrow. "Did you need me to draw you a picture?"

"No." He rolled to the side and sat up. "Friends don't do this and we shouldn't, either."

She reached out to smooth the wrinkles on his forehead. "We kissed. That's all. We admitted back in my apartment that something's happening between us. There's nothing wrong with that."

He didn't answer, so she went on, "Like I told you earlier, I'm feeling my way back to a normal life right now and you feel very good to me. I'm not sure why that is. Maybe it's gratitude. Maybe it's the pangs of a broken engagement. Maybe it's something more. Only time will tell. So stop feeling guilty every time you touch me. We're adults and we can handle this."

Eli wasn't so sure. He could handle just about anything in this world, except talking to his brothers and letting another woman into his heart. Both these things seemed to be closing in on him at once. He stood and stretched out his left hand, pulling Caroline to her feet.

"Time to get you back to the city," he said.

During the silent drive to her apartment, Caroline could feel a tension building between her and Eli. When they arrived, he got out and walked her to the door. She found her key and let them in to the dark apartment.

"See?" she said, flipping on a light. "I turned the lights off."

He stood just inside the door. "That's good. How about the night?"

"I'm going cold turkey—no lights."

"If you need me, just call." Why did he say that? He didn't want her to need him.

Her eyes narrowed on his face. "And you're hoping I won't."

He took a step farther into the room. "I don't want you to be afraid."

"It's hard not to be afraid every second of every day, but I'm managing."

Those words tightened his gut unbearably, but before he could say anything she added, "If I do feel the walls closing in, I'll call Grace. She's dying to mother me. So don't worry."

"Okay," he said, and hesitated. Why couldn't he just leave?

She stood on tiptoe and kissed his cheek, and his skin almost ached from the contact. "Thank you for a wonderful day. I'm taking pictures again and now I can go back to work. That will help a great deal."

"Yes. I'm sure it will."

She tilted her head to one side. "You have to be the nicest man I've ever met. I didn't think there were men like you in this world."

He wasn't good with praise so he said the only thing he could. "Good night, Caroline."

"Not so fast, Ranger Coltrane."

He stopped, his eyes puzzled. "What?"

"We have a deal, remember?"

He couldn't help but smile, because he knew exactly what she was talking about. "I don't think you can hold me to that. You tricked me."

"I had self-defense classes in college."

"You're a lot like Pa," he said. "He was a high school boxing champ and he failed to mention that when he challenged me."

"A deal is a deal and you're a man of your word, right?"

"Right." He agreed, reluctantly. "Caleb ask me to speak with Jane Doe, so I'll be seeing him in the morning." He paused. "I'll bring up the subject."

"Good."

He turned to go, then swung back as a thought occurred to him. "Would you like to go with me? I think it would be good for her to speak with another woman."

"I'd love to go and thank her for helping to save my life."

"I'll meet you at the entrance to the hospital about nine. Is that okay?"

"Yes. Good night, Eli."

He walked to his car with a spring in his step. He wasn't angry that he'd have to speak with Jake and Beau. It was time to bury the past. It was time for a lot of things.

THE PHONE STARTED TO RING as Caroline took her purse and camera bag to the bedroom.

"You said you'd call when you got back." Grace came right to the point.

"I just got in."

"Then you took some photos?"

"Yes. I used up a lot of film today."

"Oh, Caro, that's great. Why don't I rent a movie and come over?"

"I'm exhausted," she said. "I'm going to make a sandwich, develop some film, then go to bed. Let's do it another night."

"Okay."

"I'll talk to you tomorrow."

After a bite, Caroline went to her darkroom. The film she'd taken today turned out better than she'd expected.

The pictures of Eli were awesome. She stared at them for a long time, noting with wonder that she'd caught his sensuality, his strength. She couldn't take her eyes off this man—a man who was suddenly the center of her world.

While the photos were drying, she took a shower, then crawled into bed—with the lights on. She'd turn them off in a minute. First, she applied lotion to her arms and legs, then grabbed a novel she wanted to read off the nightstand. The book didn't hold her interest. In a minute, she'd turn the light out.

She'd just spent an hour in her darkroom, so she could do this. She'd done it last night, but Eli was here. Just another minute…

The phone rang and she almost jumped out of her skin. If that was Grace, she was going to give her an earful. "Hello," she snapped into the receiver.

"Caroline, is that you?"

Eli. She sank back against the pillows. "Yes. It's me."

"Are you okay?"

"I…ah…"

"Are the lights on or off?"

"On."

"Turn them off and I'll talk to you for a while."

"Okay." She got up and flipped off the overhead light, then the bedside lamps, feeling like a little girl needing someone to tell her what to do. But she was a big girl with a big problem. She curled up in bed with the phone to her ear. "They're out."

"Talk to me until you feel safe enough to go to sleep."

"I had a great time today and the photos are really good. I'll make copies of the ones of Sam and Dee. Tuck will love them."

"I'm sure he will."

"Eli."

"Hmm?"

"Thanks for calling."

"Go to sleep, Caroline."

She went to sleep with his voice enveloping her. She'd never felt so safe in her life.

CHAPTER ELEVEN

ELI WAITED FOR CAROLINE at the entrance to the hospital. When he saw her coming up the walk his heart skipped a beat. She was dressed in tan slacks and a cream, fitted blouse that showed off her full breasts and long arms. Her blond hair bounced around her shoulders. She smiled when she saw him.

"Good morning," she said.

He fought an urge to take her in his arms and kiss her. "Did you sleep good?"

"Yes." Her smile broadened. "I hope I don't have to talk to you every night for the rest of my life."

She'd said it in a humorous way, but he wouldn't mind talking to her every night. The thought was tempting, taking him down a road he'd been detouring for a long time—one of love, commitment and marriage. He *would* like someone special in his life, someone like Caroline. But he had to take it slow—for both of them. She was confused and needed time to get over her ordeal with Buford. Eli was helping to investigate the case, which complicated matters further.

They went through the automatic doors. "I've already spoken with Caleb," he told her, punching the elevator button. "He thinks it's a good idea, too, for you to speak with her."

There were several people in the elevator and Caroline

moved closer to Eli. She liked being near him, touching him. She liked everything about him. Grace had challenged her feelings for Eli, saying they had grown from gratitude. Caroline kept waiting for those feelings to change, but so far they hadn't. If anything, they were growing deeper.

They got off the elevator and walked down a hall where they saw Caleb McCain walking toward them. Even though Caleb was lean while Eli was muscled, they both had the same chiseled features, straight nose and dark hair. They were definitely brothers.

Eli and Caleb shook hands. "Ms. Whitten." Caleb tipped his hat to her. "I'm glad you came. I'm not getting anywhere with her. She might open up when speaking with a woman, especially one who has been through a similar experience."

Caleb was dressed in the usual Texas Ranger outfit—white shirt, tie, slacks, cowboy boots, light-colored hat, gun and badge. Eli was, too, except he wore Wrangler Riatas and his light blue shirt matched his eyes.

"Has she said anything?" Eli asked.

"Only that she doesn't know anything and for me to leave her alone."

"Maybe she'll talk to Caroline." Eli placed his hand on the door to open it.

"I spoke with the hospital administrator and had her name changed to Belle Doe. It's not so impersonal," Caleb said. "She seems pleased with it—it gives her a bit of an individual identity. So please call her Belle."

"I like it, it's much sweeter then Jezebel or Jane Doe," Caroline said, and they entered the room.

Caroline saw her immediately. She was sitting by a window in a hospital gown and robe. Her head was bent and her long, dark brown hair fell forward, covering her face.

"Belle." Caroline spoke her name softly, not wanting to startle her.

The woman raised her head and Caroline saw her eyes. They were black and spoke plainly of the pain she was in. Caroline felt a deep sadness for what she had been through.

Belle stared blankly at her.

"Hi. I'm Caroline Whitten."

The dark eyes widened. "You're alive."

"Yes." Caroline smiled at her. "Thank you for helping Ranger Coltrane. It saved my life."

Belle bent her head again.

Caroline glanced at Eli, unsure of what to do. It was clear Belle didn't want to talk to anyone.

Eli walked to her. "Belle. Do you remember me?"

She didn't move a muscle.

Eli pulled a chair forward and sat facing her. "Belle, look at me."

"Go away and leave me alone." Her voice was deep and sultry, like her eyes.

"My name is Eli Coltrane. I'm a Texas Ranger and I met you at Amos Buford's camp. Do you remember?"

Belle didn't answer.

"Do you remember me?" he asked again.

She nodded.

"You gave me a clue to help find Caroline. Why did you do that?"

"They were going to… Please go away. I can't say anything."

Eli looked at Caroline and nodded.

"It's okay, Belle," she said. "You're safe now. I am, too."

"It was so awful," Belle whimpered, so low that Caroline had to strain to catch the words.

"I know. I live with constant fear, but I'm trying to take my life back. It's not easy and…"

Eli saw Caroline was getting choked up, so he stepped in again. "Neither of you have to fear Amos Buford and his followers. They're in jail and they'll be there for a long time."

"They're evil. They're evil. They're evil." Belle jerked her head from side to side.

"Yes, they are," Eli agreed.

"They said I was evil," Belle whispered as she stopped shaking her head. "Since I had dark eyes and hair, they said my blood was tainted and I was a plague on society. They forgave me and said only hard work would atone for my sins."

Caroline moved back and Caleb knelt by Belle's chair. "You are not evil."

"Please go away. They'll beat me again."

Caroline caught her breath. Eli and Caleb exchanged a glance.

"Belle, look at me," Eli instructed.

She raised her head.

"No one's going to beat you. I'll make sure of that and Ranger McCain will, too. We only want to help you. Please try to understand that."

Belle didn't say a word.

Eli continued. "Look around you. You're in a hospital and Ranger McCain is trying to find out who you are, but you have to help him. You have to tell him what you know."

"I don't remember anything." The words were barely audible.

"Tell us what you remember."

There was a long pause.

"Please, Belle. We can't help you if you don't talk to us."

"It's okay," Caroline said, sensing that Belle wanted to talk, but was so afraid. Caroline knew that feeling.

Belle clenched and unclenched her hands, then looked at her. "I…I was walking the streets—so hungry—and a couple of men accosted me. A man with long hair and a beard told the men to leave me alone, and he said he would give me food and shelter. We traveled in a truck to their camp and that's when he…"

"Who is *he?*" Eli asked when Belle stopped.

She blinked in confusion, but switched her focus to Eli. "The prophet—he told me those things. He said they were Christians and they would help me. I cooked, did laundry in the creek and worked the fields. At night I was exhausted and they let me sleep in the kitchen area on the floor. They gave me a worn old blanket. It was so cold and once I made a fire in the cookstove. They beat me 'cause they said I had to suffer. It was my fate in life. I never made a fire again for heat, but they beat me to drive the demons from my body. I…I…"

Belle began to tremble and Caroline had to close her eyes to keep the tears from spilling out.

"It's all right," Eli said in a hoarse voice. "You will never have to endure that again."

Belle hung her head and the room became silent.

"How did you know I was looking for Ms. Whitten?" Eli asked softly.

Belle looked directly at him. "At night when everyone was asleep, I watched you from the window, hoping you might take me out of that place. But I was afraid to approach you. Then I saw you get up and search around. I knew you were looking for the woman they'd brought and I knew you'd never find her." She placed her hands over her ears. "I can't say any more. I can't. I can't. Please go away."

"It's all right," Eli said, and Belle wiped her eyes.

Caroline saw how Belle had responded to Eli. He was kind and understanding—just as he was with her. It was hard not to respond to that. *Oh God!* Suddenly she could see what Grace was trying to tell her. After what she'd been through, she needed that kindness. And she had turned it into something more when all the while Eli had just been doing his job.

He was that kind of person. No wonder he didn't want to take their relationship any further—he didn't care for her in that way. He was just too nice to say so. She had to get away from him so she could sort this out, but before she left she had to thank Belle again. Without her help, the outcome could have been very different for Caroline.

Eli stood, pushing back his chair and Caroline took a step closer.

"Thank you, Belle, for being so brave."

Belle's eyes flickered. "I'm glad you're alive."

The three of them walked from the room, leaving Belle in the company of a nurse. In the hall Caleb said, "That went well. She's said more today than she has so far." He looked at Caroline. "She seemed to connect with you. Thanks for talking to her."

It wasn't her, Caroline thought, it was Eli who Belle responded to. Caroline knew that feeling very well. She had also shared things with Eli she hadn't shared with anyone else. She had to get away right now, before she made a complete fool of herself.

"How bad was she beaten?" Eli asked Caleb.

"The doctor said her back is covered in welts and scars that are never going to go away. He said it was probably done with a rope or board. Some of the cuts were deep and left jagged wounds. I don't know how she survived it. I hope they put Buford away for the rest of his pitiful life."

Caroline couldn't listen to any more. "I've got to go. I have an appointment I can't miss."

She hurried down the hall, but Eli caught her before she got too far. "I'm sorry you had to hear that."

"No. I needed to." She forced herself not to cry. "I have an appointment at a magazine for a shoot. I don't want to be late." She walked away before he could stop her, taking the stairs all the way to the ground floor. Her chest was tight and she was panting when she stepped out into the fresh air. Sucking air into her lungs, she rushed to her car.

Amos Buford had inflicted so much pain on Belle and on herself. He would *not* do this to her. She refused to be a victim of her own fears and would deal with the fear in her own way—without help from Eli.

Resting her head on the steering wheel, Caroline tried to shake off all the doubts and insecurities inside her. She'd always been a strong person, standing up to her father and living her life the way she wanted. Now she had to find that strength again—and work was the answer. If she immersed herself in her job she wouldn't think about Eli and how she'd made a fool of herself.

She drove to the magazine and accepted an assignment. A writer was doing a story about the Alamo and how young people saw it today. The editor didn't want to pull an old photo for the article, she wanted something fresh, with young people in the shots. Within an hour Caroline was back in her apartment, packing for a trip to San Antonio.

She called Grace to let her know she'd be out of town for a couple of days, then she was on the road, putting miles between her and Eli.

You're running.

And she was. She couldn't deny that. But it was the only

way to get her head straight. Then she'd see what she felt for Eli for what it was—gratitude.

Hopefully, soon she'd believe that.

ELI CALLED CAROLINE a couple of times to see if she wanted to go to the ranch with him, but got no answer. Finally he went alone. Her presence was everywhere, though, and he had to admit that something strong was happening between them. Smiling, he hung the boxing gloves back on the nail. He'd failed to do that last night. He'd also failed to mention to Caleb about visiting Jake and Beau, and he wondered why Caroline hadn't called him about it. Where had she gone in such a hurry?

He knew she was upset about the conversation with Belle. Hell, he and Caleb were, too. Eli thought he'd just give her some time, then they'd talk, but now he couldn't find her.

When he got back to town, it was late, and he drove to her apartment. She didn't answer the door and the lights were out.

Where was she?

CAROLINE CHECKED INTO a hotel, then walked to the Alamo to get an idea from the old stone mission of the type of light and angles she'd shoot tomorrow. Photos weren't allowed inside so she had to get what she needed from the outside.

She pushed Eli to the farthest corner of her mind and concentrated on her work. There was so much Texas history at the mission and she got caught up in its allure. History or myth, what had happened on these grounds in 1836 was of epic importance to the people of Texas. The Alamo stood for fighting for what you believed in. And for freedom. Sitting on a bench with history all around her, Caroline felt the spirit of that long-ago day.

Later she went back to the hotel for dinner. She was studying the menu when a man stopped at her table.

"May I buy you a drink?"

"I'm waiting on someone. Thank you," she lied.

"Sorry to have bothered you." He inclined his head and moved on.

She was waiting on Eli.

She couldn't keep lying about that. She wished he'd walk in with his boots and hat and sit down and smile at her. Then she'd feel better. Oh, this was going to take longer than she'd thought. She didn't know if she was ever going to get over Eli.

But she had to.

In her room, she went through her nightly ritual and sat in the middle of the bed, staring at the phone. She could call Eli. He was probably worried about her. No. She wouldn't take the coward's way out. It would accomplish nothing. If he tried to contact her and couldn't, he'd call Grace and she'd tell him Caroline was on an assignment.

She had to face the night alone.

She forced herself to get up and turn off the light. Crawling between the sheets, she stared at the ceiling. Muted light streamed through the drapes, illuminating the room in a clandestine glow.

It reminded her of the yellow glow of light in the cellar. All of a sudden she could almost see Buford standing there. A scream rose in her throat, but she forced it back. It was just remnants of fear, she told herself, and she wouldn't give in to it. Still, the urge to turn the light on was strong. She didn't give in.

Instead she turned her thoughts to Belle and the nightmare she'd been through and was still enduring. Compared to Belle, Caroline was lucky. She was only afraid of the dark, while Belle had so many demons to conquer. But Eli would help her. Suddenly Caroline was jealous that someone else would get his attention.

She laughed out loud at the ridiculous thought and realized her feelings for Eli were more than gratitude. They had probably started the first moment she'd touched him in that dark room. From then on, all she could feel was Eli.

Flipping onto her side, she groaned.

Go to sleep. Go to sleep. Go to sleep.

It was close to 2:00 a.m. before she fell into a restless slumber.

ELI SAT IN HIS CAR and waited. He wasn't a natural worrier; he left that up to Tuck. But he was getting worried now. He had to make sure she was okay. He wasn't clear when he fell asleep, but it was morning when he woke up. Caroline's car wasn't in her spot. She still wasn't home.

Feeling the stubble on his face, he drove to his own place, showered and changed clothes. Then he headed for the Whitten Building. He waited in the lobby for Grace. He saw her coming through the double doors and stopped her before she reached the elevators.

"Ranger Coltrane, this is a surprise," she said, a briefcase in one hand and a purse in the other.

"Have you seen Caroline?"

Grace paused. "No. Why?"

"She's not at her apartment and I'm a little worried."

"I don't believe that's part of your job description, Ranger Coltrane," she replied with a touch of sarcasm. "Why don't you let Caroline's family worry about her?"

He took a step closer. "Don't tell me about my job description, Ms. Whitten," he said in a clipped tone. "I'm well aware of what that is." He took a quick breath. "Yesterday morning Caroline visited with one of the women from Buford's camp and it upset her."

"Why would she do such a thing?"

"Because I asked her."

"See?" Grace pointed out. "You're too involved with her and you shouldn't have ever let her go anywhere near those people."

Eli's eyes narrowed. "Where's Caroline?"

A hard mask came over her face and Eli knew he'd have to push hard to get any answers. "You know, Ms. Whitten, when I get angry I'm not a very nice person. Now where in the hell is Caroline?"

He saw a flicker of fear and knew he was way out of line, but at the moment he wasn't too concerned about that.

"She's…she's with Colin."

That took the wind right out of him. "Her fiancé?"

"Yes. So you don't have to worry."

"Thank you," he said, and walked out of the building.

Caroline was with Colin.

He was in Houston, she'd said. But maybe he was back and they'd patched things up. That didn't sound right to Eli. Of course he didn't want to believe that she was with him. It was time for him to back off and let Caroline find her way back to her life before Buford.

Before him.

Suddenly that hurt like hell.

ELI WENT TO THE HOSPITAL to meet Caleb. They were going to talk to Belle again. He sat in the lobby, thinking about Caroline as he waited. Why would she take back her fiancé? Especially after all the things she'd said about him.

What the hell did he care? Eli wondered. Oh, but he did—in a big way. If she was happy, that was all that mattered, he told himself. Now he had to convince himself of that.

Caleb came in and they went upstairs.

"Sorry to bother you on your time off," Caleb said in the elevator.

"Don't worry about it. I was at loose ends anyway."

"Ms. Whitten was pretty upset yesterday." Caleb held the door for a lady with a stroller to get on, then they continued down the hall. "How is she?"

"I don't know," Eli replied. "I haven't seen her since then."

"Oh." Caleb glanced at him. "I thought you stayed in contact with her."

"I did, but she's gone back to her boyfriend." Try as he might he wasn't able to keep that touch of jealousy out of his voice.

"Oh," Caleb said again.

"Have you spoken with Belle any more?" He changed the subject as quickly as he could.

"Yes, and she doesn't seem so afraid of me now." Caleb stopped and turned to Eli. "This morning I spoke with the doctor who was running the tests on Belle. There's a bullet lodged in her skull and he said that's probably the cause of her memory loss."

"Good God. Have they told her?"

"I was there when the doctor explained it to her," Caleb answered.

"How did she take it?"

He shrugged. "She just turned away and stared out the window."

"What is your take on this?"

"Someone tried to kill her and thought they had succeeded. Evidently she was left somewhere for dead. When she came around, she started walking the streets without a clue where she was or who she was."

"That's when Buford's followers found her," Eli murmured.

"I don't think there's a connection between Buford and the bullet in her head."

"I don't either," Eli admitted. "She's been through so much, but she's probably the only one who can nail this case shut and put Buford away forever. She was in that camp for a while and we need to know what she saw."

"God, I hate to push her."

Eli could see the turmoil Caleb was in. It was hard not to be touched by what Belle had been through. "We'll just take it slow."

Caleb knocked on the door and they went in. "Belle, Ranger Coltrane is with me."

She was sitting at the window again with her head bent.

"Hi, Belle," Eli said.

She didn't respond.

Caleb knelt down by her chair. "Belle, look at me."

"Please go away."

"Look at me," Caleb insisted.

She raised her head.

"We're law officers and we're here to help you. Everyone in this hospital wants to help you, too. No one's going to hurt you and you don't have to be afraid. Do you understand?"

"How can you help me? I don't know who I am. I don't know anything."

"Oh, but you do, Belle," Eli said. "You know about Buford and his followers and you can help us put him away so he'll never hurt another woman again."

She shook her head.

"You can, Belle," Caleb said, and she stared at him.

"Why can't you leave me alone?"

"Because we need answers and only you have them."

Eli moved closer. "Buford is saying that Ms. Whitten came to the camp of her own free will, wanting to become part of his faith. His lawyer is going to try and make a jury believe that. If he can, then Buford will be free to hurt other women."

Belle's eyes opened wide. "No. They can't do that."

"Help us, then," Eli begged. "Did Caroline come there on her own?"

Belle twisted her hands. "No."

Eli felt a moment of victory and knew he had to keep going. "How did they bring her in?"

"They…they had her in the back of the truck and they carried her and laid her by the fire."

"Who is 'they'?"

"Samuel and Nathaniel."

"Was Ms. Whitten conscious?"

Belle shook her head.

"What happened next?"

"They lit the fire and flames leaped to the sky, then they began to chant things I didn't understand. The prophet prayed, thanking God for his beautiful new wife, and he prayed she would be strong enough to pass the cleansing ritual. He knelt down beside her and ran his hands over her body to bless her and to rid her of the demons of society. Then they all walked by her to view the woman who would bear the seventh son."

Eli's hands curled into fists and he had a hard time controlling his anger.

"Then what happened?" He forced out the question.

"They carried her to the cellar to begin the ritual."

Eli turned away, unable to continue the questioning. It

was his job to keep asking Belle for information, but he found it hard to do when his heart was involved. That was the first time anything like this had happened to him, but the idea of Buford touching Caroline turned his stomach.

"Thank you, Belle," Caleb said. "Why don't you rest? Maybe tomorrow you can tell us more."

"Please. He'll beat me."

Eli swung around. "Was Buford the one who beat you?"

Belle nodded, tears running from her eyes.

"Don't cry, Belle," Caleb pleaded. "You're safe here."

A nurse came in and Eli and Caleb left.

"I feel such rage inside," Caleb said outside the door.

Eli needed a moment and he took a long breath. "Yeah, but she just confirmed what Caroline had said. That helps a lot. If we keep working with her, we might learn more. When the trial comes up, I'd feel a lot better if Belle was able to testify."

"I just wish I could find out who she is and return her to her family."

"That will probably take time, but I'll help you all I can."

"Thanks. I'd appreciate that."

"No problem. I'll see you tomorrow." Eli started off, then turned back. "After we visit with Belle tomorrow, I was thinking we might drive to Waco and visit with Jake and Beau."

Caleb seemed shocked. "Sure. That would be great."

"I promised someone I'd do that. I'll talk to you later."

He walked to his car, thinking he would do it for Caroline. A deal was a deal. If he ever saw her again he wanted to be able to say that he'd kept his word.

CHAPTER TWELVE

CAROLINE SPENT THE DAY at the Alamo snapping pictures of wide-eyed school children as they visited the historic site for the first time. She got some great shots of teenagers with their funky hairstyles and modish clothes. Some carried boom boxes, others had headsets. But the expressions on their faces were the same as they stared at a piece of Texas history—expressions of awe.

She was pleased with the shoot and she hoped the writer would be, too. She'd read the article and felt she'd conveyed the story of how the younger generations still showed reverence and respect for the sacrifice that had been made by a handful of brave Texans to gain independence from Mexico. It seemed that names like William Travis, James Bowie and Davy Crockett would never be forgotten, even by rebellious teenagers.

Exhausted by the shoot she decided to spend another night in San Antonio. Another night to gain strength for when she saw Eli again. Another night to fight the fear.

That night she went to bed without the usual battle with the light. She just turned it off and slipped beneath the sheets. It took awhile to actually fall asleep, but she didn't wake up in fear. She was getting better.

ELI WAS UP EARLY and went to the ranch to feed Sam and Dee because he didn't know if he'd be back in time to feed them tonight. He was going to keep his word for Caroline and visit with Jake and Beau this afternoon, but he wasn't looking forward to it.

He'd called Tom about the visit with Belle, and Tom met him and Caleb in the hospital coffee shop. Eli told him what Belle had said.

"She corroborates Caroline's story," Eli finished.

"Lansing will tear her to shreds on the witness stand," Tom replied. "That is if you can get her to testify, which I doubt. When I last visited with her, she was a long way from being a credible witness."

"Yeah." Eli leaned back in frustration.

Tom turned to Caleb. "Has your investigation turned up anything?"

He shook his head. "Her fingerprints aren't on record and it doesn't look like she was reported as a missing person. The doctor said her memory loss is due to trauma from the bullet in her head. It's possible that she could start to have flashbacks and gradually regain her memory. Opening up to Caroline and Eli was a big step, in my opinion. So far she's resisted our every attempt to get her to talk. Every day seems to be a step forward, though. We need more time."

"We need something now," Tom said. "The attorneys feel that it will come down to Caroline's word against Buford's, and Buford's followers will back him up—that's going to destroy our case. Eli can testify how he found her, but he doesn't know how she got in that room."

"Dammit, Tom, I know and you know." Eli couldn't contain his anger.

"Yes." Tom nodded. "But there are two cases on record

where Buford walked free because a jury believed him. We're facing the same thing now and it doesn't matter that she's Stephen Whitten's daughter. That will actually work against her. Caroline is known to be a spirited woman who defies her father, and Lansing will play that for all it's worth, believe me."

"Goddammit," Eli said under his breath.

"We need some hard, concrete evidence to make this conviction stick. Keep working with Belle and maybe we'll get lucky." Tom stood. "I'll relay what's happened to the attorneys."

They shook hands and Eli and Caleb went upstairs to see Belle, but she was in with a psychologist and would be in various types of therapy for most of the day. So they headed for Waco.

"Have you talked to Ms. Whitten?" Caleb asked.

"No. Why?"

"I thought you might have told her what Belle said."

"It doesn't matter unless we can get Belle to tell us a lot more," Eli replied, not wanting to talk about Caroline. "If you and I can earn her trust, we might be able to accomplish that."

They talked about the case until they reached Marlin. Then Caleb asked, "What made you change your mind about talking to Jake and Beau?"

Eli kept his eyes on the road. "I'm tired of being angry and if I can talk to you without resentment, I figure I could probably talk to Jake and Beau, too."

"But you didn't come to that realization on your own."

"No, actually I was tricked into it." Before he knew what he was doing he was telling Caleb about the boxing gloves.

"Ms. Whitten knocked you on your ass?" Caleb laughed.

"Yeah, and I'm sticking to the story that she tricked me."

"From what Jake has said about you and from what I've heard as a ranger, no one takes you on."

"Well, then, don't let it get around that a green-eyed blonde did me in."

Eli turned off the highway onto a country road without waiting for directions from Caleb. He knew where the Mc-Cain farm was. He'd known all his life, but he'd never been there. Green cotton fields dotted the landscape on both sides of the road. When he saw the older white house with green shutters, he turned again, up the drive.

He felt a queasiness in his stomach. This was where his father had lived. He took in the barns and farming equipment, everything that epitomized living on a farm.

As a kid, he'd hated that Jake got to live here and he had to live in a cramped apartment. He'd never wanted to be friends, despite the fact that Jake was kind, taking his side when kids said cruel things. He didn't need anyone to do that, though. He could take care of himself and he'd proved it time and time again by being tough, by being mean and rebellious.

Today he wasn't feeling any of those things. He was feeling scared. Scared of emotions he didn't know if he was ready to face.

But he'd promised Caroline.

"Drive around back to the garage," Caleb said, removing his gun and locking it in the glove compartment.

Eli did as instructed and stopped not far from the garage. He removed his own gun, handed it to Caleb and took in the scene in front of him. Jake and Beau stood waiting under a basketball net attached to the garage. A dog, part Lab, lay at Jake's feet. A bike with training wheels was off to the side, as was a tricycle, a couple of balls and a bat. Kids lived here—that was obvious. This was a home. A family lived here.

Eli drew a deep breath and got out of the vehicle. Jake took a couple of steps forward and paused. They stood staring at each other as their childhoods played before them like a reel from an old movie they'd watched over and over. Two boys with the same father—one who knew and one who didn't.

"How's the arm?" Jake asked.

Eli flexed his hand. "Great."

Jake bent and picked up a basketball and dribbled it. "Remember gym class? You could make a basket from center court with your eyes closed."

Eli laid his hat on the hood of the car. "I still can."

Jake threw the ball to him. He caught it deftly. Something about the movement, the action, released the tightness in his gut.

Caleb removed his hat. "What do you think, Beau? Can we take 'em in a game?"

"Sure," Beau replied, removing his suit jacket. "We're younger, so we have an advantage."

Eli dribbled the ball, then leaped into the air, sending the ball sailing right into the hoop. Jake grabbed the ball and jumped, making another basket.

Beau and Caleb got in on the action, playing defense, and they ran, laughed and joked until they were exhausted. Beau finally slipped and lay sprawled on the concrete, sweat stains on his starched white shirt.

Jake looked down at him. "Get up, you wimp."

"I don't think I can. I'm completely spent."

"That's because you sit in an office all day," he told him. "You need more exercise." He reached down and jerked Beau to his feet.

Breathing heavily, Beau said to Caleb, "I think they kicked our butts."

Caleb grinned. "Do I need to take you to the emergency room?"

"That's not funny, little brother. I'll get my second wind in a minute." Beau took several deep breaths. "I didn't get much sleep last night."

"Hot date, huh?" Caleb joked.

Beau wiped his brow. "Don't I wish. Macy talked me into keeping one of her strays again. I swear she picks up every abandoned animal she comes across. She found this small kitten that was starving, and since she works nights, she didn't want to leave the kitten alone. She said it would be very quiet. Wrong. The thing whined half the night, and when I closed her in the utility room, she scratched at the door."

Caleb put his arm around Beau. "Do you want me to teach you how to say no to Macy?"

"I don't think the woman knows the meaning of the word."

Caleb raised an eyebrow. "How long has she been talking you into pet-sitting? Don't you think it's time you asked the woman out on a date?"

"Are you out of your mind?" Beau shook off Caleb's arm. "She drives me nuts within five minutes. I certainly don't want to spend a whole evening with her."

"Beau," Caleb sighed. "She's lives in the condo next to yours. You see her every day. You see her more than you see your own family."

Eli didn't know who Macy was, but evidently she was someone Beau had known for a long time.

Caleb filled him in. "Macy grew up in our neighborhood. She's much younger than us and was always knocking on our door, looking for a home for some cat or dog she'd found. She had a houseful and her parents wouldn't let her have any more. Old Beau was a sucker for those big blue eyes. He still is."

"Shut up, Caleb." Beau was now able to breathe normally and he was getting angry.

Jake turned to Eli. "We'll let these two continue this fascinating conversation. Would you like to see the farm?"

"I'd love to."

They fell into step and headed for the barn. The dog trotted ahead.

"As a kid, I used to dream of being here," Eli said, surprising himself.

"As a kid, I used to dream of running away from here," Jake replied.

"Did you?" Eli was shocked.

"All the time, but Aunt Vin was here and I didn't want to leave her." They stopped by a big John Deere tractor. "She's dad's sister and she lives with us. She can't wait to meet you."

Eli didn't know if he was ready to meet one of Joe Mc-Cain's other relatives. He'd only planned to meet the sons.

"It'll be painless," Jake said, noticing his expression. "How about a tractor ride?"

"Sure."

They climbed into the big closed-in cab of the tractor. The dog jumped onto the hitch, then onto the wheel and into the cab. He obviously knew his way around a tractor.

"That's Wags." Jake rubbed the dog's head. "He's Ben's dog and he follows me around until Ben comes home. Elise is picking him up from school. I hope you'll stay until they get back."

With a turn of a key, the tractor roared to life, preventing Eli from answering. He wasn't sure how long he was staying, but his attention was diverted to the farm and the view from a tractor.

The endless cotton fields soon gave way to cornfields, where workers were busy tending to the crops.

"We'll harvest the corn pretty soon. It should be a good year," Jake said. "We had just enough rain and sunshine. Sometimes I'm not so lucky."

"But you're able to make a living?"

"Yeah, and that's great because farming is all I've ever done."

They rolled back to the barn and Jake turned off the engine.

"I used to think of this place as heaven—a place where a happy family lived." The words came out before Eli could stop them.

Jake faced him. "It was more like hell. Joe McCain abused my mother and he made me think it was her fault. When she finally got the courage to leave, I refused to go because I believed all the lies he'd told me. I didn't speak to her again until I was thirty-eight years old. I hated her for leaving me and for what I believed she'd done."

"Caleb said that Joe refused to admit Caleb was his?"

"He said that Andrew Wellman was Caleb's father and I believed it." Jake looked out across the fields. "I wouldn't have anything to do with my mother or Caleb until three years ago. That's a long time to harbor hatred."

"But you have a good relationship with Caleb now?"

Jake's gaze swung back to him. "Yes, and with my mother. I'm thankful for that. Is your mom still living?"

"No. She died when I was nineteen."

"I'm sorry."

Eli rested his elbows on his knees, his hands clasped together. "She never got over Joe McCain."

"When your mother left town, Joe stayed drunk all the time. Aunt Vin and I had to go get him several times from the bar because he was causing a scene, calling Vera's name. I blamed his drinking on my mother, but I think he really cared for Vera and missed her."

Eli took a deep breath. "She finally realized he wasn't going to marry her and she wanted to make a life for me, but by then I was happy with Uncle Jess and Aunt Amalie. She agreed to let me stay, and it was probably the best thing she ever did for me. She worked in Houston for a while, then Dallas, then Beaumont, and finally settled in a small town on the coast. But she was never happy except when she was in Waco with him."

Silence filled the cab.

"I'm glad you found a good home," Jake finally said.

"The very best," Eli answered in a quiet voice.

"I never knew what happened to you. I figured that, after stealing the principal's car, you'd end up in reform school."

Eli grinned. "Now that was stupid, wasn't it?"

Jake grinned back. "Nobody but Elijah Coltrane would do something like that. Nobody had that much nerve."

"I think it was a cry for help."

"I'm glad your life turned out so well," Jake said. "And that you didn't end up in reform school."

"Me, too."

Wags whined and pawed at the door.

"Okay." Jake rose and they got out of the cab. "Somehow Wags knows it's time for Ben and Katie to come home."

"Maybe I should be going," Eli said, thinking he'd shared enough for one day.

"Please stay," Jake replied. At Eli's silence, he added, "It's time to put our rotten childhoods behind us. We had no control over them, but we do have control of the future.

It's time to be adults, to be men and to be brothers. Because whether you like it or not, we are."

Eli still didn't speak.

"I hated for so many years that it was eating away at my soul. Beau kept at me, though, trying to make me listen, trying to get me to build a relationship with my mother and Caleb. But I stubbornly refused until I was brought to my knees over Ben's kidnapping. Then I needed my mom." He took a breath. "You're the strongest person I've ever met and I know you're fine on your own, but I hope you'll let us share a small part of your life." He held out his hand.

Eli stared at it, the past and the present battling inside him. He felt it all—the little boy who desperately wanted a father, the kid that defied everyone, the teenager learning to like himself and respect others, and the man who still yearned for family. From out of nowhere he saw Caroline's face and could hear her voice.

You can do it. They're blood. They're family.

Suddenly the past released its grip and receded into his memory. He had family, as Tuck had reminded him many times, and now he was ready to accept them without feeling any guilt about Ma, Pa and Tuck. The McCains would be an extension of that family, as Caroline had told him. It was time for forgiveness. It was time….

He reached for Jake's hand and suddenly they were hugging, holding on tight. Caleb and Beau joined them, and the four men stood with their arms around each other, letting go, accepting and bonding as brothers.

Wags jumped up and down, barking, and they finally drew apart. "I think we know what time it is." Jake wiped a tear from his eyes.

"Ben and Katie are home," Beau answered in a hoarse voice.

Eli glanced up the road, knowing there were tears in his eyes, too, and he didn't bother to brush them away. A Suburban drove into the garage and Wags raced for the house.

"You're not leaving," Jake told him. "You have to meet my wife and kids."

Eli nodded, not trusting his voice, and they made their way to the garage. He watched as a very pretty blond woman got out and opened a back door. After a moment, Ben and Katie jumped out, hugged Wags and came running toward Jake, crying, "Daddy, Daddy, Daddy."

Jake ran to meet them, grabbing them both at the same time, holding Ben in one arm and Katie in the other. "How are my babies?" He kissed Ben, then Katie.

"Fine," Ben said.

"Did you have a good day at school?"

"Yes, but Ms. Taylor said…" Ben glanced at his mother. He could see Elise mentally urging him to finish the sentence. "That…that school will be out soon. I don't want school to end. I like school."

"We're going to Disney World, remember?"

"Yeah," Ben said, his brown eyes growing big.

The only time Eli had seen Ben was the day he'd rescued him from the mobile home. He'd only had a glimpse of him as his biological mother had pushed him out the window. Ben looked healthy and happy now, and Eli knew it was because of Jake and Elise's love and care.

"What did you do at Granny Althea's?" Jake asked Katie.

Eli's eyes were glued to the little girl. She was about the prettiest thing he'd ever seen, with her blond pigtails and her big brown eyes.

"We cooked all day 'cause Granny said someone special was coming."

"Did you?"

Katie nodded. "Is he here, Daddy?"

Eli realized she was talking about him, and he was thrown for a second, but he didn't have time to respond because Elise walked up and kissed her husband. Katie and Ben slid to the ground.

"Eli, this is my wife, Elise." Jake made the introduction.

She smiled and shook his hand. "It's nice to finally meet you."

"I'm sorry," he found himself saying. "It's taken me awhile."

"We understand," she said, and he realized that they did.

Caleb put his arm around Elise's waist and kissed her cheek. "How's my favorite sister-in-law?"

"Great, Caleb. It's good to have you home."

Beau kissed her other cheek. "How about me?"

"You I see all the time, and you're spoiling my kids rotten, but I love you anyway."

"Will you two get away from my wife?" Jake teased. "I wish you'd find wives of your own."

Amid the resulting laughter, Ben tugged on his dad's hand. Jake bent down to hear what he had to say, then straightened. "Eli, I'm so sorry. I forgot to introduce you to my children. This is Ben and Katie, and kids, this is my brother Eli."

Ben stepped forward and held out his hand. "Nice to meet you, sir," he said.

Eli took the little boy's hand. It seemed so fragile in his big one. "Nice to meet you, too."

"You're my daddy's brother so...so—" he glanced at his mother, and Elise nodded "—you're my uncle, like Beau and Caleb."

Eli swallowed the constriction in his throat. "Yes. I am."

"I got lots of uncles now."

Beau ruffled Ben's hair. "You sure do."

Before Eli could catch his breath, Katie stepped in front of Ben and curtsied. "Nice to meet you. Welcome to our home." She looked up at Eli. "I 'posed to kiss you but I can't reach way up there."

Eli lifted her in his arms. She felt light as a feather and as precious as anything he'd ever touched, and when she kissed his cheek, he melted.

"Me and Granny Althea practiced all day. Did I do good?"

"You did wonderfully," Elise said before Eli could.

"Yes. You did very well," he added, feeling a lump in his throat.

Caleb hugged Ben. "While I'm here, do you want to throw the ball, champ?"

"Okay, okay. I get it." Ben ran and picked up a baseball from the grass. "I can throw good now, can't I, Daddy?"

"Like a champion."

Caleb walked off into the grass and turned. "Okay, Ben. Toss me the ball."

The boy raised his arm and threw. The ball landed midway between him and Caleb.

Caleb picked it up. "Here it comes. Try to catch it." He threw the ball gently, but Ben's hands came together after the ball landed at his feet.

"Again," Ben said, not discouraged, and tried to throw the ball back. But again it landed short of its mark.

Without thinking, Eli walked over and squatted behind the child. "Don't watch Caleb, Ben. Watch the ball. Just keep your eye on the ball. Okay?"

"Okay."

Eli nodded to Caleb.

"Watch the ball," he repeated.

Ben bit his tongue in concentration, and the ball spiraled, almost in slow motion, directly to him. He caught it clumsily, but the ball was in his hands.

"Yay, Ben!" Katie shouted.

Ben kept staring at the ball as if he couldn't believe he'd caught it.

Eli glanced at Jake and Elise. Elise had tears in her eyes and Jake's face held pure joy. Evidently this was something Ben had been trying to do for a long time.

"I caught it, Daddy. I caught it." Ben's voice rose in excitement.

"You sure did, son."

Eli knelt in the grass. "Now let's throw it back to Caleb." He wrapped his fingers around Ben's forearm. "Make a fist. Let me feel your muscle."

Ben looked at him blankly, and Eli realized he didn't understand. "Like this." He made a fist to show him.

"Oh." Ben curled his little fingers in a tight knot.

"Oh, yeah," Eli said, squeezing the small arm. "I feel those muscles. When you throw the ball, use them instead of your wrist. Do you understand?"

"I think," Ben said, frowning.

Eli squeezed again. "This is your muscle. Use it for strength."

"Okay." The boy nodded vigorously.

"Now reach back." Eli demonstrated. "Make those muscles work to send the ball where you want it to go."

Eli held his breath, so badly wanting for Ben to succeed.

The child bit his lip, reached back and threw the ball as hard as he could. It sailed through the air directly toward Caleb, who took a step forward to catch it. Ben's eyes grew enormous and he looked at his parents.

Elise couldn't contain herself—she ran over and kissed Ben. "You did it. I'm so proud of you."

"I threw it, Mommy. I threw it a long way."

"Yes. You did."

Jake hugged him. "I told you one day you'd do it."

"'Cause I got muscles, Daddy. Look." He held up his tiny arm. "I got big muscles."

"You sure do," Jake replied.

Beau and Caleb ruffled his hair and teased him, but Ben kept smiling.

Eli got to his feet and Ben looked up at him. "Thank you, Uncle Eli."

"You welcome, Ben. Just remember to use those muscles."

"Oh! Oh!" The boy jumped up and down. "We got something for you."

"Let's continue this in the house," Jake said.

Eli, unable to resist, picked up Katie and followed.

Inside, Katie wiggled to get down and Eli reluctantly let her go. As he straightened, he saw an older woman in her seventies come toward him, and he knew who she was.

"Aunt Vin, I believe," he said.

She stared at him. "My, my, you have Joe's eyes."

"Yes, ma'am, my mother told me."

"My, my, this is…" She wrapped her arms around his waist and hugged him, unable to say more. Eli hugged her back, finding it quite easy.

Aunt Vin wiped at her eyes. "Now have a seat, young man, and we'll have a snack."

Ben came from the kitchen holding a large platter and walking very carefully. Elise hovered behind him. He placed the platter on the table. "We made these for you."

Eli stared at the cinnamon rolls. "Thank you, Ben." He glanced at Jake, recalling a day in grade school when Althea had made cinnamon rolls for their class. Eli had loved them and Jake had remembered.

"Sit, sit," Aunt Vin ordered, and everyone settled at the table.

Elise tried to put Katie in her seat. "No, no," she said. "I have to tell Uncle Eli a story."

Jake lifted an eyebrow. "A story?"

"Yeah." She stood by Eli. "Aunt Vin, Granny Althea and me made these and Ben put on the icing and they're really, really good. Do you know why?"

Eli shook his head. "No. I don't."

Her eyes sparkled. "'Cause they got love in them. See if you can taste it."

Eli tried not to laugh. He reached for a napkin, picked up a roll and bit into it. It was as good as he remembered, if not better.

"Can you taste it?" Katie asked, watching him closely.

"Can you?" Ben pressed.

Eli smiled at them. "Oh, yes. I can taste it." And he felt it all around him. He saw it on their faces and in their actions, and he wondered why it had taken him so long to find his way to heaven. As a kid, he'd thought this place was heaven, and he'd been right—maybe not then, but now. Jake had made this a haven, a place to be happy, and Eli wanted that, too.

He lifted Katie onto his lap, knowing he wanted his own home, wife and kids. He'd planned that with Ginny, but life had thrown him a destructive curve, which seemed to be a pattern for him. Life hadn't been kind, and he dealt with it the best way he could. Alone. Keeping everything inside. If he didn't let himself feel, he couldn't get hurt.

But deep down he'd always longed for love and family.

Suddenly all he could see were Caroline's green eyes.

CHAPTER THIRTEEN

WHEN IT WAS TIME to leave, Eli felt a moment of sadness for the years he'd missed with the McCains, especially after Ben's kidnapping. He hadn't been ready to know them then, but now he was, and it felt so good to let all the resentment go.

He stood with Katie in his arms. Ben looked up at him.

"When you coming back, Uncle Eli?"

"I'm not sure, but I will be back." He glanced briefly at Jake and saw approval in his eyes. Eli didn't want to give Ben a date because he had to concentrate on the Buford case and he wasn't certain when he'd be free. "In the meantime you practice your throwing."

"I'll use my muscles." Ben made a fist and flexed his arm. "And Daddy and Uncle Beau will help me."

Caleb placed a hand over his heart. "I'm crushed. I've been replaced."

"Nah," Ben said, running to him and wrapping his arms around him. "I love you."

Caleb picked him up. "Love you, too, champ, and when we come back we'll all play ball."

"Okay."

Eli walked to the car, feeling more love and warmth than he'd felt in a long time. On the drive back, Caleb talked about the family and Eli listened with an open heart.

They drove to the hospital where Caleb's car was parked, and they hugged as brothers as they parted. It was an awesome feeling.

Eli didn't drive to his place—instead he found himself driving to the ranch. He hadn't planned to, but it seemed to be where he needed to go. It was dark as he pulled into the carport. He saw Sam through the beam of headlights, racing for the house thinking it was Tuck. Turning off the ignition, Eli got out and rubbed the dog's ears.

"He'll be home soon, boy," he told him, and retrieved the cinnamon rolls Aunt Vin had given him to take home. Sam curled up on his mat by the door and Eli went inside.

Flipping on the light, he laid the rolls and his hat on the table, soaking up the ambiance of the big, comfortable kitchen and den. He'd learned about life here, learned about family. Eli never wanted to lose the feeling he got when he walked into this house. Letting out a long breath, he knew he hadn't. Caroline was right. There were many facets to love, and he'd found another one tonight—the love of his brothers.

He opened the sliding door and stepped onto the patio. When he sat in Ma's rocker, Sam came and lay down at his feet. Soon Dee materialized and went to sleep on Sam. Crickets chirped and Eli stared out into the night, feeling Ma and Pa's presence all around him. He knew beyond a shadow of doubt they would have wanted him to form a connection to his brothers. If they were alive, they would have insisted on it. He hadn't recognized that until Caroline mentioned it. They wouldn't want him to continue to live with the resentment. They'd taught him better than that.

He drew in the fresh, cedar-tinged air and suddenly all his doubts and guilty feelings over loyalty vanished. He had family and he would build on the relationships he'd formed today.

Glancing up at the stars, he wondered where Caroline and Colin were tonight. Ignoring the sudden ache in his heart, he hoped she was happy and that Colin would be with her during the trial. She would need him.

Headlights flashed across the barn—Tuck was home. Sam ran for the carport and Dee disappeared into the darkness. Eli sat where he was. He didn't feel like moving.

In a few minutes, Tuck came through the patio doors munching on a cinnamon roll. "Where'd you get these?" he asked, patting Sam and giving him a bite. "They're delicious."

"You'd never guess."

"Probably not." Tuck licked his fingers.

After a long pause, Eli said, "I went to visit the McCains today."

Tuck plopped down in Pa's chair. "What? How did that happen?"

"After you left the coffee shop, I forced myself to talk to Caleb. He was very nice, didn't even mention how rude I'd been. We talked and talked. It wasn't difficult at all, like you said. Joe McCain didn't claim him, either." Eli told him the rest of the story.

"Man—I never expected anything like that."

"Me, neither." Eli leaned forward. "I thought they were this happy, perfect family."

"But you knew that Jake's mother had left Joe a long time ago."

"Yeah. But I thought the boys had a connection with their father. It seems Joe McCain didn't raise any of us. Aunt Vin, Joe's sister, raised Jake, and I met her, too. A very sweet lady."

"Sounds like Joe had problems," Tuck remarked.

"Big problems." Eli rubbed his hands together. "He was selfish and manipulative—like a lot of criminals we see—willing to do anything to get what he wanted, even if it meant hurting people who cared about him." He glanced at his foster brother. "I don't want to be like that."

"You're not," Tuck assured him.

Eli exhaled deeply. He didn't want to be so rigidly selfish and stubborn, but he had been in the past. "I resisted seeing the McCains because I already had Ma, Pa and you. I felt guilty about wanting to have another family."

"For heaven's sake, why?"

"I thought that seeing the McCains would diminish my feelings for Ma and Pa. Everything they gave me and everything they did for me."

"Eli," Tuck sighed. "You know them. They wanted you to be happy."

"Yeah." Eli glanced at the stars. "Someone made me realize that."

"Who?" Tuck asked, stretching out his legs. Sam jumped into his lap.

"Caroline."

"You've been seeing her?" Tuck stroked the dog.

Eli told him about the day he'd brought Caroline here and about the boxing gloves.

"She knocked you down?" Tuck laughed. "Would've paid a lot of money to see that."

"Don't get carried away. I didn't fight back."

"I wonder why?" Tuck mused, then asked, "How did the visit with the McCains go today?"

Eli told him every detail of the day.

"So Katie put love in the rolls?"

"That's what she called it, and she wanted to make sure that I knew. She's a little doll. She stayed with Althea while Elise was at the university. Aunt Vin went over and they cooked all day, making the rolls and practicing Katie's introduction to me. They waited until Ben got out of school so he could put the icing on. I can't believe they went to all that trouble."

"They're your family."

Eli realized he could hear that now without his insides caving in. "I'll be working with Caleb on the Buford case. We're trying to get Belle to talk so we can find out who she is and maybe get more information on Buford."

"That will give you a chance to get to know each other better," Tuck said.

"Yes." He stood. "I'd better go. I'm back in my office tomorrow."

They walked into the house. Sam and Dee followed.

"Why don't you just spend the night?" Tuck suggested.

"I need to get back to town." He wished he was going to see Caroline.

Tuck observed his face. "What's wrong?"

"Nothing."

"Yes, there is. If you tighten your lips any more, they'll disappear."

"Caroline went back to her fiancé." The words came out before Eli could stop them.

"That's good, isn't it? She's getting on with her life."

"Yeah."

"You don't say that with much enthusiasm."

"It was unexpected and I don't think it's what she really wants."

"Eli—"

"I gotta go," he interrupted. "I'll talk to you tomorrow." He tore off half the tin foil covering the rolls and divided them. Picking up his half, he left.

Unable to stop himself, Eli drove to Caroline's apartment. He wanted to tell her about today and thank her, but she still wasn't home. She and Colin had probably gone away for some time together. When she came back, she and Eli would be strangers.

And that's the way it would stay.

CAROLINE LEFT SAN ANTONIO early, eager to get home. She'd done a lot of soul searching and she felt clearer, more in tune with her emotions and her fears.

There were several things she wanted to do. First, she had to see Colin. She felt she'd been unfair to him and wanted to more fully explain her feelings. Maybe they could end the relationship more amicably. Second, she wanted to visit with Belle. She owed the woman her life, and wanted to do something for her. Third was Eli. Just Eli. She wasn't sure how she was going to explain her quick disappearance, so she'd just tell him the truth. She hoped he was ready to hear it.

The drive was long and tiring, but eventually she reached Colin's office, which was over the camera shop. His car was in his parking spot, so she knew he was there. She walked up the outside stairs and knocked, then opened the door. Colin was at his desk and Julie, a girl who worked in the camera shop, was sitting on his desk with her legs crossed, facing him.

When Colin saw her, he jumped to his feet, almost knocking over his chair. Julie stood more slowly. "Talk to you later, Colin," she said as she walked out.

"Caroline, I'm so glad to see you," he said, coming around the desk to her side.

"I'm sorry I interrupted," she replied.

"We were just going over some figures."

"Yes. I could see."

"Please don't be jealous," he begged, not missing her insinuation.

"I'm not, Colin." And she wasn't. She and Colin were wrong for each other. If not for the kidnapping, she probably would have married him. Or maybe she wouldn't have. She'd had doubts—that's the reason she couldn't set a wedding date.

"I'll close up and we can go to lunch."

"No, Colin. There were several messages on my cell phone and I just wanted to ask you to stop calling me. It's over and I'd like for us to get on with our lives."

"You've been through so much—are you sure you're thinking clearly?"

"I am," she told him. "I'm thinking more clearly than I have in a long time."

"Caroline…"

"Colin, don't." She looked around the office. Everything was in its place, nothing out of order. Everything was organized—just like at his stores. She smiled. "You know how I like to leave things out in my apartment."

"Yes."

"Well, if we ever lived together, we would drive each other crazy within a month."

"No, I—"

She held up a hand. "Grace has the same personality as you, neat and organized. I can only stay with her a few days before we start to get on each other's nerves. It would have been the same with us. Our interest in photography couldn't be the only thing to hold us together."

Colin looked down at the floor.

"And you've already moved on."

His head jerked up. "Julie means nothing to me."

"Be honest, Colin."

"Your disinclination to put things away did bother me."

That wasn't what she meant, but she nodded. "Be happy, Colin. I plan to." She moved toward the door and turned back. "I'm sorry about the ring."

"Don't worry. I had it insured."

She should have guessed he had all his bases covered. "Goodbye, Colin."

"If you change your mind, I'll—"

"I won't."

He nodded. "Bye, Caroline."

This time it was final.

NEXT SHE WENT SHOPPING. Belle was about her size and Caroline intended to buy her some clothes. She purchased gowns and a robe, slippers, panties, one bra, just to see if it would fit, a couple of pairs of slacks and a few tops. Then she bought lotion and moisturizer and a few makeup items. Belle's skin was so lovely that Caroline didn't think she needed much.

Finally she headed for the hospital. On the way, she called Grace.

"Hi. I'm back."

"Caroline," Grace said in a nervous tone. "I didn't think you'd get back this soon."

"It didn't take long to photograph the Alamo."

There was a noticeable pause.

"Grace, what's wrong?"

"Nothing. I'm just busy."

"Okay. I'll talk to you tonight. Maybe we can have dinner."

"Sure. I'll talk to you then."

Caroline hung up, thinking Grace was acting weirder than usual. She put it out of her mind as she reached the hospital.

ELI'S MORNING WASN'T going well. He met with Tom, Bill and the attorneys handling the Buford case.

"It doesn't look good," Greg Sherr, the assistant U.S. Attorney said. "Caroline Whitten spent her college career protesting everything she could."

"Why does that matter?" Eli asked.

"Because Lansing will take this evidence and devour her like a pit bull," Greg replied, looking at the papers in front of him. "Listen to this. At her school, there was a professor, James Halter, who was a Mormon and had two wives. When the university found out, he was fired. Ms. Whitten, along with several other students, protested the firing and was arrested. Of course, Congressman Whitten got her out as soon as he could. But it proves she's in favor of multiple marriages."

"It proves she's against someone getting fired unjustly," Eli muttered.

"That's not the way a jury will see it. Buford said she wanted to join their faith. After a jury hears that story, which you can bet your money Lansing will get in, it will plant a seed of doubt. That's all he needs to do."

"Goddammit. She was kidnapped," Eli roared.

"Get me hard evidence," Greg replied.

"Her word should be all you need. My word should be all you need."

"It isn't."

Eli was about to explode with the injustice of it all. Caroline didn't deserve this.

"Eli." Tom drew his attention. "You said the dark-haired woman was starting to talk. Keep working with her. Maybe we can get her to testify. That would seal the case, but she has to be credible, unshakable."

Eli took a long breath. "I'll do my damnedest."

"Caleb McCain will continue to help you," Greg said. "Get me something quick. Lansing's good, and he will use every shred of evidence he can to Buford's advantage."

Eli walked away feeling numb. He knew the system had flaws, but was feeling it personally once again. And it wasn't just about Ginny.

It was about Caroline.

He would work day and night to get something on Buford. The man wasn't going to go free, of that Eli was certain.

He wished Caroline would come back. He needed to talk to her. This time it wasn't personal. It was business.

CAROLINE WALKED INTO Belle's room and found her staring out the window again. "What do you see?" she asked, her arms full of shopping bags.

Belle swung around. "Ms. Whitten."

"Call me Caroline, please." She set her load on the floor.

"What are those?" Belle asked, looking at the bags.

"I brought some things that I thought you might need."

Belle shook her head. "You didn't have to do that."

"I wanted to." Caroline pulled out the contents of the bags and laid them on the bed. "Come look," she invited.

Belle moved closer.

"I bought you some gowns and a robe. Thought you might like them better than the hospital stuff."

Belle drew the robe closer around her thin frame. "They're okay."

Caroline knew she was making Belle nervous so decided to take it slow. She sat in a chair. "How are you?"

"I don't know," she murmured in a feeble voice. "My mind's blank. There's nothing there and it's so frightening."

Caroline's throat went dry at Belle's distress and she wanted to comfort her in some way. "The people here will help you. Just let them."

"Ranger McCain is nice."

"Yes, he is." Caroline was surprised, for she'd felt sure Belle would have said "Ranger Coltrane" instead.

The woman hung her head and was silent.

"It's all right, Belle. You're safe here."

Belle wrapped her arms around her waist. "I don't feel safe."

"Sometimes I don't, either," Caroline admitted. "I'm having a hard time sleeping in the dark, but I'm making myself do it."

"You're very brave," Belle said.

"So are you. It took great courage to tell Ranger Coltrane where I was, especially after all the beatings you'd endured."

"I have a bullet in my head," Belle said abruptly.

"What?"

"One of the tests showed a bullet in my skull. Someone tried to kill me. What kind of life did I have that someone hated me that much?"

Caroline didn't have an answer and she so desperately wanted to help Belle.

"The doctor wants to remove the bullet and…and I'm scared—scared of what I'll remember."

"Don't be," Caroline told her. "I will be here to help you face it."

Belle blinked in disbelief. "You will?"

"Of course. You saved my life. It's the very least I can do."

"Thank you."

Belle touched the clothes on the bed as if to make herself concentrate on something else. Caroline thought it was time to do that, too.

"I bought you a bra," she said. "I'm not sure what size you wear, but if it doesn't fit, I can always return it and get the correct size."

"Size 34C."

"What?" Caroline drew back in surprise.

"I wear a…" Belle's eyes opened wide as she realized what she'd said. "I know my bra size."

Caroline jumped up. "What's your shoe size?"

"Six."

"What's your name?" Caroline could hardly contain her excitement.

Belle's brow wrinkled in thought, then she placed her palms against the side of her head. "It's not there. It's not there," she cried.

"It's okay, Belle," Caroline said. "You remembered something about yourself. That's a start."

Belle removed her hands. "It is, isn't it?"

"Yes. It's wonderful." Caroline grabbed her arms in excitement and Belle jerked back.

"Please don't touch me."

"I'm so sorry," she said immediately. "I'm a toucher. I'm always doing that."

"I'm not. I never liked to be touched."

"You mean when you were with Buford and his followers?"

Belle put a hand to her temple. "I think. I didn't like it if they touched me in any way. The men would hold me down while he beat me. Sometimes the women would slap and kick me if they weren't pleased with something I'd done."

Caroline swallowed. "I can only imagine what you've been through."

"Yet sometimes I feel this need to be hugged." Belle kept talking as if Caroline hadn't spoken. "And sometimes I want to cry myself to sleep in the arms of someone who cares."

Caroline felt so much sympathy for this young woman. She couldn't even imagine living in her world, where nothing was familiar. "When you want that hug, just let me know," she said, to keep from crying.

"Okay," Belle replied, and turned back to the clothes.

"Keep these things if you want to, but if you'd rather not, I'll take them back. I don't want to make you uncomfortable."

Belle picked up a black knit top and held it against her. "I think I'll keep them."

"Good." Caroline smiled. "Try everything on and I'll return in the morning and take back what doesn't fit."

"Okay. Thank you."

Caroline picked up her purse. "I'll see you tomorrow." She turned to leave and came to a complete stop.

Eli stood in the doorway.

CHAPTER FOURTEEN

NEITHER SAID A WORD. Caroline didn't want to meet him like this. She'd planned to call and invite him over to explain why she'd left without telling him. He was dressed in Wrangler Riatas, a short-sleeved shirt and a tie, boots, hat, gun and badge, and she soaked up every nuance, even those guarded eyes staring back at her. He wasn't happy. Caroline was vaguely aware that Caleb was behind Eli.

"Caroline," he said, removing his hat.

"Hello, Eli."

"Ms. Whitten." Caleb stretched out his hand and she shook it.

"Please call me Caroline," she told him.

Caleb nodded and the room became very quiet.

"I was just leaving," she said, feeling awkward. She glanced at Eli. "Could I speak with you outside please?"

He hesitated for a second. "Sure."

She walked out the door and he followed. In the hall, she turned to him. "Belle remembered her bra and shoe size."

He frowned. "Excuse me?"

"I bought Belle some things that she might need because I knew she didn't have anything. I told her I didn't know her bra size, and she told me what it was. She knew, and it shocked her as much as it did me. I then asked her shoe size and she knew it, too. But when I asked her name, she couldn't remember. She's recalling things about herself, and that's good, isn't it?"

To say he was taken aback was putting it mildly. Eli expected a lot of things from his next meeting with Caroline, but not this. He had a hard time concentrating on what she was talking about. She'd been gone for two days and she acted as if she'd never left. He brought his thoughts back to what she was saying.

"Yes, it's good," he answered, staring into her eyes. She looked better than he'd ever seen her. Her skin glowed and her eyes sparkled. She looked happy. "How are you?" he asked her.

"I'm better than I've been since the kidnapping."

He could see that and he supposed Colin helped her cope with her fear of the dark. His gut twisted at the thought. "I better get back in there." He turned toward the door.

"Eli."

He looked back.

"Could you please stop by my apartment later this evening?"

She was asking him over? What for? he wondered. He was at a loss on how to answer her. It would be best if he didn't see her, but he found it hard to refuse.

"I'll be working late," he hedged.

"It doesn't matter. Come when you can."

"I'm not sure when I'll finish." He should just say no. Why couldn't he do that? Maybe it was her hopeful green eyes.

"Like I said, come when you can."

"Okay," he said slowly, unsure of what he was doing.

"Bye, Eli." She reached up and kissed his cheek, then she was gone.

He held a hand to his face. What in the hell was going on? He would definitely go to her apartment tonight because he had to know.

CAROLINE SPENT the afternoon getting the photos ready for the magazine. Then she went grocery shopping and cleaned the apartment. At six, she showered and changed into light blue lounge pants and a halter top. She brushed her hair, applied a little makeup and went into the living room to wait for Eli. At seven-thirty he still wasn't there and she wondered if he was coming at all. He'd been so hesitant today, and he had a right to be. But Eli was a man of his word and he'd be here. She'd just have to wait.

She checked on the steaks and baked potatoes she had on the grill. Then she went back to the living room. She glanced at her watch. Eight o'clock. Where was Eli?

She turned on the television but nothing caught her interest. As she clicked it off, the doorbell rang. Eli was here. Her heart pounded like a drum in her ears.

Opening the door, she took a steadying breath. "Come in."

He walked through to the living room and laid his hat on the coffee table. "I'm sorry I'm so late, but as I said, I'm very busy."

She looked into his eyes. "You're lying. You didn't want to come."

He inhaled deeply. "You could be right," he admitted, glancing around the apartment. "Are you alone?"

She frowned. "Yes. Who did you expect to be here?"

"Colin."

Her frown deepened. "Why would you expect Colin to be here?"

"Are you kidding me?" he asked, his eyes narrowed.

"Not that I'm aware of."

"What's going on, Caroline?"

"I don't know what you're talking about."

"You're back with Colin, right?"

"What?"

In that instant Eli knew everything Grace had told him was a lie, and anger stirred inside him. He had to get all the facts.

"When you disappeared without a word, I was worried about you. I checked your apartment and saw that you hadn't been home. The next morning I went to see Grace. She told me I had no need to worry and you were back with Colin."

Caroline shook her head. "No. Grace wouldn't do that."

"She did," he assured her. "Seems your family thinks you're getting too involved with me."

She took his hand, led him to the sofa, and they sat down. "I'm not back with Colin nor do I have any plans or thoughts of reconciliation."

"Then why did you disappear like that?"

She curled up on the end of the sofa with her feet beneath her. "I'm going to be completely honest."

"Please do."

She looked down at her hands. "That morning when we talked to Belle, I saw how she responded to your gentleness, your kindness. In that moment I realized I'd done the same thing, after my ordeal. There's just something about you that makes a woman feel safe, and I needed that. I thought that everything Grace had said was true. I was very grateful to you, and my feelings had grown out of that gratitude. I felt like a fool and just wanted to get away and sort through what I was feeling."

She smoothed the fabric of her pants. "I had an appointment at a magazine I freelance for and they wanted a photographer to take some fresh shots of the Alamo. I accepted the job and left immediately."

"By yourself?"

"Yes," she replied. "I realized, too, that I'd been clinging to you for strength, and I had to find the strength within myself to deal with my fears."

He studied the pattern on the area rug. "Did you?"

"That first night was hell. I wanted to call you so bad I couldn't stand it."

He glanced at her. "Why didn't you?"

"Because I would have been giving in to my fears—to my need for you."

He held her gaze. "From the way you look, you succeeded."

"Yes. I slept with the light off. I didn't sleep very well, but I did it. I also did a lot of thinking. I know I feel a lot more than gratitude for you."

His eyes never left her face. "You do?"

"Yes." She leaned forward and kissed his cheek, and he turned his head and caught her lips. His arms slipped around her waist and he pulled her onto his lap, their pulses igniting from a need too long denied.

He kissed her deeply and long, and her hands stroked his face and his hair as she gave herself up to what she'd been wanting for days.

"Oh, Caroline." He kissed the arch in her neck. "I've been going crazy with worry about you."

"I had to get away."

"I know. Just keep kissing me and maybe soon it won't matter so much."

She held his head with both hands and kissed him with everything in her, their tongues and lips tasting, exploring and discovering. Eli groaned and pulled her down on the sofa.

"Let's go to the bedroom," she said between heated kisses.

"Whoa. Whoa. Whoa!" Eli tore his mouth away and sat up. "This is too fast. We need to slow down."

Caroline took a breath and pushed hair from her face. "Okay. We can eat dinner. I have it ready."

He arched an eyebrow. "Wow. A woman who can cook. Every man's dream."

"But I thought you were self-sufficient, Elijah Coltrane, and didn't need a woman for anything."

The corners of his mouth twitched. "That's not exactly true."

"Then you do need a woman in your life?"

"Occasionally."

"Can I apply for the job?" She leaned forward, the scent of her perfume wafting around him, and his resistance weakened. He didn't know what he was fighting, anyway—himself or her? Still, he had to be sure.

"Caroline, you know I want you, but there's a lot we need to discuss."

"Like what?" she asked, her eyes holding his.

"So many things. We barely know each other."

She leaned back on the sofa. "Okay. Talk."

"I have a lot of insecurities about my childhood." He wanted her to know that. It was important for him to be honest.

"Do you want to compare notes?"

"No."

"I didn't have your kind of childhood, but mine wasn't idyllic, either. I deal with a lot of guilt every day because I've disappointed my parents."

"So, you're not perfect?" A grin teased his mouth.

"No one is, Eli. Certainly not me. Just go with what you're feeling now."

"You're a witness on a case I'm working," he said in a hurry. "That's a conflict for me."

She touched her lips to his cheek, his mouth, and his skin burned from the tantalizing sensation. "Doesn't feel like a problem to me."

"Caroline."

"We're two consenting adults," she whispered, carefully removing his badge. She set it on the coffee table. "Now you're not a ranger."

He watched the light in her eyes and his doubts wavered. But his need for her was stronger. He scooped her up as if she weighed no more than a feather, and headed for the bedroom.

"Your arm," she protested against his lips.

"It's fine," he said as he laid her on the bed. Then he hurriedly slipped off his boots and jeans. She raised herself to her knees and helped with his shirt, her hands running over the smooth muscles of his shoulders and the matting of hair across his chest.

He undid her halter top and her breasts fell into his hands. She lay back and shimmied out of her pants, and Eli just stared at her nakedness. "God, you're lovely," he murmured.

"You're pretty magnificent yourself." Her eyes traveled over his hard, masculine lines and an ache formed in her lower abdomen.

He smiled and found her lips again. But doubts still niggled at him. "This is too fast, Caroline. Let's talk first." He ran his tongue across her lower lip.

"No. No. I do not want to talk." Her tongue played with his.

"Caroline…" His lips traveled from her mouth to her neck, to her breasts, and his hand slid over her stomach and lower. When he touched her intimately, she moaned.

"Be very sure about this." He raised his head and looked into her eyes.

She reached for something on the nightstand and held it up. It was a packet of condoms. "If this isn't sure, I don't know what is."

He laughed and kissed her deeply as heated emotions spiraled out of control. He took the packet and ripped it open. Within seconds, he'd sheathed himself.

"You do that very well," she teased, kissing his shoulders. "I was hoping to help."

"Maybe next time. Tonight I don't…" Words clogged his throat as sexual tension mounted. He straddled her and nothing else was said as their lips, hands and bodies did the talking.

Her palms stroked every inch of him, needing to feel and touch him until the ache in her subsided.

"Eli…"

She opened her thighs and he entered her with one deep thrust. She wrapped her legs around him as his body took her on a journey she'd never been on before—a journey of sensual pleasures and sinful delights. A journey of passion.

They moved in perfect harmony until her body convulsed into a quivering mass of unequaled gratification. He trembled against her as he reached that same pinnacle.

Their sweat-bathed bodies lay entwined, and Eli kissed the damp hair from her face. "You okay?"

"Mmm." She smiled in a contented way. "I love you."

Eli stilled. Had he heard her correctly? He looked at her face and saw she was asleep. Easing to the side, he pulled her to him, feeling as if his chest was about to explode. He wanted to say those words back to her, but they were locked away so deep inside him that he couldn't manage to.

Why hadn't they talked?

The problem wasn't new. He could never say those words to Ginny, either. She'd asked if he loved her, and he'd answer, "Yes." He never actually said the words and Ginny had been fine with that. She understood him. But he wanted to say them to Caroline. He needed to.

But he couldn't.

Oh, God. Was he going to be like Joe McCain, never really able to love another person? *No. No. No.* That wasn't happening to him. He'd tell Caroline soon. He kissed the side of her face, feeling spent and enjoying this incredible gift he'd been given—the gift of her love.

He felt a sense of inadequacy, though. Caroline deserved a whole man, not someone who was afraid of that four-letter word. He had to admit that he was afraid. Love hadn't been kind to him and he was still protecting his heart from further pain. Why? He wasn't sure. Fatigue overtook him and he forgot his doubts in sleep.

CAROLINE WOKE UP to sheer bliss. She smiled as she felt Eli's arm around her and his leg across hers. This was the way she wanted to wake up for the rest of her life—with his strength and warmth enveloping her.

Before falling asleep, she'd told him that she loved him. He hadn't said the words back to her. But she knew Eli would have a hard time telling her his feelings. She would give him time because she was not letting go of this marvelous man.

He couldn't have made love to her as he had unless he felt something deep for her. She knew that, too. Last night hadn't been a casual thing for either of them. She would wait—patiently.

She stroked the hand lying against her waist.

"Are you awake?" he asked.

She turned to look at him and all she could see was love in those dark blue eyes. "Yes." She kissed him briefly, knowing she'd wait forever for Eli.

He caught her lips and deepened the kiss, then drew back before they got carried away. "We need to talk."

She sighed. "You're the only man I know who'd rather talk."

He sat up against the headboard and she rested on her knees facing him. Neither had a stitch of clothes on, yet it seemed so natural. Not in the least bit uncomfortable.

He tucked her hair behind her ear. "It's not that I'd rather…" He stopped. "Have there been a lot of men?"

She caught the hand against her face and kissed his knuckles. "Jealous?"

"I'm sorry. I shouldn't have asked that."

"A boyfriend in college and Colin," she answered. She didn't want to keep anything from Eli.

"That's it?"

"Yes." She linked her fingers with his. "And you?"

His hand tightened on hers. "I'm almost forty-two and…"

"And there's so many you can't remember them all?"

"There were a couple in high school, several in college and afterward, then Ginny. After her I couldn't be with another woman without seeing her face."

Caroline chewed on the inside of her lip, hesitating, but she needed to know. "Did you see her face when we made love?"

He stared into her eyes. "No. I haven't seen her face for a while now."

"Does that upset you?"

"No."

That was all she needed to hear. She wrapped her arms

around his neck and kissed him with all the love she was feeling. He groaned, taking her mouth with a fierce hunger, his hands stoking her back. Then he stopped and rested his forehead against hers. "We're getting sidetracked. We need to talk."

"Okay. Okay. " She snuggled against him, resting her head on his shoulder. "What time is it?"

"Almost midnight. You went out like a light and slept for a couple of hours."

She stroked his chest. "I guess we should have eaten first."

"Maybe."

"We can eat now."

He rubbed her arm. "Maybe later."

She kissed his throat. "I haven't slept very well the past two nights."

"I haven't, either," he admitted. "I've been quietly going out of my mind with jealousy."

"Oh, Eli, I'm so sorry." She made a face. "Tomorrow you might have to arrest me for killing my sister."

"She was trying to protect you. This happened so fast and I'm still trying to adjust and—"

She placed a finger over his mouth. "No regrets. No excuses."

He should tell her now, but all he could see in her eyes was love. He suddenly realized he needed that. Accepting it was the hard part.

"Okay."

She nestled against him and a peacefulness settled over him. "Aren't you going to ask about my promise?"

Her eyes glittered as she looked up at him. "About visiting your brothers?"

"Yes."

She smiled. "You did it."

"Yes."

She clapped her hands and sat up. "I'm so proud of you. How did it go?"

He told her about the afternoon he'd spent at the McCain farm, and her joyful expression was like a glimpse of the heaven he'd been dreaming about. He knew he loved her more than he'd ever imagined. But the words were still locked deep in his chest.

"Thank you for forcing me to go. It was just like you said. They're a part of what and who I am, and I know Ma and Pa would want me to have that connection with them. When I left there, all my resentment was gone."

"I'm so glad."

"Me, too."

"And you'll be working with Caleb trying to help Belle?"

"Yes." Now he had to tell her about the new developments in the case. He didn't want to take that smile off her face, but he had no choice.

He gathered her in his arms again. "I have something to tell you and it won't be easy."

Her hand curled into a fist. "Just tell me."

"Lansing, Buford's attorney, is digging up dirt on you."

"Like what?" she asked, her voice hesitant.

"He's dug up several things you did in college, where you were involved in protests."

"I was rebellious in college, trying to break free from the mold my father had planned for me. But what difference does that make?"

"The incident with Professor Halter hurts the case."

She pushed away, frowning. "Professor Halter? I don't remember…oh, now I do. He was my roommate's history professor and she said he was fired unjustly, so she gathered us all together to protest. I didn't realize what we were protesting until I was sitting in a jail cell and had to face the wrath of my father. After that I agreed to finish law school, which I did. I kept my word, but I didn't go into my father's law firm. It's been a sore subject between my parents and me. What does this have to do with my being kidnapped by Buford and his followers?"

"Buford's story is that they found you outside their fence photographing wildflowers. They talked with you and you showed interest in their faith. Later his men went to visit with you and you told them you wanted to join them, so they took you back to the compound, where you agreed to undergo the cleansing ritual. His followers are backing up his story."

"But that's a lie. That's a lie," she cried.

"I know, honey. I know." Eli pushed back her hair. "I just want you to be aware of what's going on. Lansing is a cutthroat defense attorney and he's trying to discredit you any way he can. The Halter incident proves you support multiple marriages and—"

"I do not," she spat, jerking away. "And anyone who believes that is crazy."

"Come here." He pulled her back into his arms. "Don't worry. I'm going to make sure he doesn't get away with this. Caleb and I are working with Belle and she can corroborate your story."

"I just don't understand why my word isn't enough."

"Because we live in America, where everyone is innocent until proven guilty, and we wouldn't have it any other way. We just have to stay a step ahead of Lansing."

"Then my testimony doesn't matter. It's Belle's that we have to concentrate on."

"Yes. We're sure she knows a lot more. The case hinges on Belle recovering her memory."

"I don't want to hurt her in any way—even if that means Buford goes free."

"Caroline…"

"I mean it, Eli. I don't want an attorney to tear her apart on the witness stand. She's been through enough."

He cupped her face. "You're wonderful."

"I have to be strong and sometimes I'm not sure I can be."

His heart twisted at her forlorn tone of voice. "I'll be right beside you," he promised.

"Do you believe in love at first touch?"

"You mean love at first sight?"

"No. I mean touch," she said. "When I was in that dark room and I heard your voice, I thought I was hearing things. Then I touched you and everything has been different since that moment.

"I can't explain that feeling, but it's not gratitude and I know it's never going to change for me. Just tell me you felt it, too." Her eyes begged for an honest answer.

"I felt it, too," he whispered, taking her lips in a gentle caress. But he cursed himself for not saying the words she wanted to hear.

The kiss deepened. "Love me, Eli. I don't want to think about anything or anyone but you for the rest of this night."

"I hope you bought a lot of those condoms."

She drew back. "I'd never bought them before and the selection is endless—regular, different colors, psychedelic, glow in the dark, and my personal favorite, ribbed for her pleasure." She reached for the box on the nightstand. "What's your preference?"

He pulled her down into the bed, laughing. "You're my preference."

She giggled. "You have to choose."

His lips found her breast and her thinking became cloudy.

"We'll try them all and choose our favorite."

Her eyes opened wide. "Really?"

"Well, maybe not tonight." He grinned, stroking her abdomen. "But by the end of the week, we'll have a winner."

Her senses spun as his hands worked their magic, and she eagerly reached for him, letting her worries slip away as her body responded to his touch.

She already had a winner.

CHAPTER FIFTEEN

THE BUZZ OF ELI'S cell phone woke him. Even when he was dead asleep, that sound could do so. Over the years, he'd been conditioned that way. His job came first.

He immediately slipped from the bed, careful not to wake Caroline, and found his phone in his clothes on the floor. It was Greg—there was a new development in the Buford case. Greg had an early appointment and wanted to see Eli at ten. Eli agreed and clicked off.

He looked at Caroline, her disheveled hair, her soft skin, and realized he'd made a big mistake. They'd said they'd have no regrets, make no excuses, but as daylight filtered through the blinds, he felt very differently.

What had he done? He'd compromised the best thing about him—his ethics as a Texas Ranger. He'd stepped over the line so far that he couldn't even rationalize it to himself. He wanted Caroline and he'd taken what he wanted. Like his father, he was selfish, thinking only of himself.

The fact that she'd made it easy for him didn't change a thing. Even after they'd made love and she'd said I love you, he couldn't say the words back to her. He wanted to, but they were frozen inside him. Would he ever be able to love completely?

"Eli," she murmured sleepily.

He quickly slipped into his clothes. Buttoning his shirt, he said, "We need to talk."

She opened one eye. "That doesn't sound good." She pushed herself to a sitting position, the sheet falling away, exposing her breast.

He forced himself not to look. "Last night should never have happened."

She paled, but didn't say anything.

"I was so glad to see you and happy you weren't with Colin that I lost sight of my honor and ethics as a ranger."

"We did talk about this and we both wanted the same thing."

"But I knew it was wrong."

"It didn't feel wrong."

He closed his eyes briefly. "It was selfish on my part."

Her eyes flared. "Don't you dare say that. It was loving and passionate—everything it should have been."

He took a deep breath. "Last night you said something to me a couple of times and I didn't say it back to you."

"Yes. I know."

"That's not loving—it's selfish."

She clenched her jaw. "I'll never believe that and I'll never believe you weren't feeling the same thing I was."

"What I feel for you is stronger than anything I've ever felt for any woman and yet...I can't say those words."

"Were you able to say them to Ginny?"

"No. It's just something I can't do."

"Eli." She scrambled toward him and he took a couple of steps backward. "It's okay...."

"No. It's not okay. You deserve better than that."

"Eli."

"We should've had this conversation last night," he said,

so low she almost didn't hear him. "I guess that's what I really wanted to talk about, but stronger needs took over."

"Eli."

"The one thing I'm proud of—the one thing I'm good at—is being a Texas Ranger, and now I've tarnished that." He swallowed. "I took from you without making you fully understand, and I can't continue to do that. Until this case is over, we won't have a repeat of last night. And until I can say those words to you, we won't have anything."

She trembled. "You felt differently last night. What happened between then and now?"

"Reality." He spat out the word. "Of who and what I am."

Her bottom lip quivered and Eli looked away, jamming his foot into a boot.

"You once said I could hurt you badly, but you're the one hurting me—for no reason."

He looked at her. "How long do you think you could live with a man who's so scarred inside that he's unable to say those words? They're three little words—what's the problem? Everyone says them. But I don't think I'll ever be able to. I couldn't say them to Ginny and I could tell it hurt her. I told myself she understood, but that's asking a hellva lot of a woman. I won't ask that of you. I won't put you through that."

Caroline sank back on the bed, getting a glimpse into Eli's soul. "That's it, isn't it? Ginny died before you could say those words to her. You've been grieving about it all these years. That's what this is about."

"I wanted her to know."

"She did, Eli," she told him. "She probably felt it every moment you were with her, every moment she shared with you."

"I should have been man enough to tell her."

"Eli…"

"I've got to go to work."

"What about us?" she asked in a rush.

"I'm sorry, Caroline." He hurried out the door and her heart burst into a million pieces.

She lay back on the bed and grabbed Eli's pillow and held it tight. She wouldn't cry. Not after last night. She would give him time, but she would never give up on Eli. With her arms around the pillow, she slipped into a beautiful dream where she found her Prince Charming.

She was arguing with her father and mother, the guilt eating away at her. Then she was shrouded in darkness where there was no air, no light, and the guilt wasn't important anymore. Life was. At her lowest point, her prince arrived. One touch and she was free. He wore boots, a cowboy hat and a Texas Ranger badge. He felt like Eli, looked like Eli.

Her prince was Eli.

CAROLINE WOKE UP at nine and quickly showered and dressed, with thoughts of Eli filling her head. In her teens and twenties she'd dreamed of finding Mr. Right. He would have a special touch that would ignite a passion in her she'd only ever read about. Last night that dream had come true—almost. Eli hadn't told her he loved her and that hurt.

His words this morning hurt even more, mainly because she knew he was right. She wanted him to say I love you—she needed it. Ginny probably had, too. Eli was such a special man, though, that one little flaw was easy to overlook. Except he couldn't overlook it. She loved him all the more for that.

She always knew he was a man of honor and she hated that she was the cause of his inner conflict. Their relationship had happened so fast, but she didn't regret a moment of it. She only regretted that he was torn between her and his job.

Picking up the box of condoms, she put them in the nightstand drawer, not sure when they'd use them again.

If ever.

ELI DROVE AND DROVE. He wasn't sure where he was going until he looked up and realized he was in Marlin. The McCain farm—that's where he needed to go. To understand himself he had to face one more demon from his past— the ghost of Joe McCain.

When he stopped at the garage, Jake was coming out of the house, Wags behind him. Eli got out and Jake halted when he saw him.

"Eli," he said, surprised.

"I'm sorry. I should have called."

"Nonsense," Jake said. "You're always welcome here. Come on in and have a cup of coffee."

"Thanks." Eli followed him into the house and sat at the kitchen table. He removed his hat and Jake placed a steaming mug in front of him.

"You're probably wondering what I'm doing here," Eli said after a long silence.

"I'm just glad to see you," Jake replied, sitting with a mug in his own hand. "Elise just left to take Ben to school and to drop Katie at her mom's. Aunt Vin's gone to one of her marathon bingo days."

Eli twisted his cup. "You and Elise seem to have a good relationship."

"Yes. But it wasn't always like that."

Eli glanced up. "It wasn't?"

"No. We were both in our late thirties and we got married to have a child, then we found out about Ben and everything fell apart."

"Do you mind if I ask why?"

"Elise didn't know if she could be a mother to another woman's child."

Eli took a sip of coffee. "That doesn't sound like the woman who was scared out of her mind when Ben was kidnapped. It doesn't even resemble the woman who dotes on him."

"Like I said, we got married for the wrong reasons and we both had a lot of emotional garbage. Elise had been married before and was still in love with her dead husband. I wasn't very familiar with love. I never had a lot of it in my life."

"I haven't, either," Eli murmured. "At least not until I went to live with Ma and Pa. Ma would always say 'I love you' before she went to bed and I would say 'ditto.' She'd call me Ditto to tease me, and tell me one day a woman would make me say those words and I'd be happy to do so."

"But that hasn't happened?"

"No." He stared into his cup. "I've met someone and I'm happy when I'm with her. I tell her things I haven't told anyone else, yet I can't say what she wants to hear. What every woman deserves to hear."

"I had a hard time with that, too," Jake admitted.

Eli looked at him. "What did you do?"

He shrugged. "I don't have a plan or a formula. It's something that has to come from here." He placed a hand over his heart. "It's about forgiving and accepting. I had to forgive my mother and the father who hurt me terribly, and most of all, I had to forgive myself. Until I did that I didn't have anything. I couldn't have Elise or happiness until I wiped the slate clean and started over. I had to tell Elise I loved her, and I didn't think I could do that. Rejection makes cowards of strong men and I was no exception. But I was determined to have the family I'd always wanted, and Elise made it easy."

Silence filled the room.

Suddenly Jake set his cup on the table and got to his feet. "I have something for you."

He was back in a minute and laid a chain on the table in front of Eli. A heart, split in two, was attached to it. Eli stared at the names engraved on each half—Vera on one, Joe on the other. Eli's lungs felt tight.

"After my mother left, Dad wore that all the time," Jake said. "He must have had it hidden somewhere because I never saw it before then. And I never saw whose names were on it until he died. When he knew he wasn't going to make it, he took it off and asked me to give it to someone. I didn't know who he was talking about and I assumed he was out of his head."

Eli swallowed. "Who did he ask you to give it to?"

"Someone called Thatch."

Pain shot through Eli. It took a moment then he tentatively touched the heart with his forefinger. "That's what he called me," he murmured, barely able to speak. "I had this thatch of unruly hair when I was born and…"

"I didn't realize until I found out about you that this heart had something to do with you." Jake resumed his seat. "I was going to show it to you the other day, but so much was happening that I forgot about it."

Eli picked up the chain and heart and the years rolled back. He could see Joe McCain clearly. "When I was about four or five, my mom would take me to work with her and I slept in the back room at the bar. Sometimes Joe would show up and say, 'Come on, Thatch. Let's go home,' and he'd take me back to the apartment. I slept on a sofa bed, and he'd pull it out and sit in a chair, waiting on Vera. When she got there, they usually argued, waking me up. He'd tell her that a bar was no place for a kid. And she'd tell him to do something about it. Then they'd go into her room." Eli took a breath. "Funny how I'd forgotten all about that."

"You came here looking for answers," Jake said. "But the answers you're looking for are inside you."

"Yeah." He leaned back. "I've been hating for so long that I'd forgotten Joe could be nice at times."

Jake watched him. "Aunt Vin told me something you need to know. Joe's mother used to cheat on his father. She'd meet men in motels and lock Joe and Vin in the bathroom. Aunt Vin was too young to know what was going on, but Joe did. I believe it scarred him for life. The only kind of love he understood was physical." Jake paused. "Don't let Joe McCain's inability to love scar you, too."

"We're not the sons of Joe McCain," Eli said under his breath. "We're the sins of Joe McCain."

"But we're better men than he ever was."

Eli stood. "Yes. I see that now. Thank you, Jake."

His half brother got to his feet and picked up the chain. "This belongs to you."

Eli just stared it, unable to take it.

"He was your father. Not all the memories you have of him are bad." Jake stepped closer. "If Joe had admitted you were his, he would've had to take responsibility. He couldn't let himself do that because he already had a wife. He probably really loved Vera, but didn't consider her the marrying type. In his mind every woman was like his mother—a cheat not to be trusted." He raised the chain higher. "Take it. Maybe in a small way it can help you find a measure of the forgiveness you need."

Eli reached for it, his fingers closing around the cold metal. He drew a deep breath. "Thank you."

The two men embraced, and Eli walked to his car, still feeling trapped in a mold he couldn't break.

Joe McCain kept him shackled to the past, to a little boy who craved the love of his father. How could he change that?

CAROLINE CLEANED the kitchen and threw out the food. They hadn't taken time to eat last night. Other things had occupied them completely. She let herself feel a moment's pain, then grabbed her purse. She had to get through this day.

One person was on her mind now: Grace. They were supposed to have dinner last night, but Grace hadn't called. Caroline knew why.

She took the elevator up to Grace's office and walked past her secretary.

"Ms. Whitten." The girl jumped up, but Caroline opened Grace's door and went in.

Byron was leaning over Grace's shoulder, staring at some documents on her desk. He straightened abruptly. "Caroline, it's good to see you. You look great."

"Thank you. I'd like to speak with my sister alone, please."

"Of course." Byron moved toward the door. "I'll talk to you later, Grace."

Grace stood, and Caroline walked to her desk with fire in her eyes. "How dare you tell Eli that I was with Colin?"

"I did what I thought was best for you."

"You're not my mother, Grace," she cried. "Stay out of my life."

"Okay. I overstepped, but Ranger Coltrane has, too. He's way over the line of professionalism in his dealings with you and he should be reported."

Caroline's eyes narrowed. "You do anything remotely like that and I'll never speak to you again."

"Calm down."

"I'm about as calm as I'm going to get," she said. "You should be happy I'm not pulling your hair out."

"I'm not sure how to respond to you when you're in this mood."

"How about saying you're sorry and you won't interfere in my life again?"

Not a flicker of remorse showed on Grace's face, and something snapped in Caroline. "You know, Grace, you're just like Dad—so structured and molded that human emotions can't even get through."

Grace turned a pasty-white. "You're being mean."

"I'm just getting started."

Suddenly Grace sank into her chair and buried her face in her hand, crying. At the sight, the anger in Caroline subsided. She walked around the desk and sat on it, waiting for Grace to regain control. She never lost control for more than thirty seconds.

Grace pulled out a bottom drawer and reached for a Kleenex. Caroline noticed that everything in the drawer was orderly—nothing out of place. Just like her sister, a sister she knew so well, and loved despite her proclivities.

"Why don't you like Eli?" she asked.

Grace wiped her nose. "It's not that I don't like him. I just think he's taken advantage of the situation."

"You remember how he was when we went to see him in the hospital?"

"Yes. Standoffish."

"He's been that way from the start. I have literally pushed myself on him."

"Why would you do that?" Grace asked, puzzled. "You were in love with Colin a few weeks ago."

A dreamy look came over Caroline's face. "When the nanny read us a fairy tale about Prince Charming, you and I were enthralled. Later we wondered how we'd recognize our prince. Well, now I can tell you it has to do with a feeling. When Eli touched me, I knew something magical was happening. There's no doubt in my mind." She pressed her hands together. "He's my other half, my soul mate, my prince. I love him."

Grace's eyes opened wide. "You're serious."

"Yes. I am."

"No wonder you're so angry with me." She wiped her nose again.

"Eli said you were just trying to protect me."

"He stood up for me?" Grace asked in shock.

"Yes. He's that kind of person. I wish you'd let your guard down just a tiny bit and let yourself get to know him."

"I'm sorry, Caroline." Grace stood and Caroline did, too. They hugged.

"Let's have that dinner tonight," Grace said after a moment. "I was too scared to call you last night."

"Okay." Caroline knew there wasn't any chance of seeing Eli tonight and she had best keep herself occupied. But she wondered how long she could wait.

"You look sad," Grace stated, watching her.

She blinked. "Remember that saying about love never running smoothly?"

Her sister nodded.

"Well, it's true."

"Then you and Ranger Coltrane aren't…"

"We are, but he just doesn't know it yet, and I may spend the rest of my life trying to convince him."

"Caro…"

"I've got to go." She hugged Grace again and turned away. At the door she stopped. "When you see Eli, please apologize."

"I will."

"And if you happen to see Jeremiah Tucker, could you do the same? His name means a lot to him."

Grace lifted an eyebrow. "Anyone else?"

"No. That covers it."

As Caroline hurried to her car, her cell phone rang.

"Caroline, your mother and I are in town. Please meet us for lunch." Stephen Whitten didn't bother with introductions.

She didn't want to meet them. She wanted to go to the hospital and see Belle.

"Okay." She found herself agreeing.

Walking into the restaurant, she dreaded every moment she was going to have to spend with her parents. She knew exactly what her father wanted to talk about.

She hugged them both and took her seat.

"You look great, darling," Joanna said. "I'm happy you've recovered so quickly."

"Thank you, Mom."

"If the Buford case was going that well, we wouldn't be here," her father said.

The waiter came and took their order, giving her a small reprieve. Caroline placed her napkin in her lap, bracing herself.

"I talked with Greg Sherr and it seems your past has come back to haunt you, Caroline," Stephen continued a moment later.

"Yes. I heard."

"You seem very calm about this."

"Stephen," Joanna interjected. "Don't lose your temper."

He took a deep breath.

"I can only tell my story and hope a jury believes me."

"Hal Gooden will be contacting you," Stephen said as if she hadn't spoken. "He's an attorney and will coach you on your testimony. He will tell you what to say and what not to say. Sherr will work with him, and I don't want to hear one word of objection out of your mouth."

Caroline stood and placed her napkin on the table. "I'm not twelve years old and I resent being treated that way."

Her father's eyes narrowed. "And I resent all this negative publicity."

"Then go back to Washington and let me run my own life."

He got to his feet. "You're my daughter, Caroline, and what you do reflects on me. Years ago you thrived on defying me, but I thought you'd matured."

"I have. I'm not trying to be difficult, but this has been very hard for me, and for just this once I'd like your support."

"Oh, darling, your father is only trying to help you."

"It doesn't feel like help. It feels like criticism and manipulation."

Joanna got up and put her arm around her daughter. "Sit down and let's talk this out. We only want to help you get through this."

Caroline knew that they did, but her father's controlling nature was hard to handle. She sat back down. "Okay. I'll speak with the attorney. I'll do anything to keep Buford behind bars. I don't want him to hurt another woman."

"That's my girl," Stephen said, taking his seat. "Strong like me."

After that the meal was eaten in relative peace, but Caroline was glad to finally leave. Her father had an appointment with Sherr and Gooden, and she agreed to meet with them when they called. Giving in wasn't so bad. After all, everyone wanted the same thing.

ELI HURRIED TO his appointment with Greg. Tom and Bill were already there when he arrived.

"What's up?" he asked, seeing their stern faces.

"Buford's been taken to the hospital," Greg said.

"What the hell for?"

"He began vomiting and started running a high fever. The doctor looked at him in his cell and said he had to get him to the hospital to get his fever down. He's on an IV with antibiotics and now we just wait."

"I assume he's under heavy guard."

"You bet. Lansing is eating this up."

"I have a bad feeling about this," Eli said. "A lot can go wrong in a hospital."

"We're hoping to get him back in jail as fast as we can, but Lansing will try to do just the opposite."

"And he's in the same hospital as the dark-haired woman." Tom joined the conversation.

"Why did they take him there?"

"That's where all the inmates are taken," Tom explained.

"Damn." Eli felt anger churning inside him. "If she gets even a glimpse of him, she'll shut down and we won't get anything else out of her. We have to protect her. We owe her that much."

"I've already contacted Ranger McCain," Greg said. "He's making sure she won't be taken out of her room today, and maybe we can get Buford back in a cell before tonight."

Caroline.

"I've got to go," Eli said, and rushed out the door. He tried her apartment, then her cell phone, but she didn't answer. Where was she? He had to warn her.

CAROLINE PARKED at the hospital, reached for her cell phone and realized the batteries were dead. Damn. Damn. Damn. Her father was going to think she'd done this on purpose. She put the phone on charge and got out. Hurrying inside, she found a pay phone and left a message for her father, then went up to Belle's room.

There was a uniformed officer outside the door. He hadn't been there yesterday. Had something happened? She walked up to him. "Could I see Belle, please?"

"Just a moment." He tapped on the door and Caleb opened it.

"Caroline!" he said, clearly startled.

"I came to see Belle," she told him.

The ranger stepped outside and she noticed he glanced down the hall. "Sure, go on in. She could use some company. I think she's tired of me."

"Thanks, Caleb." Caroline wanted to ask what was going on, but decided they'd tell her if it was anything serious. Inside the room she stopped suddenly. Belle came out of the bathroom in the navy slacks and yellow-navy-and-white top Caroline had bought her. They fit perfectly. Her long hair was hanging down her back. It took a moment for Caroline to recognize her. Belle was beautiful.

Almost at a loss for words, Caroline finally managed to say, "They fit."

"It feels so good to be in regular clothes," Belle said, sitting on the bed.

Caroline took a chair. "Do you like to shop?"

"I don't know. I think I would."

"My sister and I love to shop—that's the only thing we have in common, except that we love each other."

"Must be nice to have a sister." Belle caressed the fabric of the slacks.

"Sometimes it is. At other times I want to strangle her."

Belle frowned. "I know that feeling, but I don't know how I know it."

"Do you have a sister?"

Her brow creased painfully, then she grabbed her head. "Nothing is there. Why can't I remember? Who am I?"

Caroline moved over to the bed, careful not to touch her. "Don't push it. Give yourself time."

"Everyone is so nice, not like…"

"We all want to help you." After a moment of silence, she added, "I want Amos Buford to pay for what he did to me, to you and to others."

"He should pay," Belle whispered. "He's evil."

"Yes. The rangers could use your help." Caroline pushed on. "But no one is forcing you, so do only what you feel you can."

"Like what?"

"Tell them what you know so they can put Buford away. I'm afraid and I know you're afraid, but together we can make sure no other woman is victimized by him."

Belle didn't answer, just stared at her feet, which were dangling off the bed.

Eli came through the door with a worried expression on his face. He seemed to relax when he saw her.

"Hi." She smiled, her heart doing a wonderful flutter at the sight of him.

"Hi." He didn't smile back and her heart stilled. Was it going to be like this between them now?

"Could I see you outside?" he asked.

"Yes." She slipped from the bed. "I'll see you later, Belle. Think about what I said."

"I will, and thank you for the clothes."

Eli took Caroline's arm and ushered her from the room, down the hall, around a corner to a small waiting room.

"Eli, what's wrong?" she asked, noting his solemn expression.

"I glad you're okay."

She shot him a confused look. "Why wouldn't I be okay?"

"Buford has been admitted to this hospital."

The confusion quickly turned to disbelief. "What? Why?"

"He became ill and they brought him here."

"Oh, God." She trembled in sudden fear.

"I'll take you to your car. I don't want you to return to the hospital until he's back in his cell."

Caroline could see the concern and anxiety in Eli's eyes, but that wasn't what she wanted to see. She wanted so much more from him. For the first time she realized that might never happen. Eli was a prisoner himself, and she didn't know how to free him. That hurt worse than anything she'd ever felt in her life.

Through the pain she heard him say, "Don't worry. Everything will be okay."

But it wasn't. Life would never be the same again. She couldn't concentrate on that now, however. Later, when she was alone, it would torture her. Now she had to be on guard against the events going on around her.

"Oh, no," she cried.

"What?"

"Belle. She's doing so much better, and if she sees him it will—"

"We're taking care of her."

Caroline's courage crumbled. "Is this nightmare ever going to end?"

Eli looked away and took her arm. "Let's get you out of here."

They walked together to the elevators, out of the hospital, to the parking area. Neither spoke.

At her car, he said, "I'll call when Buford is back in his cell."

"Okay," she replied, feeling more than a little distracted. She wanted to kiss him so badly that she had to restrain herself.

I love you.

The words hovered on her lips as she got into her car, but she didn't say them. Eli wasn't ready.

She watched as he headed back into the hospital, and tried not to let her nerves get the best of her. Searching for her keys, she saw Grace drive into the parking lot. What was she doing here?

Grace jumped out and ran for the walkway before Caroline could get out of her car. She had a feeling something was wrong, yet she didn't want to go into the hospital again. She wanted to avoid any chance of running into Amos Buford. But it was a big hospital, and Grace was clearly upset. Taking a fortifying breath, Caroline hurried toward the entrance.

She caught a glimpse of her sister's back as she disappeared around a corner, running. Grace never ran. A sliver of alarm edged its way up Caroline's spine and she quickly followed, weaving around people, trying not to lose sight of her quarry.

Grace went straight to the emergency room and Caroline saw her talking to a nurse at a desk. By the time she reached them, Caroline was out of breath. "Grace," she panted.

Her sister swung around, her face blotchy from crying.

"Where have you been?" Grace railed. "I tried your cell a number of times. Why can't you keep the damn thing charged? That's what happened, isn't it? Your phone is dead. Sometimes you make me so angry."

Caroline put her arm around her sister's shoulders. "Calm down, okay?" She'd never seen Grace like this and knew something was terribly wrong. Taking a breath, she asked, "What's wrong?"

"Daddy's had a heart attack."

CHAPTER SIXTEEN

THE BLOOD DRAINED from Caroline's face. "What?"

"Mom called and I got here as fast as I could." Grace looked around. "She has to be here somewhere."

"I just had lunch with him," Caroline whispered, almost to herself. "He seemed fine—his usual self, demanding and giving orders."

"He's always so strong. What if he…" Grace couldn't finish the sentence, and Caroline grabbed her and held on tight.

"He'll be fine," she assured her. "He has to be."

Had she upset him? Had her defiance triggered this? The guilt kept stabbing at her. Oh, God, no. She could live with a lot of things, but not that. She and her father had their differences, but she loved him. She hadn't shown that recently, though. Neither had he. What had happened to the little girl who thought her father could walk on water? And what had happened to the man who thought his daughter could do no wrong? Suddenly all their disagreements faded away and she wanted to see her father.

A doctor walked up to them. "Your mother is waiting for you. Come this way."

They followed him down a hall and into a small waiting room. Joanna was pacing, talking on her cell phone. "Yes. Cancel everything. I will be in touch tomorrow." She clicked off and turned to her daughters.

"Oh, my darlings. I'm so glad you're here." She hugged them briefly. "Don't worry. Your father will be fine."

Caroline stared at her, hardly able to believe her eyes. She didn't seem upset and was carrying on business as usual.

"They're taking him up for surgery. I contacted Dr. Herman Miller. He's one the best heart surgeons in the country and I have a lot of faith in his ability. Now I have to call my secretary and have a statement released to the press."

"What happened?" Caroline asked, before her mother could punch in the number.

Joanna shrugged, staring at the phone in her hand. "You know your father and his temper. Sometimes he lets it get away from him, and he's been having problems with his blood pressure. He won't listen to the doctors about diet and exercise."

"Where did it happen?"

Joanna sighed. "Caroline, is this important now? I really have to make some calls."

"Yes. It's important," Caroline insisted. "Where did it happen?"

"Greg Sherr and your father got into a heated argument about how Greg was mishandling the case and letting Lansing manipulate the system. Stephen clutched his chest and fell to the floor. An ambulance brought him here. Don't worry, darling. He'll be fine." She smiled and turned her attention to her phone.

Caroline wasn't so sure. Heart surgery was serious, and her mother was acting as if Stephen would be back in his office tomorrow. What bothered Caroline the most was that it could be her fault. Suddenly she felt helpless and afraid, and she didn't know what to do.

She needed Eli.

No. She could handle this alone.

Her mother put down the phone. "We'll go upstairs now."

"Can we see him?" Caroline asked.

"No, darling," Joanna answered. "We can see him after the surgery."

Caroline gripped Grace's hand and they followed their mother, hoping against hope that their father would make it.

ELI HURRIED BACK to meet Caleb, breathing a little easier now that Caroline was out of the hospital. He didn't want there to be any chance encounters with Amos Buford. She'd suffered enough at his hands.

Eli wanted to tell her he was sorry about this morning, but he'd already done that. There wasn't anything left for him to say until this case was over and he could do what Jake had done—put his past behind him, forgive and move on. Eli was still grappling with how to do that.

All his life people had told him how strong he was, but he didn't feel strong. He felt weak and vulnerable. He didn't like himself very much. Now he had to concentrate on his job. Tonight he'd deal with the pain. Deal with what he'd done to Caroline and with the fact that he was a scarred man. And pray that love would find a way to heal.

Caleb stood outside Belle's door, waiting.

"How's Belle?" Eli asked.

"I'm not sure," his brother said. "To tell you the truth I hardly recognize her."

"What do you mean?"

"She's dressed in the clothes Caroline bought her and she's so different. She's really beautiful. I can't believe that there isn't someone out there really missing her."

Eli cocked an eyebrow. "You say that like you don't *want* anyone missing her."

Caleb frowned. "I feel a lot of sympathy for this woman and I just want to get her back to her family."

Eli saw a look in Caleb's eyes that said he felt a lot more than sympathy for Belle.

"Let's see if we can jog her memory," Eli said, and they entered the room.

Eli noticed the difference Caleb was talking about. Belle was out of her hospital gown and nicely dressed. It seemed to give her confidence, a boost she needed. And she was beautiful—even he could see that.

Yep. There had to be someone missing Belle. But who? And how had she ended up with Buford and his followers?

For the next thirty minutes they talked about a lot of things and Belle wore a perpetual frown, not able to remember anything about her past life. Eli could see she was getting upset, so he decided to shift the questions from her to Buford.

"Do you know how long you were at the camp?"

Belle shook her head. "Seems like forever." She tried to think. "It was cold, really cold, when they took me there. That's why I built the fire in the wood-burning stove. I wasn't used to sleeping in the cold."

"You weren't?" Eli caught the reference to her past and hoped she'd keep talking, keep remembering.

"No. We had central air and heat."

Eli glanced at Caleb and continued. "Who is we?"

Belle looked at him, her eyes dazed. "What?"

"You said *we* had central air and heat."

She frowned. "I did?"

"Yes," Caleb interjected in a whisper.

Belle closed her eyes and her forehead creased in thought. "Yes." She ran her hands up her arms, her eyes still closed. "It was nice and comfortable. I can feel my big bed. He bought me Egyptian cotton sheets and I said it was too extravagant and he laughed and said nothing was too good for his girl. He spoiled me rotten and I liked it. No one ever…" Her eyes shot open and she clasped her cheeks with her hands. "How do I know that?" she asked in desperation.

"It's all right, Belle," Caleb told her. "Your memory is starting to come back. Just take it slow and easy and soon you'll remember who *he* is."

"Yes." She gave a small smile. "I'm starting to remember. Oh, that's wonderful."

There was silence for a moment and Eli knew they'd probably pushed her enough for one day. Still…

"Do you feel up to talking about Buford?" he asked.

Belle linked her fingers together. "Caroline said I should help you."

"We'd appreciate it," Eli said. "To keep Buford behind bars we need more evidence."

Belle bowed her head. "What do you need?"

Eli and Caleb shared a relieved glance. "You were there for several months so you saw what was going on."

She nodded. "But I stayed out of the way when I was doing their chores because I didn't want them to beat me again."

Eli swallowed. "How long had they been preparing for the wedding?"

"Since…" She paused.

"Since when, Belle?" Eli prompted.

"Ever since I was there and when the other one—please, I can't talk about it."

Caleb got up and sat on the bed beside her. "I know this is hard, but talking about it may help you to deal with it."

"It was horrible," she breathed.

"Tell us what was horrible." Caleb's voice was gentle, soothing.

"They…they brought another woman in, blond like Caroline and very young. The prophet prayed over her and touched her, thanking God for the great gift he'd been given. The others joined in with chanting and praying, then they took her to the cellar. A few days later they brought her out and she was lifeless and limp."

"Was she dead?" Eli asked after a moment of pained silence.

Belle shook her head. "I don't know. I hope so."

Eli and Caleb shared another glance.

Belle started talking again. "They told me to stay in the kitchen, but I peeked out the window. They placed her body on a bed made of wood and straw. I didn't know what they were doing and I was so afraid. I tried running away once and they beat me until I lost consciousness. But I wanted to run again because I could feel something bad was about to happen. I guess that's why I kept looking."

She took a ragged breath. "Every night they'd build a fire and he preached. That night they marched to the piled logs with her body. The prophet prayed for mercy on her soul, saying the demons had taken over her body and it had to be destroyed. They lifted her body to the top of the logs and then they…they lit it and I…I couldn't look anymore. I cowered in a corner, knowing this was evil. I didn't have a memory but I knew this was evil like I'd never seen before."

Eli had heard and seen a lot in his law career but he was having a hard time handling this. It was worse than he'd ever imagined.

Caleb was silent and his face had turned a sickly white.

"That's why I had to tell you where Caroline was. You had to get her out of there before they did that to her."

Eli cleared his throat. "Was that the only burning you saw?"

Belle nodded. "Yes. From the first day I was there, all they talked about was the prophecy and how it had to be fulfilled."

Eli stood. "Thank you, Belle. This will help a great deal."

"I just don't want them to do that to another woman."

"Don't worry." Caleb got to his feet. "We'll make sure they don't. Now try to get some rest."

"I am tired," she said, and stretched out on the bed.

Eli and Caleb walked outside and stood staring at each other. Neither spoke for a second. "We got him," Eli said. "Sherr wanted hard evidence. Well, this is it."

"Yeah." Caleb shook his head as if to rid himself of the images. "It's just hard to believe."

"Mmm." He couldn't dwell on that part. He wanted Buford and now they had evidence to work with, evidence that Lansing couldn't poke holes in. "Let's go over to Sherr's office so we can get a forensic team out to the camp ASAP. All we need to find is human remains in the ashes. Hopefully we can find enough to identify someone and to put Buford away for the rest of his insane life."

Eli's cell phone buzzed and he clicked it on. "Yes. We're on our way." He glanced at Caleb. "Sherr wants to see us. I'll meet you there."

Within minutes they were headed to Greg's office. Bill and Tom were there, too. Greg held up a plastic bag that had a diamond ring inside.

"The digging crew found it—Caroline Whitten's engagement ring. It wasn't discovered in Buford's hut. They found it about twenty feet under the ground. Exactly where Eli said the cellar was."

"That's damn good work," Tom said. "It proves they're all lying."

"Yes," Greg agreed. "But I'm sure Lansing will have a way to explain it. It's good, but I'd like to have more."

"We have more," Eli declared, and told them what Belle had revealed.

Greg laid the bag down, his eyes narrowed. "Is she sure about this?"

"Get a forensics team out there and find out, because I have a feeling Belle knows exactly what she's talking about," Eli said solemnly.

"I was hoping for a break, but this is horrific." Greg's expression spoke volumes.

Eli's phone buzzed again and he turned away to answer it.

"Eli, it's Caroline. I just wanted to let you know that I'm not at my apartment in case you call. I'm at the hospital."

Eli didn't hear a thing but those last four words. "Why?"

She didn't answer.

"Caroline?"

"Daddy's had a heart attack." The hysteria in her voice twisted his gut.

"I'll be right there."

"There's no—" Eli clicked off, cutting her short.

"Is that about the congressman?" Greg asked.

It took a moment for Eli to realize he was speaking to him. All he could hear was her trembling voice. "Yes… yes."

"How is he?"

"I don't know. I've got to get back to the hospital."

"Me, too," Caleb said. "I don't want to leave Belle too long."

"I'll get everything set in motion. Keep me posted about the congressman," Greg called as they walked out.

"Is something wrong?" Caleb asked in the hall.

"I'll tell you later." Eli hurried to his car.

He didn't hear Caleb's reply. His mind was on Caroline now. The traffic was heavy and his temples throbbed with a need to just get to her. At the hospital, a nurse told him the congressman was in surgery. Security had the family waiting in a private room to avoid the press. Eli showed his ID and the nurse made a call. Soon he stepped onto the designated floor. He saw Caroline immediately.

She was pacing back and forth by the nurse's desk. Turning, she saw him and stopped. They stared at each other and he could see all the pain in her eyes. His ethics, his problem seemed trivial compared to what he felt for her. He walked to her and took her in an embrace.

She wrapped her arms around his waist and for a moment neither said a word.

"How is he?" Eli asked, his voice thick.

"He's in surgery now. The waiting is awful."

He stroked her hair. "How are you?"

She drew back. "Better now that you're here. I just had to touch you." Her hand splayed across his chest. "Now I can handle it."

"But not alone."

They gazed at each other and both knew they had to talk.

"It's just so scary, though," she said. "I thought he was invincible."

"The doctors can do wonderful things these days."

"I hope so." She glanced at the floor. "I have so much

to say to him. We haven't talked in years. When I was younger, we talked all the time."

"He has an important job." Eli tried to comfort her. "His life must be very hectic and demanding. Family are the ones that lose that precious time."

"Yeah." She brushed her hair back in a nervous gesture. "I'd better go sit with Mom and Grace. The hospital arranged for us to have a private room, to keep us away from reporters. I was waiting out here because I didn't want to miss you."

"I'll stay for a while."

"You don't have to do that. I just wanted you to know why I wasn't at my apartment."

He caught her arms and made her look at him. "Yes, I do."

"Eli," she sighed. "You can't say we have no future, then want to be here for me. I can't deal with that." She blinked back a tear. "You were right this morning. I want to hear those words from you. This relationship happened so fast, but I know what I want. You have to make up your mind what *you* want. And to hell with your ethics." She turned and walked into a room.

His stomach clenched tight and he wondered if he was deliberately trying to hurt her…and himself. This was destructive behavior. Destructive behavior from a troubled childhood.

His legs felt weak and he sank into a chair. Jake's words came back to him. *The answers you're looking for are inside you. It's about forgiving and accepting. I had to forgive my mother and the father who hurt me terribly, and most of all, I had to forgive myself.*

How did he do that? By making a conscious effort. The answer was plain as day.

All this time Eli had been dealing with the pain inside him and wondering how to make it stop. *By forgiving.* By forgiving Joe McCain—and himself. Looking back over the years, he realized it had been important to him to hate Joe McCain—that's what had made him strong. But he couldn't live that way any longer because he couldn't continue to hurt Caroline. Or himself.

Ever since Ben's kidnapping, events in his life had been spiraling toward this moment. Getting to know his brothers had been the catalyst and now he had to follow through. He reached into his shirt pocket and pulled out the chain.

Either Joe and Vera had bought this together or Vera had given it to him. The heart split in two pretty much symbolized their relationship—and Joe McCain's life.

He'd been in love with two women at the same time and had made some lousy choices for himself, his kids and the women involved.

Joe wasn't good at intimate relationships. Eli wasn't, either. But the Tuckers had shown him what love was all about so he couldn't keep blaming his father for his inability to love. It was time to take responsibility for his behavior.

The chain felt light and warm in his hand. Joe wanted Eli to have the chain and split heart. That meant he'd been thinking about him. He hadn't forgotten. He knew Eli was his and maybe this was his way of letting Eli know.

He inhaled a deep breath and then let it out. As his diaphragm expanded he glanced toward the door Caroline had gone through. He knew what he wanted.

His hand closed around the chain and he could almost hear Joe saying, "Thatch, you're gonna be a big boy. Thatch, you have to watch out for your mother. Thatch, make your mother proud." All Eli could hear were the good things his father had said to him. From somewhere deep inside, he felt Joe would've been proud of the man he'd become. In that moment, he forgave Joe McCain.

I forgive you.

Still clutching the chain, he felt the words run through him like a victory cheer from a long-fought game—powerful and uplifting. Nurses and other staff rushed by him. Life went on. No one seemed to notice that a miracle had just happened.

He got to his feet, wondering how he'd forgive himself. That might take time. His past wouldn't just miraculously disappear, but he could accept it now and move on. He didn't know a lot about love, but he knew he wasn't leaving Caroline. He followed her into the room.

Her mother was on the phone and Grace and Caroline were sitting in chairs. Caroline's eyes widened when she saw him.

Joanna put down the phone. "Ranger Coltrane, I believe."

He removed his hat. "Yes, ma'am. I'm sorry about Congressman Whitten."

"He'll be fine," Joanna declared, to Eli's surprise. "Stephen is strong as a horse."

Eli wasn't sure how to respond to that so he said nothing. When Joanna took another call, he sat beside Caroline.

She didn't say anything—just stared at him. He wanted her to touch him. He needed that, but he didn't deserve it.

Destructive thoughts.

Yes, he deserved it. As he sat there staring at Caroline, his heart began to beat faster with that wonderful realization. He deserved it. He deserved her. And just like that, he forgave himself for all the hatred, the bitterness and the rebellion. He felt winded, out of breath, surprising himself at this sudden change. All because he loved Caroline. A life without her was unthinkable.

"Hello, Ranger Coltrane," Grace said.

"Hello." He nodded briefly.

There was a tense moment, then Grace added, "I'm sorry I lied to you about where Caroline was."

"I'm sorry you lied, too." Eli knew he'd answered, but all he could think about was getting Caroline alone. Her family needed her, though.

The doctor came in, preventing further conversation. They got to their feet. Joanna kept talking on the phone and the doctor waited, until finally Caroline nudged her and she hung up.

"Oh, Dr. Miller. I'm sure you have good news for us."

"Your husband came through the surgery, but he's not out of the woods."

"What are you talking about?"

"We did a quadruple bypass and Mr. Whitten's blood pressure is so erratic we had a hard time finishing the surgery. In short, your husband is not in good shape. We'll watch him closely during the night and hope for the best."

Caroline turned white and Eli put his arm around her waist. Grace had tears in her eyes, but Joanna stared at the doctor with a calm expression. Then, just as calmly, she said, "I'm sorry. You're services are no longer required. I'll be contacting another doctor to take over Stephen's case."

Dr. Miller's eyes narrowed. "Pardon me?"

"Mom, what are you saying?" Caroline asked.

"He botched the surgery. I'm calling in another doctor." Joanna picked up her phone, but Caroline took it out of her hand.

"No. You said Dr. Miller was one of the best in the country, so please try to focus on what he's saying. Daddy needs us to be strong and levelheaded."

Joanna took a couple of steps backward, shaking her head. "This wasn't suppose to happen to us. We…we…" She began to cry openly. "I can't survive if something happens to Stephen. I…I can't."

Caroline wrapped her arms around her mother and held her. Grace joined them and for a moment nothing else was said. Then Joanna's cell phone buzzed.

Caroline reached for it. "My mother is not to be bothered for twenty-four hours. Just take care of things until she calls you." She laid the phone down. "That was your secretary. Now let's just concentrate on Daddy." She looked at the doctor. "What are Dad's chances?"

Dr. Miller hesitated, then said, "About fifty-fifty."

Caroline bit her lip and Eli saw how hard she was trying to control her emotions for her mother's sake. He felt such intense love for her—a deep feeling he'd never experienced before. It was there and he could feel it.

"Fifty-fifty." She turned to her mother. "That's a done deal to Daddy. The odds against him were greater in his first election and he won. He'll beat this, too."

"Yes." Joanna hiccupped. "Your father's a fighter."

"Can we see him now?" Caroline asked the doctor.

"Yes. But only for a few minutes and, please, don't try to talk to him. He won't hear you and we want to keep him quiet."

Caroline linked her arm through her mother's. "Ready?"

"Yes," Joanna replied, linking her other arm through Grace's.

They followed the doctor out the door.

Eli felt very alone at that moment, but he took a seat. He'd wait.

In a minute Caroline was back. Eli got to his feet with

a worried frown. Before he could say anything, she said,
"I don't think I can do this."

"Sure you can."

"It's my fault he had the heart attack."

"What?"

"I upset him at lunch and he got into a big argument
with Greg Sherr. I…I just—"

"Listen to me. You're not the cause of your father's
poor health and you certainly didn't cause his heart attack."

"Then why do I feel so guilty?"

"Because you're you." His eyes clung to hers. "Now go
see him. Your mother and sister need you."

She turned and left. Eli resumed his seat, knowing this
was going to be a long night. He would be with her, though,
every step of the way. That's what love was all about. He
was learning.

A NURSE TOOK THEM to Stephen. The three women just
stood and stared at the man in the bed. Caroline had to take
a deep breath. There were tubes, IVs and monitors, but her
eyes were glued to her father's face. He looked older and
so unlike himself. His face was slightly swollen and he was
pale. So very pale.

"Oh, my God." Joanna knees buckled and Caroline and
Grace held her up. After a moment, they helped her from
the room.

Throughout the night they took turns going to check on
Stephen. Eli went to get coffee and sandwiches, but they
ate very little. They drank the coffee and Eli went back
for more.

"I like Eli," Joanna said while he was gone.

"Thank you," Caroline said. They were sitting on the
small settee in the private room. "I like him, too." The fact

that Eli was still here was a good sign. She'd hold on to that. She needed it. She needed him.

"He's strong like your father."

Caroline had never made the connection, but she could see they had similar qualities. They were both fighters and it seemed as if there was nothing they couldn't handle. Similar yet so very different. Eli had a softer quality he didn't show to many people. She loved that about him, but his strength was what attracted her.

"I don't deserve you girls." Joanna's words penetrated her thoughts.

"Why would you say that?" Caroline asked, rubbing her mom's arm.

"Because I haven't been a very good mother."

Caroline and Grace didn't say anything.

"It's not easy to have to choose between your kids and your husband. When your father wanted to go into politics, I knew that someday I would regret not being at home with my children."

"We're okay, Mom," Caroline said.

"Yes," Grace added.

But Joanna kept talking. "It wasn't so bad when Stephen was a judge, but I was busy with your father's career even then. I had to delegate parts of my life. I couldn't take you to school or pick you up, and I missed so many of your functions. I regret that. Your childhood is gone and I can't get it back. And now your father…"

Her voice trailed away and Caroline saw a side of her mother she'd never seen before—her vulnerable side. She was always so in control of everything in her life. Today, though, that control had been shattered, and Caroline saw a woman torn with conflicting thoughts and emotions. Caroline had never felt so close to her.

Joanna patted her daughters' hands. "I'm so very proud of the way both of you have turned out. And, Caroline, I know your father has been unhappy with some of your choices, but they're *your* choices and it's your life. From this day forward we will not interfere again, except to support you."

Emotions jelled in her throat. "Thank you, Mom," she finally managed to say, feeling the years of resentment slowly ebbing away.

Eli came back with the coffee and Caroline got up to take it from him. "Why don't you try to get some rest?" he suggested.

"No. I can't sleep." She didn't want to be woken up to hear that her father had died.

She tried to get Eli to go home, but he wouldn't, and she knew it was useless to argue with him. He removed his hat, sat in a chair and stretched out his legs. He was here for the duration and Caroline couldn't have loved him more.

She, Grace and Joanna talked about the good times they had shared, the vacations and holidays. Times they'd forgotten. Times they needed to remember to endure the long night.

As dawn crept through the window, a nurse came into the room. "Dr. Miller would like to see you, please."

"Oh, God," Joanna cried.

Caroline tried to breathe normally. "Let's just go and see what he has to say."

They got to their feet. Caroline looked at Eli and she saw a lot more than concern in his eyes. Her heart tripped. Later, they would talk. Now…she reached out and took his hand. If she was hearing bad news, she wanted him with her.

CHAPTER SEVENTEEN

As soon as they saw Dr. Miller, they knew it was good news. He was smiling.

"He's awake and all his vital signs are good. You can speak to him for a moment if you want, but he's very groggy. We weathered the worst and, baring any complications, I'm expecting a full recovery."

"Thank you, Dr. Miller," Joanna said. "I'm sorry I lost it yesterday."

"I understand, Mrs. Whitten. This is going to be a long recovery and he has to slow down and take better care of himself."

"I will see to that. You can count on it."

Eli waited at the desk while they went inside.

Joanna stepped to one side of the bed and Caroline and Grace walked around to the other. Stephen's eyes were closed and he still seemed frail, though his color was better. Joanna leaned over and kissed his forehead.

"Hi, honey," she whispered.

He moved his head. "Jo..." he breathed.

"Yes. It's me." Joanna combed her fingers through his gray hair.

Stephen licked his lips. "Where are...the...girls?"

"They're right here," Joanna told him. "Open your eyes and you can see them."

His eyelids fluttered weakly, then opened. His eyes had a dazed quality and Caroline felt her chest tighten.

"Hi, Daddy," she said, her voice hoarse.

"Daddy." Grace's voice was even hoarser.

He just stared at them, and Caroline grasped his free hand. He squeezed gently and closed his eyes.

"That's enough for now," Dr. Miller said. "You can visit at intervals during the day."

Outside the CCU, Caroline went straight to Eli. "He's better. Thank God."

"That's great," he said.

Caroline brushed away tears. "Now go to work. I know you have lots to do."

"Are you sure?"

"Yes." She smiled. "I'll stay here with my mom and I'll let you know if anything changes."

Nothing ever came between Eli and his work—until Caroline. Now he didn't want to leave her. He had so much to share with her. But he could wait. They had a big break in the Buford case and he should let Caroline know what Belle had told them. He couldn't, though. She had enough to deal with. He'd tell her later.

On the walk to the elevator, he said, "They recovered your engagement ring."

"Oh. I didn't expect that."

"It's evidence right now, but you can get it back."

"I won't need it—ever." Her eyes sent him a message.

He inclined his head. "Later," he whispered, not trusting himself to say anything else.

"Later," she echoed as he stepped onto the elevator.

ELI NOW HAD TO concentrate on his job, so he called Caleb as soon as he got into his car. They planned to meet at

Sherr's office. Eli hurried home for a quick shower, shave and a change of clothes. In record time he was walking into Sherr's office. Caleb had beat him there.

"How's the congressman?" Greg asked.

"They think he's going to make it," Eli replied.

"Thank God." Greg sighed. "That was a terrible scene—not one I want to repeat anytime soon."

Eli took a seat. "It's really hard on the family. The congressman was always a strong man."

Greg grimaced. "Don't remind me."

"Have you heard anything from the forensic team?" Eli asked. He knew a group had gone out yesterday to start the search for remains.

"I got a call late yesterday evening from Martin, head of the team that's out at the camp. It's a slow go because they don't want to miss anything. But they found teeth and a bone—what looks like a thigh bone, he said. It and the teeth have been sent to the lab to determine if they're human."

"They are," Eli said.

Greg frowned. "Do you think they burned more than one woman?"

Eli rubbed his hands together. "Probably."

"This is just horrendous." Greg leaned back in his chair.

"It's brutal," Caleb agreed. "This man has to be stopped."

"If those remains are human, Amos Buford won't see the light of day again."

"Are they taking Buford back to a cell today?" Eli asked.

Greg shook his head. "No. His fever spiked during the night. They say he has an infection, but they can't isolate it. Until they can get him stabilized, he's staying at the hospital."

"Dammit." Eli got to his feet. "I don't like this."

"It gets worse," Greg said. "The Wessells are in town. They brought Ruth and Naomi to see Buford."

"You're allowing this?" Eli's voice rose in disbelief.

"We argued in front of a judge yesterday, but since Buford hasn't been convicted of anything, the judge is allowing his family to see him."

"How in the—"

"Calm down, Eli." Greg pushed his chair forward. "We can't deny this man his rights. If we do, Lansing will get him free on a technicality, and I certainly don't want that to happen."

"Caroline and Belle are in that hospital and if they see those women…" He stopped.

Greg shifted in his seat. "I can assure you I have this situation under control."

"How?"

"A guard will escort Ruth and Naomi to see Buford and there will be heavy security. The judge agreed to it. The visit is at two o'clock this afternoon and the guard at Belle's door has been alerted not to let her leave her room until the women are gone from the building. And I'm sure you can handle the Whitten situation."

"You're damn right I will." He swung toward the door.

"Eli."

He looked at Greg.

"The system sometimes doesn't work in our favor, but we got him this time. Thanks to you."

"I'd just feel better with Buford in a cell."

"Maybe soon." Greg nodded and Eli left.

Caleb caught up with him. "I'll stay around Belle's room until this fiasco is over."

"That's probably a good idea," Eli said. "I'll catch you later."

CAROLINE DIDN'T understand what Eli was doing back at the hospital, and he hedged and lied until he couldn't do it anymore. Then he took her down the hall to a small waiting room. Luckily, they had it to themselves. They sat on a sofa and Eli told her about Ruth and Naomi's visit.

She gasped. "They're allowed to see him?"

"Yes. The visit is at two, so stay on this floor until they leave the building. I'll let you know when they do."

Her eyes flew to his. "What about Belle?"

"Caleb is taking care of her."

"Good. She doesn't need to see them."

"Neither do you."

She folded her hands in her lap. "I'm fine. I really am."

"I can see that—especially last night when you were handling the situation with your mom. You were wonderful."

"My mother has always been so strong, so in control, and last night I saw a vulnerable side of her. I felt a connection that we'd lost. All these years my parents and I have been at loggerheads over the same thing. My father wanted me to show my love by going to law school and working in his firm. I, on the other hand, wanted them to show they loved me by letting me live my own life. We wanted to feel that love, but we were too stubborn to acknowledge it."

"I think everyone wants to feel love," he said.

"Do you?" Her eyes demanded a response.

The question hung between them and Eli knew his answer. He cleared his throat, but before he could say what he was feeling, some people came into the room. He'd never felt so frustrated in his life. He wanted to tell her, needed to, but he'd have to wait. He took her arm and they went into the hallway, where Grace came toward them.

"I'll be back," he said. "Just remember what I said."

"Don't worry, and tell Belle I'll visit her sometime today."

Eli hurried toward the elevators, cursing the circumstances, the situation and his inability to do anything about it. But now Caroline's safety and Belle's took precedence. He went down to Belle's room, and Caleb told him everything was quiet. Eli relayed Caroline's message, then headed down to Buford's room. For his own peace of mind he had to see how sick the man was. The guard looked at his badge and ID and Eli went inside. Another guard was in the room and Eli nodded to him. Then he riveted his eyes on the man in the bed.

Amos lay very still. An IV was in his arm and he was hooked up to a heart monitor. He still had the long hair and beard, but his skin had a grayish tinge to it. He looked old, and Eli knew there was no way he could fake this.

"How long has he been asleep?" he asked the guard.

"He drifts in and out, talking about prophecy and fulfillment. It's spooky as hell in here."

"Is he lucid?"

"Not that I could tell."

"Thanks," Eli said, and walked out. He went down the hall and waited, glancing at his watch. At two o'clock he saw them get off the elevator. Ruth and Naomi wore long black dresses, their hair tied in a knot at their nape. Two guards were with them along with an older couple, which had to be their parents, the Wessells.

They walked by Eli without a second glance. They didn't recognize him and that was good. The group went into Buford's room, and soon the couple came out. They were nervous and upset. He could see that. The Wessells walked down the hall and sat in chairs, waiting for their daughters.

Eli waited, too, watching the clock. An hour later the

women came out and their parents joined them. They all left and Eli made his way back to the room.

"What happened in here?" he asked the guard.

"A lot of praying and chanting, willing the bad spirits out of his body."

Eli glanced at the sleeping Amos. "Did he wake up?"

"For a few minutes."

"What did he say?"

"I didn't understand a word. This is all very weird."

"Yeah," Eli agreed. "Just be on guard."

The rest of the day went smoothly and Eli was able to relax. He went back to see Caroline and she was all smiles. Congressman Whitten was continuing to improve. Eli told her about the Wessells and Buford, then went to his office to check his messages and do paperwork.

As he was getting ready to leave for the hospital again, Greg called.

"Just wanted to let you know that more teeth and bone fragments have been recovered. From the number of teeth, it has to be more than one person."

"Good God."

"My sentiments exactly," Greg replied. "The visit by the Wessells went well, I was told."

"No problems, but..."

"But what?"

"I just have an uneasy feeling that I can't explain."

"Maybe you're too closely involved," Greg suggested.

"Maybe," Eli admitted.

"To put your mind at rest, I just got a call from the doctor attending Buford, and the report wasn't good. They've isolated the infection to his heart, but he's not responding to the antibiotics."

"He looked bad when I saw him."

"Buford's not in any shape to cause more trouble. He's fighting for his life right now. So relax, Eli, and try to get a good night's rest. I'll be in touch."

Eli hung up, still feeling uneasy, but he shook it off and headed to the hospital. The Whitten women were spending the night there again, in the room the hospital had provided. There were two twin beds and a cot there. He left knowing Caroline needed this time with her family.

He planned to get a good night's sleep, but tossed and turned with worries he couldn't define or explain. Staring into the darkness, he wished Caroline was here in bed with him so he could touch her skin and feel her body next to his. He wanted her. Because he loved her. *He deserved love.* Finally, he could believe that with every part of him— even his heart. Soon they'd be together again. But that time seemed so far away.

Sometime before dawn he got up and called Tuck. He was always up early, so Eli didn't worry about waking him. They talked for a few minutes and Eli felt better. Tuck had a sensible way of looking at things. "If it ain't broke, don't fix it." Pa lived by that philosophy and Tuck did, too. There was no need to worry because Buford wasn't able to hurt anyone else.

Eli went to his office and Caleb stopped by. Before they could discuss anything, the phone rang.

"Get to the hospital immediately," Greg said.

Eli was on his feet. "What is it?"

"Don't worry, Eli. It's not Caroline. It's Buford. The doctor called and said we need to get over there."

"I'm on my way." Eli hung up, explained to Caleb and ran to his car. Caleb rushed to his. Within minutes, they were at the hospital. Several people were standing in the hall. Eli recognized Lansing, Tom, Bill and Greg.

Greg walked up to them. "Buford died a few minutes ago."

The news didn't take Eli by surprise. Maybe this was what he'd been expecting. "I guess God has his own kind of justice for Amos Buford."

But he felt an odd sense of disappointment. He wanted Buford to pay for what he'd done to Ginny, Caroline and a number of other women. He'd spent years keeping tabs on his activities so one day justice could be done. It seemed Buford had gotten off easy. Hell was a horrific place, though, befitting a man like Amos Buford. Nothing on earth could equal that punishment.

All Eli could do was stop other men like him.

"I'll go tell Belle," Caleb said. "I know she'll be relieved."

He walked off and Tom and Bill came over.

"Lansing is going to sue the hospital on the Wessells' behalf because Buford didn't get proper treatment," Tom said.

"Yeah, right," Eli replied. "I'll tell Caroline this is finally over."

"Not quite," Greg warned. "We have a lot of evidence to gather and identify. When it's over, maybe some families can put their daughters to rest."

"If you need any help, you know where to find me." They shook hands and Eli went to find Caroline, desperately needing to see her.

The Whitten women were coming out of the room. "I'd like to borrow Caroline for a minute," he said.

"Sure, Eli," Joanna said. "But don't keep her too long. Her father is waiting."

"Yes, ma'am," Eli replied as he and Caroline moved off down the hall.

"What is it?" she asked. "You seem excited."

"Buford died a little while ago."

"What?" Her eyes were enormous.

"It's finally over," he told her. "He can't hurt another woman."

"Oh, Eli." She threw her arms around his neck, almost knocking his hat off. "I never thought I'd feel good about someone's death, but I do. He's hurt so many women— Belle, Ginny, me and others."

Ginny. Her ghost was finally resting in peace. Not because Buford was dead—but because of Caroline.

"Are you spending the night?" he whispered against her face.

She drew back. "Mom refuses to leave, so Grace and I are going to take turns staying with her. Tonight Grace is staying. I will meet you at my place at eight o'clock and we'll talk. Date?"

"You bet."

She grinned. "And don't be late."

"Eight o'clock," he said, and walked away smiling.

Caroline turned as Joanna and Grace came out of the CCU. She didn't know what the night was going to bring, but she was optimistic. Very optimistic.

"Your father wants to see you, darling," her mother said.

Caroline walked into the room feeling a knot in her stomach. Her dad was awake.

"Hi, baby," he said, his voice much stronger. He hadn't called her that in years and she felt like his little girl once again.

"Hi, Daddy." She kissed his cheek. "You look much better."

"I feel like hell, but I'm grateful to be alive."

"I'm glad you're alive, too."

"Are you?" he whispered.

"Yes," she answered without hesitation.

They were silent for a moment, then Stephen said, "I've been very hard on you—even unfeeling at times."

"Daddy…"

"It's true, and it's funny how you can see things so clearly when you've been taken down so hard that all you want is to see your kids' faces again. I thought that in the emergency room when they were working on me. I just wanted to see my girls one more time."

She pulled up a chair and took his hand. "I'm right here."

"My dream was for you and Grace to follow in my footsteps, but that was my dream, not yours. I devoted my life to public service and I was proud of my work even when I was criticized and judged for my decisions. But when I was staring at those pearly gates, I wasn't thinking about the work I'd done. I was thinking about what I hadn't done for my kids, for my girls."

Caroline chewed on her lip and didn't say anything. "We had a good life, Daddy," she finally said. "I'm not sure when things started to change."

"When I became an ass and demanded and bullied until I got my way." He looked at her. "I'm sorry, baby."

"Oh, Daddy." She stood and gently hugged him.

"You remember when I used to take you and Grace fishing?"

"Yes. I loved it." She brushed away a tear. "Except putting the bait on the hook."

"When I get better, let's do that again. Just the three of us—a day fishing."

"Okay. I'd like that."

He gripped her hand. "I can be a better father."

"Daddy, please." She could hardly take any more. "I was stubborn and rebellious, too."

"Then let's have a new beginning."

"Oh, yes." She hugged him again and years of guilt disappeared. Then she slipped out of the room before she cried like a baby.

Joanna and Grace were waiting for her.

"He's so different." Caroline blinked back tears.

"He's more like the Stephen I married," Joanna said. "He's not so driven. I think our lives will change now."

Caroline felt the same way. She was eager to get to know her parents, to feel their love and to love them in return. She wasn't so naive to believe that her father's controlling nature would completely disappear. But now they would understand each other better.

"I have a ton of calls to make." Joanna's voice penetrated her thoughts. "But I think I'll sit with Stephen for a bit." She hugged her daughters. "You girls go home for a while."

"I need to go to the office," Grace said. "But I'll be back later to spend the night."

"I'm going to see Belle." Caroline looped her arm through her mother's. "But after that, Mom, you're stuck with me for the rest of the day."

"You girls are so wonderful." Tears gathered in Joanna's eyes.

They hugged tightly and Grace left.

"I want to freshen up before seeing Belle," Caroline told her mother. "I'll be back in a little while."

"Thank you, darling."

Caroline went to the hospital room, wiped her eyes and applied a touch of lipstick. She grabbed her purse and stopped dead in her tracks. Ruth stood inside the door in a long black dress. She looked different, but Caroline knew who she was. Fear seized her.

What was Ruth doing here?
What did she want?

CHAPTER EIGHTEEN

"WHAT ARE YOU DOING HERE?" She forced out the question.

Ruth stepped farther into the room. "You have to pay."

The words sent a shiver down Caroline's spine, but she fought the panic rising in her. "Please leave. My mother will be back any minute."

Ruth lunged for her and grabbed her by her hair, clamping a hand over her mouth. Caroline wrestled like mad, kicking out with her arms and legs, and they tumbled to the floor. Then someone grabbed her around the neck and her body writhed as she wheezed for air.

Ruth got to her feet, staring at Caroline's face. "Listen, you bitch," she snarled. "My sister is going to release you, but if you scream or do anything I don't like, Naomi will walk into CCU and plunge a knife into your father's heart."

Naomi loosened her grip and Caroline sucked in oxygen. Her panic turned to hysteria and she felt herself choking in response to Ruth's words. She tried to breathe normally and focus on the woman still holding her.

"Do you understand me?" Ruth asked.

Caroline nodded. She didn't have much choice. She knew Ruth meant what she'd said and there was no way Caroline would risk her father's life.

Naomi removed her arm and got to her feet. Caroline rubbed her throat, her eyes on her captor. Fleetingly she noted how much Naomi looked like her sister, but it was the knife in her hand that held Caroline's attention.

"Now, we're leaving the building very quietly. Do exactly what I tell you. Naomi is staying behind in case you try any last-minute heroics. You alert anyone and your father dies. Do you understand?"

Caroline nodded again, any hopes of getting away dwindling with each second. But someone would see them. Someone… She slowly stood, and as she and Ruth walked from the room, she spotted her purse where she'd dropped it when Ruth grabbed her, its contents scattered all over the floor. The furniture was also helter-skelter from the struggle. *Good,* she thought. Eli would know something was wrong. Eli would find her. She had to stay strong.

Ruth pulled her toward the stairs and they went down them quickly to the ground floor. They saw no one, not a soul, and the fear inside Caroline grew. Ruth guided her to a side entrance and they stepped out into a warm June day. A van was parked nearby and Ruth opened the back doors.

"Get in," she ordered.

Caroline saw two men standing on a loading dock, which was obviously a delivery area. All she had to do was scream and they'd hear her. But the other woman was still on the CCU floor, and if Caroline alerted anyone it would mean her father's death. She couldn't do it. The price was too high.

She got into the van and Ruth followed, tying Caroline's hands with a small rope. Soon Naomi jumped into the driver's seat and the van sped away. Caroline didn't know what they had in mind for her, but she knew it wasn't good.

Just like before.

Sitting on the floor of the van, cramped and uncomfortable, she prayed for strength and she prayed Eli would find her.

Eli, please find me.

ELI WENT TO SEE HOW Belle was doing and met Caleb coming out of her room.

"Did you tell her?" he asked Caleb.

"Yes, and I could almost see the fear being lifted from her. This will help her recovery."

"Yeah," Eli sighed. "And maybe each day she'll remember a little more about her life."

"The doctors are talking about removing the bullet from her head. They think it might help her to recover her memory, but she seems hesitant."

"I'm sure it's very frightening for her."

"I know," Caleb said. "I was thinking about putting a photo of her in all the big newspapers to see if someone might recognize her. I mentioned it before, but she was still so afraid she didn't want to. She might agree to it now."

"That's a good idea."

"Do you have any plans for lunch?" Caleb asked before Eli could walk away.

"Why?"

"I'm having lunch with Jake and Beau and thought you might like to join us."

He had big plans for tonight. He planned to buy flowers, champagne and chocolate. This night was going to be special. But he had some time now—he could have lunch with his brothers.

And it felt so right.

"Sure. Tell me where."

Thirty minutes later he was sitting in a steak house with

the McCains, talking and laughing as if they'd known each other for years. Jake spoke about Ben and Katie, and Eli realized he wanted children. He could admit that now. Children with Caroline. That family he'd been wanting was just within his grasp.

Tonight he would tell Caroline he loved her. And it wasn't frightening at all. Tonight.

"I've been reading in the papers about Amos Buford," Beau was saying. "It's a horrible story."

"Yeah." Eli twisted his tea glass. "No telling how many bodies we'll find in the ashes. I just hope DNA can identify them."

"Thank God you got Caroline Whitten out of there when you did," Jake said.

"I'm not letting her far out of my sight in the future." The words came out before Eli could stop them. He saw the puzzled look on Beau's face and recognition on Jake's.

"I knew it," Caleb laughed. "You're in love with Caroline."

Eli stared at his glass. "Yeah, but telling her has been difficult. I'm not one to love easily." He couldn't believe he was revealing his private emotions, but they kept coming out of his mouth.

"I think, as McCains, we're all like that," Jake said. "Joe never showed us any type of love and we're afraid of it, we don't trust it. But once you find that special person and realize you can't live without her, the words will come. Trust me on that, Eli. I'm an expert."

"He is," Beau confirmed. "I spent years trying to break through that rock-solid pride of his, and Elise did it without much effort."

Eli took a sip of his tea. "All my life I've felt like the forgotten son, and I wanted it to stay that way. Needed it to stay that way. There wasn't any chance of getting through that barrier of pride that I had built and strengthened over the years. Not until a green-eyed blonde knocked me on my ass and shattered every defense I ever had."

"Here's to kick-butt blondes." Caleb raised his glass with a broad grin.

"Here's to brothers," Jake added.

"Brothers," they echoed.

And Eli meant it.

JOANNA WALKED INTO the private room and stopped short. Caroline's purse was on the floor with its contents scattered everywhere. The beds were pushed together, up against the wall.

"Caroline?" she called, looking in the bathroom, but it was empty. She walked outside to the nurse's station. "Have you seen my daughter Caroline?"

"No, ma'am," the nurse answered. "I haven't seen her for a while."

"Thank you." Joanna went back to the room, staring down at Caroline's checkbook, cash, keys and makeup. Then she saw the scuff marks on the floor. There had been some sort of struggle. Her fingers shook as she picked up the small address book. What had happened here? She didn't know, but she was afraid. She quickly looked for Eli's number. Something was wrong and Eli would find out what. He would make sure her daughter was okay.

Caroline had to be okay.

"WE NEED TO MAKE THIS a monthly event," Beau said, sitting back in the restaurant booth.

"I agree," Jake replied. "A brothers' meeting once a month."

"Sounds good," Caleb stated.

"I think so, too," Eli declared.

"Then I nominate Beau as secretary," Caleb joked, "to keep the minutes of our stimulating conversations for future generations to read."

"What generations?" Jake couldn't keep a straight face. "I'm the only one with kids."

"Then you get to be the secretary," Beau told him.

Eli's phone buzzed and, smiling, he pulled it out. "Eli Coltrane."

"Eli? This is Joanna Whitten."

"Yes, ma'am."

"I hate to bother you because this might be nothing, but I'm a little concerned about Caroline."

Eli sat up straight. "What is it?"

"I came into the room at the hospital and Caroline's purse was on the floor. Her things are scattered all over the place and I can't find her."

Eli was on his feet. "I'll be right there. Don't touch a thing." He turned to his brothers. "Sorry guys, I've got to go. Caroline might be in trouble." He ran for his car.

Caleb was a step behind him. "What is it?" he asked, climbing into the passenger's seat.

Eli told him what Joanna had said, trying not to let his imagination run wild. "Call Tom and Bill and get them to the hospital," he added. "I'd rather be safe than sorry."

Caleb talked on the phone as Eli roared through traffic, weaving in and out. He parked in front of the hospital and the two men ran for the elevators. One was available and Eli poked a button. Seconds later they reached the CCU floor and Caleb went to check on Belle.

Joanna met Eli outside the room and Eli took in the scene in a glance. Something was very wrong, and the fear he'd been pushing back surfaced.

"Caroline wouldn't leave her purse like this," Joanna said.

"No," he agreed as Tom and Bill entered the room. Eli nodded to them and they stepped back out into the hall.

Caleb joined them. "Belle is fine and she hasn't seen Caroline," he reported.

"What are you thinking, Eli?" Tom asked.

"I'm thinking someone took her by force. The question is who."

"Buford is dead and his followers are in jail," Bill said. "This doesn't make sense."

"His wives aren't in jail," Eli pointed out.

"They're in the custody of their parents and not in the area," Bill added.

"Ruth and Naomi were here yesterday. Make sure they're in Houston with their parents."

"Eli," Tom sighed. "This is ridiculous. There has to be a reasonable explanation."

"Do it," Eli shouted. "And do it as fast as you damn well can."

"Okay." Tom gave in. "I'll call the Wessells if it will make you feel better."

"Get agents in here to question people, find out if anyone's seen her."

Tom and Bill shared a glance.

"Do it," Eli said between clenched teeth.

Bill glared at him, but grabbed his phone.

Joanna came out of the room with a worried expression and Eli went to her.

"What is it, Eli? Where's Caroline?"

"I don't know, but I'll find her."

Her hand trembled against her mouth and tears gathered in her eyes. "You don't think…"

"I'm not sure what to think right now," he said, not

wanting to alarm her any more than necessary. "Why don't you call Grace and get her over here?"

"Yes, yes. I'll call Grace." She hurried back into the room.

Eli stared at Caleb, striving for answers among the jumbled thoughts flooding his mind. "Remember that story Belle told us about the burning?"

"Sure."

"I feel in my gut that Ruth and Naomi have taken Caroline."

"But why? Buford is dead."

"He told them something before he died, and I'd bet my life that he told them to kill Caroline."

"Again, why?"

"The prophecy, that goddamn prophecy. Caroline is the reason it's not going to be fulfilled, and in their warped minds she has to…" The word stuck in his throat and he couldn't say it.

"Good God."

"We have to get to that camp and fast." Eli ran for the elevator.

"You think they're doing this at the camp?" Caleb asked, following on his heels.

"Yes. That's the only place it could be."

"But the forensic team is still out there," Caleb reminded him.

"Ruth and Naomi don't know that." Eli reached for his phone and called Greg.

"Is the forensic team still at the site?" Eli came straight to the point when the man answered.

"No. I talked to Martin about an hour ago. They found a couple of big bones and more teeth and they're bringing them to the lab and closing up for the day. Why are you asking?"

Eli told him his suspicions about Caroline.

"I'll call Tom and Bill immediately," Greg said.

"They're here, but thanks."

"Keep me posted."

"Will do."

"The team has left," he told Caleb. "We have to get there fast."

"It's all locked up, Eli. I don't see how they could get in there, but if you feel we need to go then I'm with you."

Tom met them at the elevators. "The Wessells don't answer so I had a patrol car check out their house. We should hear something shortly."

"We're going to the camp," Eli said. "I think that's where they're holding Caroline. Get as many men as you can and follow us."

Tom hesitated. "Eli, this doesn't—"

Tom's phone buzzed and he clicked it on. He listened, then hung up with a solemn expression. "The officers found Mr. and Mrs. Wessell dead, their throats slit."

Eli swallowed hard and got on the elevator, stabbing the button with his finger. There was no time to lose now. Seconds counted. Deliberately he shoved away the fear that he was about to lose everything he'd ever wanted—for the second time. He didn't know if he was that strong. He didn't know if anyone was.

"We're right behind you," Bill called as the elevator doors closed.

Eli and Caleb ran to the car, which was still parked in front. Caleb barred the driver's side, arm outstretched. "Let me have the keys. I'm driving."

"Get out of my way."

Caleb didn't budge. "For Caroline's sake, let me drive. You're in no condition. Think about Caroline."

Hearing her name had a calming effect on Eli, and he handed over the keys. Soon they were on the highway, heading out of Austin.

Eli didn't think. He kept his mind a blank. He had to. That was the only way he could deal with this.

He wasn't a praying man, even though Ma had taught him how. But now he was praying like he never had before.

Please let Caroline be alive.

CAROLINE SAT ON the ground with her hands tied, watching the women as they piled the wood high. They were at the camp, she knew.

They'd waited in the van for a long time. Someone had been here and they couldn't drive in immediately. She'd heard the Wessell sisters talking about forcing their way in, and she'd assumed the gate was locked. She didn't know how they opened it, but they had.

She had very little memory of the camp—just the darkness of the cellar and the escape through the woods. The small shacks were in a circle around her. She hadn't been aware of them as she and Eli had sprinted for the woods, only of the moon and stars.

What did these women have in mind for her now? The cellar had been caved in, so they couldn't put her back in there. Thank God for that.

The rope on her wrists was cutting into her flesh and she moved slightly to ease the pain. The ground was cold and hard and a pungent smell filled the still air. The only sound was the clatter of wood as Ruth and Naomi stacked it onto a large pile of ashes, which Caroline assumed had been their campfire.

She glanced toward the thick woods that surrounded them. Where were the bird sounds? The rustling of the trees? Everything was unnaturally quiet, and fear tightened its grip. But she wouldn't give in. Her life depended on that.

The van had been hot and she was sweaty, but she stayed focused on one thing: she was not going to die. She would fight to her last breath. All she needed was a chance—one small opportunity to escape.

Ruth and Naomi were bigger and older, and Caroline was hoping she could outrun them. Her feet weren't tied, and if she just had an opening...

The sisters started to chant in a dialect Caroline didn't recognize, and they circled the wood, waving their arms and bowing to the ground. Over and over they chanted, keeping up the strange ritual.

This was it. Caroline raised herself to her knees. Dusk was blanketing the camp and she had to make a move soon.

Ruth threw a match on the fire and screeched ominous sounds as flames leaped to the sky. The heat from the fire was scorching, and Caroline knew her time was running out.

Ruth and Naomi fell to their knees and began to pray. Slowly Caroline rose to her feet, then sprinted for the woods.

ELI AND CALEB SAW the smoke as they turned onto the dirt track.

"Oh, my God," Eli cried, feeling his insides cave in.

Caleb pressed his foot down and the car flew through the woods. When they reached the gate, he didn't even slow down. The vehicle burst through it, sending wire and boards flying in all directions, and came to a stop about twelve feet from the fire.

Eli and Caleb bailed out with guns drawn, but no one was in sight and the sizzle of the fire was the only sound. Eli's heart thudded painfully against his chest as he looked for Caroline. They walked around the fire and didn't see anything but an old van. It was getting dark and hard to see.

Eli heard a sudden swishing sound and turned quickly. Naomi lunged at him with a knife. He sidestepped and grabbed her outstretched arm, wrestling her to the ground with one hand, while he held his gun firmly in the other.

He squeezed until she dropped the knife, then he placed the gun against her head. "Where's Caroline?"

"In the fire where she belongs," Naomi spat. "The demons have taken her. She belongs to the demons."

"Where is she?" he yelled, fury ballooning inside him.

"Eli," Caleb said soothingly, "I can't see anything in the fire, so Caroline still has to out here somewhere. Ruth's not here, either. Eli, can you hear me?"

Caroline wasn't in the fire.

Eli loosened his hold and got to his feet, while Caleb quickly put handcuffs on Naomi. Eli handed him his own cuffs and Caleb clicked them on her feet. The woman began to chant and rock to and fro.

"Enjoy the fire," Caleb said, straightening.

Cars of FBI agents arrived and Caleb filled them in. Eli had only one thing on his mind. "We have to start searching now," he said. "Caroline and Ruth are somewhere in these woods. Let's find them."

The darkness was almost complete. Eli knew it was going to be hard, but he wouldn't rest until he saw her face again. He closed his eyes briefly as a weak feeling came over him. He'd had this same fear when he'd been searching for Ginny. He'd wanted to see her, to tell her he loved her. But he had been too late.

Was he too late again?

His belly tightened with a cold, sick fear.

Tom was shouting orders, and Eli ran to the woods, calling her name. "Caroline. Caroline. Caroline."

Bushes and vines clawed at him, but he kept going.

CAROLINE RAN UNTIL HER chest was tight with fatigue. She couldn't stop, though. She could hear Ruth lumbering through the woods behind her. Suddenly Caroline's foot caught on a root and she stumbled to the ground. The woman was on top of her in an instant.

"Get up, you bitch," she snarled, wielding a knife. She held the blade to Caroline's throat. "I could kill you here, but your spirit has to be taken by the fire never to live again."

Caroline gasped for air, hardly able to believe what Ruth had said. "You're going to burn me in the fire?"

"That's our faith. All evil has to be destroyed by fire."

"Amos Buford is evil," she cried. "And you're evil, too, if you can do something like that."

"Shut up," Ruth said, and jerked her to her feet by her tied hands.

"It's true," Caroline insisted. "He's brainwashed you. You're like an automaton, doing what he tells you even from the grave."

Ruth slapped her across the face. "You have to die for your sins!" Her voice rose in anger.

Caroline staggered, but didn't go down. "You're already dead," she yelled back. "You can feel it, can't you, Ruth? Amos stole the life from you, took other wives, had other children. And when it was time to fulfill his crazy prophecy, he chose another woman, not his head wife."

"Shut up. Shut up. Shut up."

Caroline was going on a woman's instinct now, thinking about how having multiple wives would affect Ruth. The woman didn't like it; that was obvious by her agitation. Caroline kept the conversation going, anything to buy time.

Eli, please find me.

"You should have been the one to bear the messiah. You deserved that honor for your faithful service to him." The words tasted bitter in her mouth, but they were the only weapon she had.

"Yes. It should have been me."

"But he wanted someone younger, someone prettier."

"Shut up. Shut up!" Ruth hurled herself at Caroline and they tumbled backward into the bushes, where sharp twigs and branches dug into her back and arms. Ruth straddled her, holding the knife to her throat. "You have to die. You have to die," she chanted.

Caroline fought her terror, trying to stay calm, trying to stay alive.

Eli. Eli. Eli.

"They had to die, too. The prophet said so. They were filling our heads with evil ways."

Caroline took a breath, her tied hands hurting from Ruth's weight on them. "Who, Ruth? Who had to die?"

"Our parents."

The Wessells. Oh God.

"Ruth…"

"Shut up," she screamed, and Caroline could see she was losing what little sanity she had. "You have to die."

"Ruth, listen to me. The prophet is dead and there is no more prophecy. You are free. Do you even know what that means?"

"You have to die. The prophet said so."

"No, Ruth. I don't."

"Shut up." The knife trembled against her throat.

Caroline closed her eyes and prayed.

"Caroline! Caroline!"

She heard Eli calling and hope spiraled through her. She screamed his name with every ounce of strength she had left.

Within minutes the FBI had them surrounded. Eli stepped forward, a gun in his hand. "Put the knife down, Ruth," he coaxed.

"She has to die," Ruth said, the knife shaking in her hand.

Caroline swallowed hard. "Give him the knife, Ruth. It's over."

"She has to die. She has to die. The prophet said so." The knife wobbled against Caroline's skin and she drew a hard breath, not thinking or feeling, just focusing on the knife and Ruth.

Eli slowly moved closer, then in the blink of an eye grabbed Ruth's wrist. The knife fell to the ground.

The agents grabbed the woman and quickly handcuffed her. "She has to die. She has to die," Ruth chanted as they led her away.

Eli fell down by Caroline and gathered her in his arms. He was shaking and so was Caroline.

"My wrists," she gasped.

He drew back and saw that her hands were tied. Reaching for the knife, he cut the rope, and Caroline flew into his arms.

"Hold me. Hold me," she cried, burying her face in his shoulder.

"I'm never letting you go." He stroked her hair. "Are you okay?"

She nodded, unable to stop the tremors.

"I was so afraid I'd find you…like Ginny."

"I'm alive." She kissed his throat.

He took a deep breath. "I…I love you," he whispered in an aching voice.

The horror, the night, the woods, the agents—everything faded away. All she could hear were those words, holding her together, making her stronger. For a moment she thought she might be imagining them, but she knew she wasn't. They were as real as the man in her arms.

She rubbed her face against his, knowing how hard this was for him, and loving him all the more. "I love you, too."

Eli sat on the ground with her in his lap and they clung together. Neither was the least inclined to move.

He gently caressed her hair, her shoulders and her arms. "I'm sorry. I'm sorry I couldn't say that to you the other night. But I've been so afraid of love—even when it was good, like with Ma, Pa and Ginny. Somehow I felt I didn't deserve it. I just couldn't expose that part of myself—that vulnerable part. The heart of that little boy who felt no one loved him."

She touched his face, wanting him to feel her love—always.

He caught her fingers with his mouth, then kissed her palm. "Instead I held those feelings inside, hurting myself, hurting others. But when I saw the pain in your eyes at the hospital, I knew I couldn't keep doing that. I loved you and I deserved a life with love. I was going to tell you tonight, but…" He gripped her tighter. "I thought I was too late again. Oh, Caroline, Caroline. I love you."

She kissed his cheek, his lips. "I know."

"Eli," Caleb said.

He glanced up.

"We have to get Caroline to a doctor."

"Oh. Yes." Eli rose to his feet with her in his arms. Caroline didn't protest. She was exhausted.

As they headed back to the camp, suddenly torturous screams filled the night. Eli quickly hustled her into the back seat of a car and Caleb took the wheel. Soon they were leaving that gruesome place behind. She didn't look up. She didn't want to see what was going on.

Eli held her tightly and she rested against him. Neither spoke as they traveled through the night. Once they reached the hospital, Eli carried her inside and laid her on a gurney. A nurse whisked her away and Eli followed.

"The doctor will examine her," the nurse said. "You'll have to wait outside."

Gently, he brushed back Caroline's hair. When he saw the bruises on her face, his stomach churned with fears he'd been feeling most of the night. *She's alive,* he reminded himself, and he kissed her forehead.

She raised her hand to touch his face and he saw her wrists, with their rope burns and bruises. He cleared his throat. "I have to go tell your mom you're okay."

"Yes," Caroline murmured as exhaustion overtook her.

"Do not leave her alone," he told the nurse.

"Yes, sir."

Eli left the cubicle and walked to the waiting area. He stopped when he saw who was there—Tuck, Jake, Beau and Caleb. They immediately embraced him, all of them at once. His knees buckled and his brothers held him up and he knew what family was about—having someone to lean on when the world caved in. It took a moment, but he gained control.

"You okay?" Tuck asked.

"Yeah. She's alive. I was so afraid I'd find her dead— like Ginny."

The room became very quiet as the men realized they were witnessing a first—Elijah Coltrane admitting to being afraid.

"I'm okay," he added, noting their worried glances.

"How's Caroline?" Jake asked.

"She has some cuts and bruises and she's exhausted, but she's alive." He couldn't seem to stop saying that.

They heard high heels clicking on the tiled floor, and Joanna and Grace hurried in.

"Where's my daughter?" Joanna asked Eli.

"They're checking her over," he replied. "She's fine."

Joanna hugged him. "Thank you, Eli. Oh God, thank you." She brushed away a tear. "Can we see her?"

"Go through that door." He pointed and they quickly left.

Eli saw Tom and Bill walk in.

"How's Ms. Whitten?" Tom asked.

"Shaken up, but alive," Eli answered running both hands through his hair. He'd lost his hat somewhere, he realized. "What was the screaming about?"

Tom and Bill glanced at each other, then Bill said, "We took the cuffs off Naomi's feet and stood her up to get her in a car. While we were waiting for the vehicle, she and Ruth started talking and chanting weird stuff. Before we knew what they were planning, they both jumped into the fire. We tried to reach them, but the flames were too hot." He exhaled a breath. "God. It was awful. Been an agent for fifteen years and never had to deal with anything like that."

"I haven't seen anything like this, either," Tom added. "Nor do I ever want to again."

Eli didn't wish to hear any more about Buford and his followers tonight. He just wanted to get back to Caroline.

"I'd better go," he said. He embraced his brothers again, then walked away, feeling richer than any man on earth.

Joanna and Grace came out of the cubicle. "She seems tired," the older woman said. "So we'll wait outside and let her rest."

Eli went in and watched Caroline for a moment. She lay on her side, her eyes closed, and it was the most beautiful sight he'd ever seen. He sat down at the side of the small bed, realizing his clothes were torn and dirty. But it didn't matter. All that mattered was that he had her back.

He had a second chance.

"Eli?" she whispered.

"Hmm?"

"What time is it?"

He glanced at the clock on the wall. "Ten after nine."

"You're late."

"What?"

"We had a date at eight o'clock."

He smiled. "I was busy saving a woman who has suddenly become my whole world."

"Oh." She rolled onto her back. "Thank you, Eli." She touched his face with her hand, and he noticed her wrists were bandaged.

"You did that the first time I rescued you from Buford's camp, and I knew you were a woman who liked to touch and be touched."

"But you didn't like me touching you." She trailed her fingers down his arm, feeling his scars, a reminder that would be with them always.

"No."

"And now?"

His eyes held hers. "Now I don't want you to ever stop touching me."

"Say it," she said, her eyes never leaving his.

He knew what she meant. They both did.

"I love you." The words came out slow and husky. Jake was right. It was easy.

She sat up and wrapped her arms around him, and he held her in a fierce grip. "I love you, Eli," she whispered. "I knew it the first moment you touched me."

He kissed her deeply, cupping her face in his hands. "Then let's make this legal."

She lifted an eyebrow. "By legal, Ranger Coltrane, do you mean marriage?"

"Yes, ma'am. I do."

"Does this proposal have anything to do with ethics?"

He grinned. "Not one thing."

"Then yes, yes, I'll marry you. Anything to keep you an honorable man," she teased with laughter in her eyes.

He smiled, seeing clearly what he wanted—home and a family with a woman he loved. He'd never thought that would happen for him, but now he was accepting and giving with everything in him. The past would haunt them occasionally, but they would face it together. And they had a big family to support them. He didn't feel alone or forgotten anymore.

He felt loved.

EPILOGUE

Six months later

THE COUPLE CIRCLED the dance floor, and all eyes in the ballroom watched the groom in his tux and boots and the bride in a beautiful white gown. Eli held Caroline like a priceless piece of china and she sparkled in her husband's arms.

"How much longer?" he whispered against her forehead.

She smiled up at him. "Not too long now. You're doing great."

Caroline had never planned to have a big wedding. She'd thought she'd leave that to Grace. That had been the defiant Caroline, doing the opposite of what her parents wanted. Since the horrible incident with Buford and his followers, and her father's heart attack, she had a clearer understanding of herself and her family. She didn't need to do a thing to get her parents' love—it was there, and she'd learned to accept it, to compromise and talk when they disagreed.

Her father, being in a better frame of mind, helped tremendously. He had actually made the last six months enjoyable. He hadn't retired from politics, but had changed his diet, his bad habits and had slowed down. They seemed to have needed to experience these bad times before they could accept who and what they were.

Caroline was a congressman's daughter and she knew her behavior reflected on him. After almost losing him, she didn't want to cause him any more pain. Those attempts were petty and she was above that now.

When she and Eli had talked about marriage plans, she'd realized he wanted the wedding to be as simple as possible. Her parents, on the other hand, wanted a big wedding. But Eli's wishes came first.

Being an extraordinary man, he'd sensed that she was torn, and said that, since he planned to get married only once, they might as well do it right. And they had. It had been a fairy tale day with family and friends.

Now Eli was ready for the honeymoon. She was, too.

Eli had also gone through changes. Accepting his brothers had been a turning point for him. It had removed the curse of the past, allowing him to love and accept love. That had never been easy for him, since he'd felt so unloved as a child. The Tuckers had shown him love, but he never knew quite how to handle it. Now he did.

He had so many inner conflicts about his father and his love for Ginny. But talking to his brothers had helped to heal those deep wounds. These days Eli didn't have a problem with those three little words. He made sure Caroline heard them every morning when she woke up and every night before she went to sleep.

They had weathered the past and were stronger for it. They'd learned about family and love, they'd discovered their strengths and weaknesses. Caroline was happier than she'd ever been in her life, and she saw that happiness mirrored in Eli's eyes.

The song ended and Stephen walked toward them.

"I guess I have to relinquish you to your father," Eli said, his voice reluctant.

She touched his face. "Just one last time, then I'm yours forever."

"That sounds about right." He stepped away and gave Caroline's hand to Stephen.

While the bride danced with her father, Eli danced with Joanna, then with Aunt Vin and Elise. As the wedding went on, he danced with just about every female but his wife. After an hour or so he finally stepped to the side, and Tuck brought him a beer.

"Thanks. Everything set?" Eli asked, taking a couple of deep breaths.

"Yes. Caroline doesn't know?"

"Not yet."

Tuck watched Grace talking to one of the waiters. "You must be very sure of her reaction."

"You bet…." He noticed Tuck's gaze. "Why are you staring at Grace?"

"Because if she starts my way, I'm disappearing."

Tuck and Grace had not gotten along from the start, and all through the wedding preparations the tension between them had been obvious.

"Cut her some slack."

"If she tells me to do one more thing, I might strangle her."

Eli laughed at easygoing Tuck getting his feathers ruffled. "As best man and matron of honor you have certain duties, but I don't think strangling each other is one of them."

Tuck took a swallow of his beer. "I'll try to remember that."

They watched Caroline sail by in Beau's arms.

"Our lives are changing, Eli," Tuck murmured.

He caught the forlorn note in Tuck's voice. "I'm not dying. I'll be living right next door to you."

He and Caroline had started construction on the house he'd always planned. They would live in her apartment until it was finished.

"I like that," Tuck said. "Ma and Pa would, too."

Eli felt the same way.

He patted Tuck on the back. "There's a lot of beautiful women here tonight. Ask one of them to dance, and have a good time. You love to dance."

"I might just—"

"Jeremiah."

"Damn. She caught me unaware," Tuck whispered to Eli as Grace walked up to them.

"Did you distribute the confetti I gave you for the bride and groom's departure?" Caroline's sister looked directly at Tuck.

"Yes, ma'am." He saluted and clicked his heels. "Mission completed."

"I don't find that funny," Grace said in a haughty voice.

"Neither do I," Tuck replied, and walked off.

Grace frowned. "He really is very rude sometimes."

Before Eli could respond, Caroline slipped her arms around him and rested her head on his shoulder. "I'm tired."

He kissed her forehead. "I think it's…"

He paused as he saw Ben and Katie coming toward them. They were the ring bearer and the flower girl and looked adorable. Ben bowed in front of Caroline. "May I have…have this dance, please?"

Eli squatted down. "Are you trying to steal my wife?"

Ben giggled. "No. I'm too little. But…feel my muscle." He held out his tiny arm. "It's getting bigger and I throw…throw better. Daddy said so."

Eli squeezed the thin biceps and felt a muscle the size of a jellybean. "Just keep practicing, champ."

"That's what my daddy says." He looked at Caroline. "I gotta dance now."

Caroline took his hands and they walked onto the floor. Eli stared at Katie in her white dress. She looked like an angel.

"If you hold me, I'll dance with you," the little girl said, her face serious. "That's how I dance with my daddy."

Eli picked her up and twirled onto the floor. "You look beautiful today."

"My daddy says I look like a princess."

Eli kissed her cheek. "Definitely a princess."

They danced until Jake and Elise found them.

"I danced with Uncle Eli," Katie said.

Jake took her. "Now it's time to dance with Daddy. And I think it's time for you to go," he whispered to Eli.

Eli hugged him. "Thanks for never giving up on me."

"You're welcome," Jake replied.

Beau put his arms around both of them. "Wow. What a party. I'm going to pick the prettiest woman that will have me and spend the rest of the night—"

Elise cleared her throat.

"Watching a movie," Beau finished without missing a beat, and everyone laughed. "Come on, munchkin, let's dance." He took Katie and danced away.

Elise hugged Eli. "Have a wonderful honeymoon."

Eli grinned. "I plan to." He glanced around. "Have y'all seen Caleb?"

"He's over there." Elise pointed toward the band. "Goodbye," they called as Jake and Elise took to the floor.

Caleb leaned against a pillar, his eyes trained on a table in a corner where Belle sat with an older lady. Eli knew it bothered Caleb that he hadn't been able to find out who she was, but he and Social Services had found her a home and a job. Mrs. Gertrude Parker was elderly and quite wealthy, but her eyesight was bad and she couldn't drive anymore. She'd taken Belle into her home, and Caleb had helped to get her a driver's license so she could chauffeur Mrs. Parker wherever she needed to go.

Gertrude sponsored several charities and attended many social functions. The arrangement was working well, but Caleb still didn't have any peace. Belle had had the bullet removed from her skull without any effect to her memory. She had flashbacks now and then but still didn't remember who she was.

The photo in the papers hadn't turned up anything, either. Belle was in limbo. And so was Caleb.

The Buford case was still going on. Three sets of teeth had been recovered from the fire and three women identified—all under the age of twenty-one. Now their families had some peace.

Greg had determined that the other wives hadn't participated in the killings, so he hadn't charged them. The five men in jail were charged with capital murder and the first trial was in three months. Eli and Caroline had put it behind them and left the case in the court's hands. They worried, though, that Belle would have to testify.

She and Caroline had grown very close. She was even a bridesmaid, at Caroline's insistence. Belle had resisted every step of the way.

Eli hoped that one day she would remember who she was. He didn't know how that would affect Caleb, for it was very clear that she had had a husband or boyfriend. Caleb definitely had feelings for her.

Eli walked up to him and gave him a big bear hug. "Thanks, Caleb."

Caleb lifted an eyebrow. "Did I do something?"

"Yes. You became my brother."

"I didn't have any choice in that, but I'm awfully glad about it." He smiled. "And thanks for inviting my mom and Andrew."

"The past is over and I'm not harboring any more resentment." Eli followed Caleb's gaze to Belle. "Why don't you ask her to dance?"

"I have and she's not very comfortable with it."

Eli patted his shoulder. "Then make her comfortable."

Caleb took a deep breath and walked toward Belle.

Caroline rushed up to Eli. "It's time."

He took her hands and held her for a moment, giving Caleb time to dance with Belle.

"I thought you were ready." Caroline looked at him, puzzled.

"I'm so ready," he whispered in her ear. "Just wanted Caleb to have a little time with Belle."

"Oh. You're wonderful." She smiled.

The band stopped playing and everyone headed for the entrance. Eli and Caroline ran through the throng of people throwing confetti. The two of them were covered with colorful hearts and stars as they climbed into the waiting limo.

Eli waved to his brothers, and the last thing he saw was Tuck frowning as Grace jabbered at his side. Yep. This was going to make an interesting family. But he'd think about that later.

He took his wife in his arms and kissed her. "Oh, yeah. This is what I've been waiting for," he murmured. The last two weeks had been so hectic that they hadn't had any time together.

When they came up for air, Eli noticed a package on the seat. "What's that?" he asked, kissing her nose, her cheek.

"I don't know," Caroline said, breathing heavily. "I saw it when I got in. Think I should open it?"

"Why not? Later you'll be too busy doing other things."

She kissed him quickly and tore into the package. Her eyes opened wide at what was inside.

"What is it?" Eli asked.

Grinning, she pulled out the worn boxing gloves. A note fell out, as well.

Eli picked it up. It read For when you disagree, these are a great equalizer. Tuck.

Eli laughed out loud.

"You didn't know about this?" Caroline asked, laughing with him.

"No," he replied, "but it's a great way to tell you something."

"What?"

"You haven't asked where we're spending tonight."

"I assumed we'd be staying at my apartment, then catching the plane to Hawaii in the morning."

He cupped her face. "We're spending the night at the ranch. Tuck has the house ready with flowers, champagne, the works."

"Oh, Eli. I'd love that." She threw her arms around his neck.

"I thought you would." He kissed the side of her face. "It's a good way to start our life together. We can drink coffee in the morning and watch the construction on our house before we leave for the airport."

"I love you," she whispered.

He raised his head and gazed into her eyes. "I'll love you forever."

Eli took a deep breath, feeling love like a warm glow in his heart. Never again would he be alone or forgotten. He had everything and all it took was three little words.

Words he would never forget to say.

Not ever.

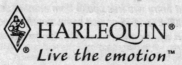

If you enjoyed what you just read,
then we've got an offer you can't resist!

Take 2 bestselling love stories FREE!

Plus get a FREE surprise gift!

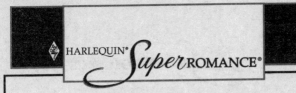

HARLEQUIN *Super*ROMANCE®

**A new book by the critically acclaimed
author of No Crystal Stair**

Heart and Soul
by Eva Rutland
Harlequin Superromance #1255

Life is both wonderful and complicated when you're in
love. Especially if you get involved with a business rival,
as Jill Ferrell does. Scott Randall's a wealthy man and his
background is very different from hers. But love can be
even more difficult if, like Jill's friend Kris Gilroy, you fall
for a man of a different race. She's black and Tom's white,
and her family doesn't approve. But as both women learn,
the heart makes its own choices....

Available in February 2005 wherever Harlequin books are sold.

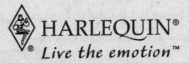

HARLEQUIN®
Live the emotion™

A six-book series from Harlequin Superromance

WOMEN in Blue

Six female cops battling crime and corruption on the streets of Houston. Together they can fight the blue wall of silence. But divided, will they fall?

Coming in February 2005, *She Walks the Line* by Roz Denny Fox (Harlequin Superromance #1254)

As a Chinese woman in the Houston Police Department, Mei Lu Ling is a minority twice over. She once worked for her father, a renowned art dealer specializing in Asian artifacts, so her new assignment—tracking art stolen from Chinese museums—is a logical one. But when she's required to work with Cullen Archer, an insurance investigator connected to Interpol, her reaction is more emotional than logical. Because she could easily fall in love with this man...and his adorable twins.

Coming in March 2005, *A Mother's Vow* by K. N. Casper (Harlequin Superromance #1260)

There is corruption in Police Chief Catherine Tanner's department. So when evidence turns up to indicate that her husband may not have died of natural causes, she has to go outside her own precinct to investigate. Ex-cop Jeff Rowan is the most logical person for her to turn to. Unfortunately, Jeff isn't inclined to help Catherine, considering she was the one who fired him.

Available wherever Harlequin books are sold.

Also in the series:
The Partner by Kay David (#1230, October 2004)
The Children's Cop by Sherry Lewis (#1237, November 2004)
The Witness by Linda Style (#1243, December 2004)
Her Little Secret by Anna Adams (#1248, January 2005)

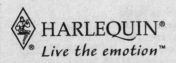